D0364801

BY JAMES ROLLINS

Subterranean
Excavation
Deep Fathom
Amazonia
Ice Hunt
Sandstorm
Map of Bones
Black Order
The Judas Strain

BY JAMES ROLLINS WRITING AS JAMES CLEMENS

Wit'ch Fire
Wit'ch Storm
Wit'ch War
Wit'ch Gate
Wit'ch Star
Shadowfall
Hinterland

INDIANA JONES™
and the
KINGDOM OF
THE CRYSTAL SKULL™

LUCAS
BOOKS

EBURY
PRESS

JAMES ROLLINS

Based on the story by George Lucas and Jeff Nathanson,
and the screenplay by David Koepp

Indiana Jones and the Kingdom of the Crystal Skull is a work of fiction. Names, places and incidents either are products of the author's imagination or are used fictitiously.

This edition produced for the Book People Ltd,
Hall Wood Avenue, Haydock, St Helens, WA11 9UL

1 3 5 7 9 10 8 6 4 2

Published in 2008 by Ebury Press, an imprint of Ebury Publishing

A Random House Group Company

The Random House Group Limited Reg. No. 954009

Addresses for companies within the Random House Group can be found at
www.randomhouse.co.uk

A CIP catalogue record for this book is available from the British Library

The Random House Group Limited supports The Forest Stewardship Council (FSC), the leading international forest certification organisation. All our titles that are printed on Greenpeace approved FSC certified paper carry the FSC logo. Our paper procurement policy can be found at

Printed in the UK by CPI Cox & Wyman, Reading, RG1 8EX

ISBN 9780091926670

To buy books by your favourite authors and register for offers visit
www.rbooks.co.uk

Book design by Katie Shaw

To George Lucas and Steven Spielberg,
for turning geeks like me into heroes in the dark

ACKNOWLEDGMENTS

For a book written under a cloak of secrecy, there are a surprising number of people who were instrumental in making this project a thrill to write. First, I must thank Sue Rostoni at Lucasfilm for walking me through the entire process, from start to finish, along with Leland Chee, who toured me through the Lucasfilm campus and taught me the incantations necessary to delve into the rich database that covers the history of Indy, from past to present. There are many others at Lucasfilm who were also invaluable in answering countless queries: Stacy Cheregotis, Jill Hughes, Stephanie Hornish, set coordinator Ryan Wiederkehr, and Frank Parisi, who shared his valuable insights. I must also express my appreciation to screenwriter David Koepp for both the inspiration and the generous counsel he offered along the way. And it's always good to have a partner in crime. In this case, that would be my counterpart in the young-adult literary world, James Luceno.

Closer to home, I must thank a group of friends who have been behind this writer from the start of his career, a writer's group any author would be proud to have at his back. They were not allowed to critique this novel due to confidentiality, but their support and years of guidance and criticism still echo behind each word written. So let me acknowledge them here, too: Penny Hill, Steve and Judy Prey, Dave Murray, Caroline Williams, Chris Crowe, Lee Garrett, Jane O'Riva, Michael Gallowglas, Denny Grayson, Leonard Little, Kathy L'Ecluse, Scott Smith, and Dave Meek. Beyond the group, Carolyn McCray and David Sylvian stand to either side of me and keep pushing me forward to loftier heights.

And finally, a special thanks to my editor and champion at Del Rey, Shelly Shapiro, for all her hard work, stalwart support, and steady stewardship of this entire project. I started my career with Del Rey, so she made it a little like coming home. And of course, I must acknowledge my friend and agent, Russ Galen, who was as excited as I was to put some small fingerprint on the rich history that is Indiana Jones.

INDIANA JONES™
and the
KINGDOM OF
THE CRYSTAL SKULL™

Return . . .

Francisco de Orellana stumbled the last steps toward the cliff's edge. At the lip of the precipice, he fell to his knees. The wide desert plain spread far below him. As the sun sank, he stared across that parched and rocky landscape, a reflection of his own soul. From this height he saw strange pictures carved into the desert floor, monstrously large, stretching many leagues across the rocky plain, giant figures of monkeys, insects, snakes, along with flowers and strange angular shapes.

It was a God-cursed and demonic land. He should never have come.

Francisco tore the conquistador's helmet from his head and tossed it behind him. While the sun gave up its last light, he planted his sword deep into the hot, sandy soil. The Spanish pommel and grip formed a cross against the setting sun.

Francisco prayed for release, for forgiveness, for salvation.

El dios querido, me perdona.

But there could be no forgiveness for the murder he had committed.

Blood bathed his gilded armor, dripped from his sword, and soiled his breastplate. The blood came from his own men, slaughtered at his own hand.

With his gold dagger, Francisco had slit the throats of the twin brothers, Iago and Isidro. He had used his sword to gut Gaspar like a pig and had come close to cleaving Rogelio's head clean from his wide shoulders. He had stabbed Oleos in the back as he tried to flee; the same with Diego, cutting him off at the knees. The last man's screams had chased Francisco to this perch atop the cliff.

But all had fallen silent.

The slaughter was complete.

Return . . .

Francisco clawed at his face and dragged deep gouges. The command filled his skull. He sought to dig it out, cursing himself and the trespass he had committed. It would not let him go. The urge cut through his entrails like a rusted hook. It dug deeper than his spine, hooking him and trapping him.

For weeks he had fled that cursed place, sure he had escaped with a wealth to challenge kings, with wonders that would make queens weep. He had chests of gold and silver, another full of rubies and emeralds. A boat waited only a few days away, ported in a deepwater cove.

So close.

Return . . .

He sank around his sword, begging for release. As this day had dawned, he had finally succumbed to the command etched into his bones. With each step away from that accursed valley, the word had grown louder in his skull. There was no escaping it. At last he found it impossible to continue, to take another step toward his ship. He became trapped in amber, unable to move forward. Only one path was left.

His men felt no such compunction. They chattered like boys, excited to return home, reveling in how they'd spend their wealth, full of grand schemes and great dreams. They would not listen when he spoke of going back. They had fought him, urged him, and swore at him. They meant to take the treasure and continue to the ship, even if it meant leaving him behind.

And Francisco would have let them.

But in their greed, the men moved to take that which belonged to Francisco alone. That could not be! In a blind rage, he had cut them down like a scythe through wheat. Nothing must stop him, not even his own men.

Return . . .

Now he was alone at last.

Now he could go back.

As the sun dropped below the far horizon and night fell, he gained his feet, retrieved his helmet, and pulled his sword from the soil. He turned, ready at last to obey the command. He headed down the dark slope—but movement drew his eye.

Below, figures shifted out of shadows and from behind tall boulders. They rose from holes and crawled from the limbs of twisted trees. They climbed toward him from all directions. He heard the knock of naked knees and the clop of stony heels.

An army, stripped of flesh . . . *made of bones.*

He paled and backed away, knowing now he was truly cursed.

The living dead closed toward him.

Come to drag him to Hell.

Where he truly belonged.

Still, he screamed to the night sky—not in terror, but in anguish, knowing he was forever damned. For he had failed, failed to obey the command burning in his skull. Merciless, relentless, the dead advanced toward him. His scream ripped into the night, but all Francisco de Orellana heard was one word.

Return . . .

PART ONE

DOOM TOWN

Yucatán Peninsula, 1957

EACH STONE told a story.

He edged on his stomach across the circular floor. Its surface had been carved into a Mayan calendar: a massive wheel made up of concentric rings of glyphs dug deep into the rock. Ahead, in the center, rose a large statue of a serpent's head, cowled by stone feathers, its fanged mouth stretched wide, ready to swallow the unwary. The opening was large enough for a man to crawl through.

But what was in there?

He had to know.

If only he could reach it . . .

He tried to go faster, but the roof pressed against his back. He could not even lift up onto an elbow. The chamber required the supplicant to slither across the floor like a snake, perhaps in representation of the Mayan god, Kukulkan, the feathered serpent. Except this current worshipper wore no feathers, only scuffed khaki pants, a faded leather bomber jacket, and a battered brown fedora.

Covered in mud, he crawled across the limestone floor. It had been raining in the Yucatán for the past week. The sun was just a distant memory. And now a tropical storm was due to strike this night, threatening to drive them away from the jungle-covered Mayan ruins that hugged the Yucatán coast.

"Indiana!" The call came from the stairs behind him.

"Little busy here, Mac!" he yelled back.

"The sun's gone down, mate!" his friend urged, his British accent thickening with worry. "The winds are kicking up fierce. A coconut flew right past my head a minute ago."

"It's only a tropical storm!"

"Indy, it's a *hurricane*!"

"Okay, so it's a *big* tropical storm! Still busy down here. I'm not leaving till I see what's hidden in the center of that statue. It has to be important."

Indy had discovered the secret entrance to the temple two days earlier. It lay beneath a Mayan city complex on the central coast of the Yucatán. Hours of careful digging had been required to open the chute that led down to the inner chamber. Jungles still shrouded most of it, keeping it hidden for centuries from prying eyes and the sticky fingers of robbers.

Indy read the calendar wheel as he worked across the floor. The outer ring told the genesis myth of the Maya, as related from the Popul Vuh, the sacred book of the Maya. It listed the birth date of the world as:

13.0.0.0.0 4-Ahwa 8-Kumk'u

In the Gregorian calendar, this corresponded to August 13, 3114 BC. The inner rings continued the story of the K'iche Maya tribe, who had mostly settled Guatemala. Their writings were never seen this far north. The tale told of the birth and rise of Kukulkan, the feathered serpent god.

Indy ignored the ache in his knees and continued his crawl toward the innermost ring and the strange sculpture in the center.

The last ring spoke of the end of the Long Count calendar, the end of the world itself: *December 21, AD 2012.*

Fifty-five years from now.

Would the world truly end that day?

He continued onward. Plenty of time to worry about that later.

Indy reached the snake god's head and lifted his lantern between the stone fangs. A small chamber opened beyond the mouth—but it had no floor. A pit dropped, like the dark throat of the stone serpent itself. It was deep, too dark to see the bottom, but a whispery rush echoed up to him.

Indy squirmed into the mouth and lowered his lantern. He caught a glint of silver, but it was still too dark to make out any details.

"Indiana!" Mac called from the stairs. "What are you doing?"

"What does it look like I'm doing?"

"It looks like you're being swallowed by a snake!"

Indy shuddered at the thought. It was his worst nightmare. He twisted around and loosed his bullwhip from his shoulder. He tied the end around the handle of his lantern and lowered the light into the pit. The darkness fell back as the lantern descended. The walls of the well appeared to be raw polished limestone.

At last his light revealed the source of the silvery glint: water flowing past the bottom of the pit. The hole opened into one of the numerous underground rivers that ran through the porous limestone peninsula of the Yucatán. Hundreds of miles of such rivers and tunnels riddled the underworld here. The Maya considered such openings to be pathways to the next life.

Indy lowered the lantern a bit deeper. The river surged fast and fierce, storm-fed by the weeks of rain and the current typhoon. But through the rush of crystal-clear water, his lantern's glow revealed a final glyph, carved into the bottom of the river channel.

He could almost make it out.

Indy sidled farther into the statue, half hanging into the pit, his arm outstretched. The glyph came into better focus. Indy recognized it. He had seen the same carving on the lintel above one of the temples outside. It was a figure of a man, upside down as if falling, symbolizing mankind's birth into this world.

Or maybe it was more literal: a warning to be careful.

Too late. The lip of stone broke away under Indy, and he went tumbling down into the pit. His heart jammed into his throat, choking back a yell of surprise and fear. His hands scrabbled against the walls, his legs splayed, trying to stop his plunge. But the walls were too smooth.

"Indy!" he heard Mac scream behind him.

The lantern hit the water first and was doused. Then he struck. The icy chill cut to the bone, tried to squeeze the air from his chest. He forced himself to hold his breath as the hard current grabbed him and shot him down the river tunnel. He rolled and turned in complete blackness. He fought to keep his legs out in front of him as he was swept along.

That's what I get for playing with snakes.

The small army crept through the dark, storm-swept jungle. Winds battered palm fronds and whipped branches from trees. Rain pelted like hail, stinging any exposed skin—then the next moment, the downpour fell in heavy sheets that threatened to drown a man with a single breath. It was a torturous slog, but the lights of the camp glowed through the forest, beckoning them onward.

Dressed in goggles, helmets, camouflage, the assault team moved like clay soldiers, half melted by the storm.

Nothing must stop them.

The leader of the team had his orders.

Secure the key.

Kill everyone else.

Flushed through total darkness, Indy held his breath.

Lights began to dance across his vision. At first he thought it was due to the lack of oxygen. His lungs screamed for air. Why keep fighting? Then he realized that the light was real. It glowed ahead, something brighter than the pitch darkness of the storm-swollen channel.

Since falling down the pit, Indy had held on to one slim hope.

The coast.

The jungle-shrouded ruins lay only five hundred yards from a remote section of the Yucatán shoreline, set high atop steep cliffs. There was a good chance that the underground river emptied into the sea somewhere along the coast.

He forced himself to keep holding his breath, banking on this one hope.

Suddenly the darkness fell away into a murky storm-light. The tunnel widened into a small cavern. The top was high enough for Indy to get his nose above the water. He gulped air into his starved lungs. He also caught a brief glimpse of an opening ahead, the end of the river. Stormy skies filled the view, framed by jungle vines. The water poured out of the rock in a heavy falls. He heard its roar over the rumble of thunder and pound of heavy surf.

He was still high up.

There was no fighting the current. Like a cork in a champagne bottle, Indy blasted out of the exit, shooting from the face of a sheer cliff. He caught a brief glimpse of sharp rocks and churning white water below.

Swinging in midair, Indy twisted and lashed out with his bullwhip. The lantern had long been shattered away, but he had kept a death grip on the whip's leather handle. With a skill that was born as much of panic as practice, Indy snapped out for a tangle of stubborn tree roots protruding from the cliff face, exposed from years of erosion by rain and wind.

With a satisfying *kuh-rack,* the whip lashed onto the roots. Indy clutched the handle with both hands and swung back toward the cliff. He got his legs up in time to bear the brunt of the impact. Still, he smashed hard, bruising his entire left side.

He hung there, gasping.

Wind and rain thrashed at him. Thunder boomed, felt down to his aching bones. He had no choice but to keep moving. Indy fought his way up, climbing and hauling. The storm pounded his back and sought to rip him from his perch. Black skies churned overhead. The cliff was deeply pocked, offering decent footholds. Still, it took him a quarter hour to reach the summit and beach himself atop the cliff.

He lay facedown, hugging the earth.

He pictured his course on the river underneath him: first swallowed down the serpent's maw, then swirled through its snaking belly, and finally shot out its end. The waterway formed the complete shape of a serpent.

Indy shuddered as he remembered Mac's words. *Looks like you're being swallowed by a snake.* Well, perhaps he had been. He glanced behind him, picturing his dramatic exit out the back end of the snake. Mac would not let him live this one down. He suspected his British friend would use a word more colorful than *shot* to describe Indy's explosive exit from the snake's rear end.

Still, he was out.

Indy groaned and pushed to his hands and knees.

He'd definitely had his fill of snakes for one day—slimy ones or stone ones.

With every fiber of muscle on fire, Indy gained his legs and headed away from the cliff. His back ached, and his legs wobbled. He had taken a couple good knocks to the head, too. He'd be feeling that ride for a few days.

As the storm worsened, he slowly made his way across the ruins. Step pyramids and stone homes spread out in a complicated pattern. His camp lay on the far side of the temple complex, buried into the edge of the dense jungle. With the wind wailing at his back, Indy hiked toward the flickering lights. Thunder pounded, and massive raindrops hit the ground and exploded like mortar shells. He skirted the edge of the ruins and headed straight for camp. Mac would be sick with worry.

At least, his friend would be thrilled to see him.

Bone-tired, deafened by the storm, Indy had entered the camp before he realized anything was wrong. He almost stepped on the first body, sprawled facedown in the mud and half buried in it. He fell back with a gasp.

The sharp *crack* of a rifle blast cut through the thunder.

It came from the center of the small camp.

Followed by a chatter of automatic fire.

Had to be grave robbers or a local guerrilla group.

Indy cursed and retreated to the jungle's edge. He had no weapon, except for his whip. If he circled, ambushed a straggler, maybe he could steal a pistol or rifle—

As he turned, darker shadows slipped from the rainy forest. Soldiers, muddy, wearing goggles, pushed into view. Weapons leveled at his chest. A figure was shoved out into the open. The man fell to his knees, bloodied, clothes torn.

It was Mac.

He was followed by a giant of a man wearing a helmet and goggles and layered with mud. He bore no insignia, but he was clearly in charge.

Still on his knees, Mac gaped up in shock. "Indy! How . . . ? I saw you swallowed by a bloody snake!"

"Apparently I gave it indigestion."

Indy crossed to Mac and helped him to his feet.

Mac sighed as the soldiers closed in all around them. "I think you were better off with the snake."

Nevada

THE DESERT killed the unwary.

One learned that lesson early or not at all.

Sergeant Jimmy Wycroft ground the scorpion under his boot heel. It squashed with a satisfying crunch. He stood with two other army MPs in the shadow of the dusty guard shack. One hand shielded his eyes against the late-afternoon glare. Beyond the shack's tiny square of shade, the sun baked the Nevada desert into a searing plain of redrock spattered with sagebrush and cactus. Nothing moved out there except wind-spun dust devils and the occasional prairie dog or sidewinder.

So it was no wonder the dramatic desert chase held all the men's attention.

A mile away two rooster tails of dust sped across the landscape, spat up by a pair of vehicles drag-racing down the distant two-lane highway. The pair made for a strange competition: an antique 1932 Ford roadster against a large army personnel carrier.

On Wycroft's left, Corporal Higgins held a pair of binoculars fixed to his face and called out color commentary, as if he were reporting on the Kentucky Derby.

"The Ford is making her move . . . she's going wide around the truck. They're neck and neck."

Near the door of the guard shack, a rock pinned down a pair of sawbucks.

A gentleman's wager.

Wycroft allowed a thin smile. He had placed his money on the Ford, though that meant he was betting against the home team. Army insignia were emblazoned on the side panel of the truck; the same with the Ford staff car and two jeeps that followed the pair. The army group made up a convoy, most likely headed here to the remote military outpost. Then a few minutes before, the roadster had sped up out of nowhere and passed the convoy with the whoop of its driver and passengers—clearly joyriding teenagers, their shouts bright enough to echo across the desert to the lonely guard post. The army personnel carrier had given chase, the truck driver clearly as bored as they all were out in the middle of the blasted desert.

"But wait, my horse is making her move!" Higgins continued. The corporal had bet on the modern army truck against the antique car. "They're passing the Atomic Café."

Wycroft pinched his eyes. He watched the two rooster tails, one larger than the other, shoot past the old diner with its missile-shaped neon sign.

"The roadster fishtails . . . the truck takes the lead! It's anyone's race!"

"Sir, shouldn't we be radioing the convoy?" the last guard asked. Private Mitchell was new to the base, nervous about infractions, boyish behind a set of thick black eyeglasses. He glanced toward the chain-link fence topped with barbed curls of concertina wire. The gate was padlocked closed. "Aren't we locked down until further orders?"

Wycroft waved down his concern. He had been stationed in the desert for five years. He knew to take his pleasure where he could. "Up my bet to twenty. The roadster to win."

"All right!" Higgins cheered. "I'll take those odds!"

The two vehicles raced down the highway, going faster and faster. They were dead even, and it became impossible to discern one from the other with the naked eye.

Higgins kept his binoculars glued to his face. His voice faltered. "The roadster has the lead again . . ."

Wycroft's smile grew broader. Though the Ford roadster was older by twenty-five years, he had worked on such beauties at his father's garage in Muncie, Indiana, when he was a teenager. The roadster was equipped with an in-line six-cylinder engine and a counterweighted crankshaft. It could rocket from zero to sixty in just under seven seconds. Wycroft saw no need even to watch the finish.

Higgins swore, marking the final defeat.

Across the desert, a whoop of teenage victory echoed faintly to them.

"How'd you know, Sarge?" Higgins asked, lowering his binoculars, defeated.

"Wisdom comes with age, Corporal."

Wycroft bent down, lifted the rock, and collected his winnings. Pocketing the bills, he dusted off his desert fatigues, shaded his eyes, and stared back out over the desert.

Off in the distance, the army truck slowed with a wash of dust and exhaust. It trundled up to an unmarked exit and veered off the highway. The narrow road climbed in switchbacks up toward their remote outpost. The rest of the convoy caught up with the truck.

"We got company, boys," Wycroft said needlessly. "Look lively."

They didn't have long to ready themselves.

The truck, along with the Ford staff car and two jeeps, rumbled up toward the guard post. Diesel smoke choked, and gears ground and popped.

Wycroft stepped out of the shade of the shack and into the road. He lifted a palm toward the truck as it pulled up to them. He kept his face stoic, professional.

The heavy vehicle ground to a halt with a complaint of its brakes.

As it idled, Wycroft circled toward the passenger side. Higgins and Mitchell stayed by the shack on the driver's side. Mitchell adjusted his eyeglasses more firmly in place.

The passenger window was down. An elbow rested on the doorsill.

Wycroft called to the truck's occupants, his voice crackling with command. "Sorry, bad news, gentlemen. This whole area's off limits for weapons testing. We're on twenty-four-hour lockdown. That means everyone."

Behind the truck, the Ford staff car's door popped open with a puff of sand and dust. A tall figure unfolded from within. Well over six feet, thick with muscle . . . a good 260 if he was an ounce. His face was as hard as the desert rock, icy and cold.

The man strode purposefully toward him.

Wycroft stumbled back a step—not from the man's size. Instead, he was startled by the silver eagles on the stranger's shoulder, marking him as an officer of the army. Wycroft cracked off a crisp salute, elbow out. "Colonel, sir."

The officer stepped toward Wycroft, silent, his demeanor hardening further.

Wycroft's gaze flicked to his men. The pair had also snapped to attention. Mitchell had shifted so fast, his glasses had slipped down the bridge of his nose.

Wycroft refused to look daunted or cowed. He had his own orders. "Colonel, sir. I'm afraid that goes for you, too. CENTCOM sent out revised deployment oh dark thirty this morning. It cannot be countermanded."

The colonel's thin lips curled, half amusement, half sneer.

"Sir . . . ," Wycroft said, hating the plaintive sound of his voice.

The colonel took another step toward him. Closer now, Wycroft noted the feral glint to his pale blue eyes. The man still hadn't said a word. Something was definitely wrong with this whole situation.

Wycroft's hand went for his holstered sidearm.

A loud crash sounded from the back of the paneled truck. Its rear dropgate had slammed down. Soldiers piled out, moving with a deadly swiftness, weapons, outfitted with silencers, held high.

Wycroft yanked his pistol free.

Too late.

The strange colonel swatted his arm aside. It felt like being struck by a wrecking ball. Wycroft's entire arm went numb, and his pistol flew out into the desert.

Off balance, he felt odd rabbit punches to his chest—but no fist touched him.

Pain bloomed outward as flashes of gunfire, eerily quiet, erupted around him.

He toppled to the sand and rock. Blood poured from his chest.

Off to the side, he saw Higgins fall. No sign of the boy Mitchell. He craned to see more, hoping the boy had run. Then he spied something under the truck to its far side. Behind a massive tire, a pair of legs in desert fatigues lay unmoving. On the other side of the tire, a pair of black eyeglasses reflected the sun. One lens shattered and broken. Both of his men dead.

Why . . . ?

A pair of heavy boots stamped into view, blocking the sight. The colonel leaned down and tugged on his arm, as if trying to pull him up. But he was only removing Wycroft's MP armband. He tossed it toward one of his men, along with the sergeant's helmet.

Another soldier crossed to the gate with a crowbar in hand.

The lock snapped away with one fierce crank.

The gate swung wide.

Nearby, the truck engine roared back to life. The vehicle lurched into motion, followed by the staff car and two jeeps.

Wycroft coughed blood. "No . . ."

He was ignored. The convoy rolled past him and headed through the gate. As his vision faded, Wycroft noted the sign on the fence, naming what he and his men had been posted to guard: HANGAR 51.

He had failed.

A scorpion skittered past his nose, reminding him.

It wasn't only the desert that killed the unwary.

Seated in the truck's passenger seat, the large colonel took off his cap, ran a thick palm over his shaved scalp, and pointed toward the rise. As the road crested the hill, he sat straighter. A desert valley stretched wide and flat ahead, shimmering with heat. The sun blasted the landscape into iron reds and broken scrabble.

Who lived in such a place? The colonel's home was much colder, a place of snow and hard winters, of ice and brittle forests. No wonder the Americans hid their secrets here, where only snakes and tarantulas lived.

Down below, a long airstrip split the valley, a black stripe of tarmac that ended at an impossibly massive hangar. It could easily hold a fleet of jumbo jets, but he knew it held much more.

Despite the miserable heat, he allowed a smile to thin his lips.

They had made it.

It would not be long.

Beside the hangar, a smaller bunker sat atop a hill outfitted with blast doors. A single set of railroad tracks ran out into the deep desert and disappeared among the rocky dunes.

The colonel turned his attention back to the tarmac below and nodded toward their destination. The truck followed the road to the airstrip, leading the convoy to the hangar. They crossed the tarmac and braked before a set of giant steel doors, four stories tall. Etched and painted into the steel was the number 51.

Engines idled, waiting for the colonel's order.

He heard the whisper of his men in the truck bed behind him, anxious, worried at being so deep in the enemy's heartland. In the rearview mirror, he spotted the Ford staff car. Inside that vehicle was the key to unlock the treasure hidden within the hangar.

It had cost him blood and men to obtain it.

The colonel shoved open the passenger door and climbed out. Other soldiers followed suit, ready to set up a perimeter defense in case their cover was blown. He motioned to two men with toolboxes, indicating the hangar doors' circuit box. The doors had to be opened as quickly as possible.

In the meantime he had another duty.

In large strides he crossed to the staff car and nodded to the guards posted at the rear. One leveled a rifle, while another popped the trunk. Two more hauled out a flailing man and set him on his feet. He was tall but slightly paunchy around the middle; he sported a thin gray mustache. His red face streamed with sweat. Bruises marred one side of his face, and a swollen gash blackened one eye. Despite the rifle pointed at his face, he kept a stiff-backed demeanor, even straightening his rumpled brown jacket with a few swift tugs and pats.

The colonel stepped past him, ignoring him.

This one was not important.

One of the soldiers held a picture next to the battered face of the man. "Is that not the professor?" he whispered to his neighbor in Russian.

The colonel silenced the soldier with a glare. Now was not the time for mistakes. In the desert, voices echoed and carried far. It would not be good for voices to be heard speaking Russian on a secret American military installation.

With a wave from the colonel, a second prisoner was dragged out of the trunk, a battered sack of a man. His hair was salt-and-pepper, his beard grizzled over the hard planes of his cheek and chin. He was slammed up onto his battered boots. *Three* rifles leveled at him. No one dared take any chances. Ignoring the threat, the second prisoner searched all around him. His face was just as bruised as the first man's, only bloodier. He had fought them at every turn.

"So he's the one," the soldier with the photo said in Russian.

The key to it all, the colonel added silently. The man was vital to their mission. Under strict orders not to fail, the colonel had plucked the man out of the jungle and brought him here.

Another guard reached back into the trunk and removed an old brown fedora. He mashed it atop the prisoner's head.

The first prisoner rubbed at his mustache. He glanced at the sky, the desert, then back to his fellow captive. He spoke with a crisp British accent.

"Well, Indiana Jones, at least you're back home."

MARCHED AT GUNPOINT across the tarmac, Indy blinked away the sun's glare. The heat scorched and shimmered in waves across the blacktop. With each step, his head pounded from whatever they'd drugged him with. His mouth felt waxy, bitter with a hint of almond and apple. An unfortunately familiar taste . . .

Sodium Pentothal.

The sedative was also used as truth serum.

That couldn't be good.

Indy scratched at the injection site in his neck. How many days had passed? He remembered the attack in the jungle, a long ride in a jeep over muddy roads, an airplane sitting on a remote airstrip. Then they'd drugged him. From the corner of his eye, he sized up the forces around him.

They were heavily armed . . . *too* heavily. These men were no ordinary thieves, nor even rogue mercenaries. They were a military force.

Noting his attention, his fellow prisoner stepped closer and lifted an eyebrow toward their captors. George McHale was a former operative with British intelligence whom Indy had known for nearly two decades. His friend had plainly made the same assessment as Indy about the armed men. He felt a twinge of guilt. Mac had been visiting Indy at the Mayan ruins and had been caught up in the crossfire. The Russian commandos had murdered all the indigenous workers at the camp with a callous brutality. But to what end? What did they want? He still didn't know.

Mac rubbed at his neck. So he'd been drugged, too.

"How you holding up, Mac?" Indy muttered.

His friend shrugged. "I've had better days." As they were marched at gunpoint, Mac lowered his voice and tilted his head toward one of the soldiers. "They're Russian. From the look of them, I'd say Soviet special forces."

"Spetsnaz?"

Mac nodded. "This won't be easy."

"Not as easy as it used to be."

Indy had a hard time hiding his limp. It felt like someone had poured sand into his hip joint. The long trek in the trunk of a car hadn't helped matters. He bit through the agony and forced his back straighter. All he needed was a hot bath, a fistful of aspirin, and he'd be at full steam.

Each painful step sought to convince him otherwise.

"We've been through worse, Indy," Mac said with his usual British aplomb.

"Yeah? When?"

"C'mon, Indy. Don't you remember Flensburg? There were twice as many then. We made it through. There's *always* a way out."

"We were younger then, Mac."

"*I'm* still young."

Indy stared at his old friend. Mac looked like someone had washed him and put him away wet. And it wasn't only the fists that had battered him into this present sorry state. Passing years had been just as cruel. Of course, Indy didn't imagine he looked any better. Still, a spark of Mac's former vigor shone in his old friend's eyes. Plainly fire remained in that old warhorse.

The same couldn't be said for Indy.

It had been a *hard* couple of years.

Motion drew his attention to the left. Over one of the guards' shoulders hung a familiar bit of property. His leather bullwhip. Scarred and frayed, it had also seen better days. Indy felt naked without it. Without any weapons, he had no choice but to cooperate with the Russians for now. Grinding through the pain in his hip, he continued to the hangar.

Indy muttered to Mac as they marched. "And remember, back in Flensburg we had guns."

"Details," Mac said with a dismissive wave. "Five hundred bucks says we get out of this just fine."

Before the wager could be struck, a giant stepped across their path, blocking them. He wore army greens, decorated with the silver eagles of a colonel. Indy recognized him from the assault among the Mayan ruins.

The leader of the Russian stormtroopers.

"Uh, better drop it to *one hundred* on that wager," Mac said.

Off to the side, a second staff car moved down the airstrip toward them. No one seemed surprised or concerned at its approach. Whoever was coming was late to the party.

The colonel moved closer to Indy. He gestured at the massive hangar ahead. A Russian accent weighted down the man's tongue, along with a dark threat. "You recognize this building, *da*?"

"Go to hell," Indy answered, but there was little heat behind his words.

Still, he studied the hangar. In fact, the building *did* look strangely familiar. Indy picked through his memories.

Distracted, he failed to see the Russian's other arm swing at his face. The fist smashed into his chin, cracking his head back. Indy tasted blood as his legs went out from under him. He crumpled to his knees.

Supported on one arm, Indy wiped his split lip while glaring up at the Russian. Fire lit his words now. "Sorry . . . I meant to say go to hell, *comrade.*"

The giant snatched Indy by the shirt collar and hauled him higher, his other arm cocked back, fingers curling into a fist.

A sharp voice cracked out like a pistol shot. *"Prasteete!"*

The arriving staff car braked off to the side. The back door popped open and a slender figure stepped out, rolling smoothly to her feet. Indy was surprised to see it was a woman. Like the others, she was dressed as a US Army soldier, only her uniform fit tighter at the hips, and her boots rose to her knees. Her jet-black hair was bobbed at her shoulders, with bangs cut straight across her forehead. She approached with a leonine grace, all sleek muscle, predatory.

The sword and scabbard belted at her waist accented her threat.

The Russian giant pulled Indy to his feet and straightened to meet her. The colonel saluted the newcomer with no condescension. In fact, Indy noted a flicker of fear in his pale eyes.

That can't be good.

She spoke in English to the tall colonel, as if wanting to be understood by all. "You did it, Colonel Dovchenko. Very good."

So the man *was* a colonel—a Russian colonel.

"Where did you find Professor Jones?" the woman asked.

"In Mexico, digging in the dirt. For this junk."

From over his shoulder, Dovchenko shrugged a satchel into view. Indy recognized his own bag. Dovchenko upended it. Indy lunged forward, but another guard forced him back. From out of the bag, ancient pre-Columbian potsherds shattered on the tarmac, along with a Mayan fertility idol and a chunk of stone carved with rare glyphs. They were all—or had been—priceless pieces of history.

Indy winced. Seven weeks of meticulous work.

He shook his head at the loss and faced the woman. Despite the desert sun, her complexion was snowy and without a drop of sweat. "Let me guess," he said. "You're not from around here."

"And where is it you would imagine I'm from, Dr. Jones?"

He eyed her up and down. "The way you sink your teeth into those *w*'s, I'd say eastern Ukraine."

Her eyes sparkled. "Highest marks to you, Dr. Jones." She held out her hand. "Colonel Doctor Irina Spalko."

Indy refused to shake her hand.

Her face registered no offense. Her wrist turned, and she motioned to the large Russian brute. "You've already met Colonel Antonin Dovchenko."

"Charming fellow. We'll all have to share some borscht. So why don't you tell me what this is all about?"

She cocked her head. "Patience, Dr. Jones. Three times I have received the Order of Lenin, also medal as Hero of Socialist Labor, and why? Because I am assigned to *know* things. To know them *before* anyone else, and what I need to know now—" She reached over to Indy and tapped a slender finger to his forehead. "—is in here."

"Lady, I don't know—"

She leaned closer, catching his gaze with hers. Her eyes were an arctic blue, almost white, with flecks of silvery ice. She stared deeply back at him, intense, disquieting. He did not flinch from her hypnotic attention, which seemed to both disappoint and intrigue her. She stared for a long moment into his eyes, then pulled back. A shadow of a smile haunted her lips as she straightened.

"You are a hard man to read, Dr. Jones. Very interesting. So it seems we must do this the old-fashioned way. You will simply have to tell us. Help us find what we seek."

A loud snap of electricity interrupted, drawing everyone's attention. Off by the hangar, smoke billowed from the power box, and a grind of huge gears sounded. Cheers rose from the men gathered there. To the side, the hangar doors started to rumble open on their tracks, splitting down the middle, straight through the 5 and the 1.

"Now we shall see," Spalko whispered with a hint of hunger.

The party was led toward the yawning entrance. The doors continued to pull back wider and wider. Indy no longer needed the guns at his back to keep moving forward. Curiosity drew him to the hangar. Inside an immense open space beckoned. Lady Liberty herself could have strolled there without lowering her torch.

High above, hanging among the immense steel rafters, ceiling lamps flickered to life—starting with those closest to the door, then spreading down the breadth of the hangar, stretching to an impossible distance. The light revealed an endless expanse of crates stacked to the rafters.

Indy craned his neck and allowed himself to be prodded inside.

Stepping over the door track, he felt a chill of recognition. Even the smell—old wood and diesel oil—took him back. He gaped at the row after row of warehouse shelving, stretching deep into the hangar and to either side. Though he'd never seen the *outside* of the hangar before, he had been *inside* it. A decade earlier, he'd been driven in a bus with blacked-out windows to this location, brought here under high security and secrecy.

Now here he was again.

Indy searched around. Stacks of crates of all sizes, each stamped TOP SECRET, each coded in cryptic government ciphers. This is where Indy's adventures usually *ended*—not started.

What mess had he gotten himself into now?

FOUR

SPALKO WALKED at the American's side. The army personnel carrier and two jeeps trailed their party into the hangar with a rumble of heavy engines, spewing diesel exhaust.

Spalko used the moment to study her captive. He looked older than she had imagined, even from the photographs taken recently. Yet she noted his concentration as he scanned the shelves, the crates, even his sidelong glances at her stormtroopers. He was always thinking, always calculating. Despite his age, there remained a sharpness to the man, along with something hard as steel. She was not daunted. She had broken harder men. She would learn how to *temper* that steel, to bend it to serve her mission. She had never failed before. She didn't intend to now.

She gestured toward the heart of the hangar and led the way forward. "This warehouse, Dr. Jones, is where you and your government have hidden all of your secrets, yes?"

He shook his head. "I've never been here before in my life."

A lie.

They both knew it.

She did not even bother arguing. She counted off what she knew on her fingers. "The object we seek is *a rectangular storage container.* Its dimensions are *two meters by one meter by two hundred centimeters.* The contents of the box are of particular interest—*mummified remains.*"

The American stumbled a step next to her, then caught himself. She did not fail to note the flash of recognition in his eyes, nor the flare of worry across his face. After just a few minutes, she was already learning to read him.

Raising an arm, she stopped him and faced him. "What I described. This is no doubt familiar to you?"

"What makes you think I have any idea what box you're talking about?"

She let her voice ice over with her deadly intent. "Because, Dr. Jones, ten years ago you were part of the team that examined it."

"Listen, sister, even if I knew what you—"

With the swiftness of a striking snake, she whipped the rapier from her scabbard. Silver flashed in the darkness, and the tip of her sword came to rest over his carotid. She held it steady. Studying the pulse of that artery, she noted his heart rate spike. But her adversary kept his face hard, unimpressed. Still, a trickle of sweat on his brow betrayed him. What the face hid, the body revealed.

Spalko smiled coldly inside, satisfied. It wouldn't be long until she could read the man as easily as Tolstoy's *War and Peace.* All it took was attention to detail . . . and patience.

She punctuated her next words with incremental increases of pressure. "You will. Help us. Find it!"

A single drop of blood welled around her sword point. It rolled to the hollow of his throat.

His expression remained icy to match her own.

"Killing me's not gonna solve your problem."

She did not lower her sword. "Perhaps you are correct."

She already knew where the prisoner was most tender, where he could best be harmed. For Dr. Jones, threats would not work—at least not threats against himself. She barked an order.

One of the soldiers swung around and slammed a fist into the ample belly of Dr. Jones's companion. George McHale doubled over with a cough of pain and dropped to his knees. Another two soldiers grabbed him under the arms and dragged him toward the idling army truck. The soldiers forced McHale to the floor and jammed his head behind the rear tire.

Spalko nodded to the driver. With a crank of gears, he slipped the truck into reverse. Before he could hit the gas, the American held up both arms.

"Okay, okay!"

She lowered her sword. "The box, Dr. Jones? Where is it?"

He stared into the enormity of the space. "Lady, I don't have a clue. It could be anywhere in here."

Spalko turned back to the driver and lifted her arm.

"Wait!" Dr. Jones barked at her. "Give a guy a chance to think already! There must be a way of finding that box."

He searched around, turning in a slow circle. She noted that his eyes held a spark of panic—but also deep concentration.

Dovchenko stepped toward him threateningly, but she waved the colonel back. She was dancing a delicate game of force and manipulation with this American. She would not have Dovchenko interfere. At least not yet.

Spalko continued her study of the man. She watched his breathing, the set of his shoulders, the rub of a finger under his chin. She picked out telltale facial tics—including a slight widening of his eyes.

Dr. Jones suddenly snapped his fingers. "I need a compass," he ordered and thrust an arm out, his palm up.

No one moved closer. A few soldiers glanced at one another in confusion.

"A compass!" he demanded. "You know, *north, south, east*?"

"And *west*!" his friend added with a shudder as he was pulled from beneath the truck.

"What kind of soldiers are you?" Dr. Jones pressed. "Nobody's got a compass?"

The American searched the blank faces. His gaze settled upon Dovchenko's gun.

"Give me your bullets," he ordered, holding out his hand.

Dovchenko laughed with a curl of his lip, but Spalko had recognized the dawning realization in the widening of the American's eyes, in the dilation of his pupils. It was no ruse.

Dr. Jones continued, "Listen to me. Do you want my help or not?" He waved an arm out toward the warehouse's depths. "The contents of the box out there are highly *magnetized*."

She nodded to Dovchenko. "Do what he says."

Moments later Indy knelt beside an open toolbox provided by one of the Russians. He grabbed a pair of pliers and twisted off the top of one of the bullets. He hoped this would work, because he had no other ideas.

Mac leaned over him and rubbed his neck with worry. "Do you know what you're doing, Indiana?"

"What I'm doing? I'm keeping that pretty little head of yours on your shoulders."

Indy shook the bullet casing and dumped the gunpowder into his palm. He repeated the process with several more bullets.

"Well, if nothing else, you're at least slowly disarming them," Mac said with a tired smile. "One bullet at a time."

Finished, Indy stood up. He felt the woman's eyes upon him, watching his every move. Her gaze itched across his skin as he crossed to an intersection of warehouse aisles.

She came up beside him.

"If the contents of the crate are still magnetized," he explained, "the metal in the gunpowder should point the way."

He lifted his hand and blew into his open palm. A plume of fine gunpowder wafted up into a diffuse cloud. Hanging in midair, it began to coalesce, drawn together by unseen forces, like iron shavings in the presence of a magnet. As everyone watched, the powder settled to the cement floor. It formed a perfect line, aiming down one of the aisles.

He turned for acknowledgment of his ingenuity, only to find Spalko hurrying down the aisle ahead of him. So much for appreciation. With a grumble, Indy followed after her. She eventually slowed, searching both sides. Wooden crates and boxes climbed toward the rafters.

"But which one?" she cried out in frustration. "There are still thousands in this direction."

Indy pointed to a soldier with a shotgun. "Pellets. I need one of the shells."

Spalko stared at him, her eyes narrowed. Then she turned and shouted crisp orders. The soldier frowned at the strangeness but obeyed. He ejected a shotgun shell and handed it carefully to Indy.

Stepping to the side, Indy promptly bit through the shell's cardboard casing. He grimaced at the taste of black powder, then dumped the shell's contents on the floor. The number eight iron birdshot bounced like tiny ball bearings across the concrete floor—then one pellet rolled to the left, drawing others with it. A trickle became a rush, picking up speed down the aisle and following the lines of magnetic force.

Or so he hoped.

Indy and Spalko chased after the birdshot.

The stream of metallic pellets raced through the warehouse. Even running at full speed, Indy and Spalko were hard-pressed to follow them. The jeeps trailed behind, filling the space with their exhaust. It was the strangest chase of Indy's life.

At last, the pellets reached the base of a stack of crates ahead.

By now Indy was breathless, limping hard. "That must be—"

The birdshot wasn't done. The pellets climbed the side of the stack and began disappearing through the space between two crates.

"Hurry!" Indy called out. "Give me a hand!"

Dovchenko came to his aid. Together they hauled the outermost crate off the shelf and heaved it to the floor. It cracked open, spilling dossiers marked EYES ONLY. Indy ignored them and stared into the hole created by the now broken crate. More wooden boxes—all identical—still blocked the way. The pellets were nowhere in sight.

"Clear out more!" Indy shouted, pointing.

Other soldiers tugged and heaved, stacking boxes in the aisle. The shelf space cleared and widened. Spalko shone a flashlight into the depths. Near the back, the face of a crate quivered—covered with metallic birdshot.

It was the crate they sought.

Indy glanced at the Russian woman. In the reflected lamplight, her eyes glowed as she backed away. She waved two soldiers to pull the crate out. With a bit of grunting and swearing, it was hauled out into the open. Indy noted that the hands on one of the soldiers' wristwatches spun erratically then settled to a stop, pointed at the crate. The box was of the exact dimensions that Spalko had described: the size of a small coffin, only a bit thinner. Her intel was spot-on.

Spalko grabbed a prybar from one of the soldiers. Indy knew she would not let anyone else open the crate. Her eyes were wild with expectation.

"*Moyo zolotse . . .* ," she muttered to herself in Russian, as if it were a prayer.

Digging the bar into a corner, she cracked the wooden lid of the coffin. Indy caught a glimpse of stenciling, half burned away. He made out a few letters and numbers.

swell, N.M. 7–9–47

It was the right crate.

As the slats were pulled away, a stainless-steel tank was revealed, cushioned and packed in hay. A curved lid sealed the tank's upper side. With a nod from Spalko, one of the soldiers fitted a crowbar into a slot at the top of the lid. He cranked on it and broke the seal with a hiss.

A thick, bluish gas escaped, swirling upward.

Overhead, the lamps in the rafters swung like compass needles, all pointing toward the open crate.

The lid slid fully open. Inside lay a shape cocooned in silvery metallic wrapping. The strange covering seemed to both reflect and absorb the light, like oil on water. Indy felt subtle emanations that made the hairs on the back of his neck quiver.

Seemingly oblivious to whatever it was that Indy was feeling, the soldiers knelt to either side and carefully teased back the crinkled shroud. There were layers of it, like an onion. Again the hands of their watches spun. One man's timepiece was even ripped from his wrist and pulled to the highly magnetized wrapping. Stray shotgun pellets also flew and glued themselves to the surface.

No longer able to contain herself, Spalko leaned forward.

She peeled the last layer from the mummified remains herself. The others gathered more tightly around the coffin. Indy couldn't see what lay within the box. But as Spalko straightened, he saw her lift free the inner layer of the metallic shroud. It held, fixed to the shape of the coffin's contents: a silvery death mask of a humanoid head. Only this skull's cranium was elongated unnaturally, and the zygomatic arches framed an oversized pair of eyes, almost insect-like in appearance.

Others gathered for an even closer peek.

This was what they all had come to find.

But not Indy.

He eased to the side and slipped behind two soldiers. He had another goal in mind. He edged toward his target.

Spalko must have sensed something. She turned sharply and fixed him with a hard stare. Their eyes met for a moment—then a shout rose to her lips, calling out a warning.

Too late, sister.

Indy had found what he was looking for. He grabbed the handle of his bullwhip, still hanging from a soldier's shoulder. The warm leather fit his grip like a tailored glove. The soldier turned toward him, but Indy shoulder-blocked the man to the floor and yanked the whip free.

The Russian guarding Mac shoved his pistol toward Indy.

Not today.

Indy snapped out his arm, and the bullwhip unfurled with a fierce crack. The lash struck the soldier's wrist and wrapped tightly around it. Surprise lit the man's face.

That was one advantage of age: plenty of time to practice.

The soldier on the floor scrambled his rifle around.

Indy flicked his wrist with a twist, causing Mac's guard to fire his snared pistol. The shot struck the rifleman in the chest and knocked him dead to the ground. Without pausing, Indy yanked hard on the whip and hauled Mac's guard toward him. The soldier lost his balance and came spinning into Indy's arms.

Indy snatched the pistol with his free hand and tossed it to Mac, who fumbled but caught it. Indy shoved the guard into Spalko and the other soldiers.

Backing, Indy scooped up the dead man's rifle into his own hands. The remaining soldiers finally brought their own guns to bear, but Indy had joined Mac. They stood back-to-back against the Russians.

Just like old times.

Indy kept his weapon leveled at Spalko, who stood a yard away.

"Guns down!" he shouted. "Put 'em down or the colonel doctor is dead."

The soldiers began to obey. Only Dovchenko refused. The massive horse pistol clutched in the colonel's fist remained pointed at Indy.

"Do it!" Indy warned, but he suddenly sensed something wrong.

Especially when Spalko crossed her arms and smiled, all ice and amusement. He felt Mac shift behind him. Indy had a sinking feeling in his gut.

It can't be . . .

Indy turned in disbelief.

The barrel of Mac's gun was pointed at Indy's head.

FIVE

INDY WATCHED MAC STROLL OVER to join Spalko and Dovchenko. His friend at least had the decency to look embarrassed, hanging his head, not meeting Indy's hard stare. Anger and grief warred in Indy's heart. He could barely form words.

"Mac? Why?"

His friend of two decades only shrugged. "What can I tell you, Indy? I'm no Communist, if that's what you were thinking. Just a good *capitalist*. And they paid. Paid very well."

The war in Indy's heart settled on anger. "Are you kiddin' me? After all those years we were *spying* on the Reds?"

Mac shrugged again, cocking his head with a shamed half smile. "Had a bad run of cards, mate. Awful. *Legendarily* awful." He glanced up at the stacks of crates. A hunger shone in his eyes as he clearly contemplated the wealth of secrets here. "Can't go home empty-handed all my life."

Dovchenko stepped forward. He cocked the slide back on his massive handgun, his intent plain. He was going to enjoy what came next.

Spalko rested her hand on the pommel of her sword. "No defiant last words, Dr. Jones?"

He thought for a moment and came up with something suitably patriotic in the face of the sting of betrayal. Simple was best.

"I like Ike."

Dovchenko was not amused. He raised his weapon. "Put gun down. And whip. Now."

Indy lifted his arms in surrender. "You got it, pal."

He pitched the weapon high, underhanded, straight into a thicket of Russian soldiers who bristled with automatic weapons. The rifle struck the floor with a bang, firing off a round. The shot sparked off the concrete floor—but not before ripping through the foot of one of the soldiers.

A shocked scream of pain rang out. The injured soldier flailed back. But as Indy had hoped, pain evoked a reflexive response: Fingers tightened in agony, including a *trigger* finger. As the soldier fell, bullets sprayed from his automatic weapon, flying all around, pinging off the idling jeeps nearby, peppering crates. Soldiers ducked for cover.

Even Dovchenko and Spalko.

Indy spun and ran for the nearby pile of discarded crates. He mounted them like a wooden staircase, leaped to the shelving overhead, and scrambled up. He heaved himself up on the shelf—then dropped flat, catching his breath. His lungs were on fire.

Grimacing, he searched for a means of escape. Around him a sea of crates spread in every direction, staggered in height, riddled with dark gaps.

Not good.

Risking a look below, he spotted Dovchenko and Mac rising to their feet. Other soldiers followed suit. Weapons aimed at his hiding place. Before he ducked away, a sharp shout drew his eyes.

Spalko.

She fled down the row, yelling to two soldiers who were loading the strange coffin into the back of an idling jeep. Spalko jumped into the driver's seat, hit the gas, and sped off down the aisle. The lamps in the rafters swung to follow her path, pointing after her, drawn by her magnetic cargo.

A second jeep followed her.

No you don't, sister.

Rising into a low crouch, Indy ran along the top row of this aisle's crates. Bullets chased him, shredding the boxes at his heels.

As he reached the end of the aisle, the hanging lamp overhead swung like a compass needle. Spalko's jeep raced just ahead.

Now or never.

Indy leaped from the end of the shelf, cracked out with his whip, and snagged the swaying lamp. Behind him, the last crate exploded under a fusillade of gunfire. Holding tight with one hand, Indy soared over the heads of the stunned Russians. The arc of his swing aimed straight for Spalko's fleeing jeep.

Or so he thought.

As he reached the end of his swing, the heels of Indy's boots danced along the top of the coffin in the back of the jeep—only the vehicle sped onward while he swung back.

Toward the Russians.

Overhead, his bullwhip unraveled with a sickening lurch.

This was not going to be pretty.

He plummeted toward the floor—and crashed smack into the front seat of the jeep trailing Spalko's. He landed between two startled Russians.

"*Damn,* that looked closer," he said and threw an elbow into the face of the passenger, then sucker-punched the driver in the ear. The two Russians fell out opposite doors.

Indy slid into the driver's seat, punched the gas, and clutched tight to the wheel. He sped after Spalko's jeep, then drew up alongside it.

Hearing the roar, the woman glanced over. Indy enjoyed the surprised look in her eyes.

She hadn't been expecting *that.*

Nor *this.*

Indy jerked his wheel and slammed into the side of her vehicle. She lost control and crashed into a nest of crates. The impact sent her flying out of the jeep and tumbling into the pile of broken boxes.

Indy braked to a stop and leaped from his jeep and into hers.

Sorry, sister.

He threw the jeep into reverse, cleared the boxes, then slammed on the gas. Burning rubber on the concrete, he shot toward the distant exit. He glanced over his shoulder to make sure the coffin was still in back.

Good.

He could not let the Russians get ahold of it.

Behind the jeep, he noted Spalko picking herself out of the debris, unharmed.

Not so good.

He swung back around in his seat and aimed for the exit. But as he crossed an intersection of aisles in the giant warehouse, one of the Ford staff cars swung into view, blocking the way, and shot directly at him.

Indy yanked the wheel and raced down another alleyway—only to find the aisle blocked by the massive army personnel carrier. The heavy truck barreled toward him. In his rearview mirror, the staff car rounded the corner with a squeal of rubber.

He was trapped.

Indy searched for the only direction open to him.

Up.

Ahead, one of the steel I-beams that supported the massive roof ran low across the aisle. Indy gunned the engine and rocketed straight for the truck in a deadly game of chicken.

Keeping the jeep in gear, he edged up onto his seat, loosed his whip, and held his breath. The headlights of the army personnel carrier speared toward him.

At the last moment, he snapped out with his bullwhip. The lash cracked like a gunshot—and wrapped snugly around the beam above.

And not a second too soon.

Holding tight to the whip, Indy was yanked out of the jeep, and momentum carried him high into the air. The sudden jerk strained his shoulder with a rip of fire, but he dared not let go.

Below, brakes and drivers screamed.

The personnel carrier and staff car collided with Indy's jeep at the same time, crumpling the vehicle between them like an accordion. The carrier and staff car spun off to the sides and smashed into stacks of crates. Wood exploded, and top-secret contents blasted into the air.

Indy landed amid the debris. He quickly shook loose his whip, but a glint of gold caught his eye. It shone from a cracked crate, damaged during the collision. Indy spied a familiar gold handle to a bejeweled box. He froze.

Could it be?

The Ark of the—

He leaned closer. "Geez, will ya look at that."

Bullets ripped past his nose and chewed across the bank of crates. Indy fell back. No time for gawking. He dove behind some boxes for cover, but not before he noted Mac climbing out of the staff car.

A pistol in his hand.

The two men made eye contact, staring across the wreckage of the smashed vehicles—and the wreckage of their friendship.

Mac lifted the gun. "Stop, Indy. There's no way out of here."

Indy returned his friend's earlier words. "There's *always* a way out, Mac!"

Indy ducked out of sight and hightailed it for the open hangar doors. He aimed for the glow of daylight across the gloomy hangar. It was still a long way off. He would have to be careful—and quick. With his ears ringing from all the gunfire, he ran through the shadows toward that light.

As he crossed the mouth of another aisle, he didn't hear the jeep until it was too late. It blasted straight at him. There was no getting out of the way in time. Indy leaped straight up. Not high enough this time. The front of the jeep struck his boots and sent him flying across the hood. He crashed into the windshield. Dazed, he clung to the glass like a splattered fly.

A familiar face stared back at him from the driver's seat.

Dovchenko.

With his view blocked by Indy's body, Dovchenko struggled to control the jeep's careening course. Indy twisted around in time to see the vehicle sailing straight for a tunnel in the back wall of the hangar.

No, not a tunnel.

It was a set of cement stairs leading *down*.

Indy braced himself, fingers clutching the edge of the windshield.

This was not going to be good.

SIX

DOVCHENKO DIDN'T UNDERSTAND the danger until it was too late. One minute he was racing along an aisle, and the next his jeep was bouncing down a wide set of stairs. It rattled his molars and sought to shake him out of his seat. He clenched the steering wheel with an iron grip.

With a final jarring impact, the vehicle crashed to the bottom of the stairs and came to a skidding stop in a huge subterranean chamber. Dovchenko breathed hard, his heart hammering, his arms trembling. He glanced around.

A flatbed railcar rested in the middle of the room, clamped to a set of tracks that led off down a subterranean tunnel. Staring at the rails, Dovchenko realized where he was. Earlier today he had spotted railroad tracks heading out into the desert, leading off from a hilltop bunker that neighbored the hangar. He must have crashed into that bunker.

A groan drew his attention. The American slid off the jeep's hood. Jones gained his feet, wobbling and unsteady, and began backpedaling away.

No you don't.

Dovchenko unclamped his hands from the steering wheel and climbed out of the jeep. He stalked after the man and slammed bodily into him, shoving out with his arms. The American sailed backward and fell heavily onto the open flatbed of the railway car.

Closing in on the man, Dovchenko frowned at the strange car. Someone had crudely bolted a jet engine to the rear of the flatbed. Before he could gain any understanding, Jones stirred and sought to pull himself back up. His fumbling hand brushed a control panel on the car.

A red light flashed, and an alarm rang out.

To Dovchenko's right, light began to stream into the room, brighter and brighter. A set of blast doors trundled open at the far end of the railway tunnel. Daylight flooded inside. Jones turned toward the brilliance and struggled to his feet.

There would be no escape that way.

Dovchenko climbed atop the railway car.

The American swung a fist at Dovchenko, hard, with more strength than the Russian had thought Jones could muster. Still, he barely felt it. He lunged forward and pinned Jones against the rear engine cowling. It took only one hand to hold him in place and the other to throttle him.

Dovchenko slowly squeezed his fingers as Jones struggled.

He enjoyed watching the man's face turn blue, then desperate.

This is how you die, Jones.

His captive's eyes went wild. Mashed against the cowling, Jones sought some means of escape. Not this time. Sudden movement at the stairs drew their attention. George McHale stumbled into view down the steps, a pistol raised and ready. The Brit took in the situation with a glance.

"Colonel Dovchenko," McHale called out. "Irina wants Jones alive. You know that!"

Dovchenko read the hope in Indy's eyes. With a sneer of satisfaction, he squeezed harder.

"Dovchenko!" McHale barked.

Strangling, Jones cast out a silent appeal to the man who had once been his friend. Dovchenko noted Jones staring hard at McHale, specifically at the pistol—then back at Dovchenko.

Begging for help, begging him to shoot.

Instead McHale lowered his pistol and looked away. "I'm sorry, Indy."

Dovchenko felt the heart go out of his captive. This last betrayal had killed him more than any throttling fingers.

Then a loud crash sounded from behind the railcar. A second jeep burst through the door to a narrow access tunnel, carrying three Russian soldiers. There was no escape.

It was over.

Dovchenko tightened the fist around Jones's throat. He leaned forward and whispered in his ear with disdain. "Good-bye, *comrade.*"

As Dovchenko straightened, he saw that the defeated look in the man's eyes had flamed to fury, and he noted where Jones now stared. Before Dovchenko could react, the American's foot lashed out and kicked a throttle hidden alongside the control panel.

The jet engine roared to life. Rippling white fire blasted out the back of the rocket, incinerating his fellow soldiers and exploding the jeep's fuel tank. Dovchenko fell back, letting go of Jones, who slid to his knees, gasping in the heat. The British traitor dove for the cement stairs, chased by flames.

Dovchenko turned just as the engine *fully* engaged.

The railcar detonated down the railroad tracks, turning into a *rocket sled.* Both men were thrown to a cushioned shield at the back of the car.

The sled dove into the tunnel. The walls blurred as thrust pinned the men in place. Dovchenko's ribs squeezed toward his heart. Lights strobed into a blur. Then in a fraction of a second the sled shot out the blast doors and headed across the desert, straight for the setting sun. The light was blinding, but Dovchenko couldn't close his eyelids; g-force and wind held them peeled open.

The sled continued to rocket across the blasted landscape.

But to where?

A minute later, Spalko stood with George McHale by the hangar. The back of the man's clothes still smoked. She stared across the twilit desert. A moment earlier, she had witnessed a streak of fire lancing low across the desert.

A sonic boom had followed a second later.

She had not understood what it meant until George McHale had arrived, half burned. "They were both aboard?" she asked again. "Dovchenko and Jones?"

He nodded and waved the smoke from his charred clothes with a wide-brimmed hat.

"Could they still be alive?" she asked.

He shrugged, but she still read the concern in his eyes as he stared off toward the fading sun. Though the man had betrayed his friend, there remained something between them, something that weighed on his heart—even if it was only the passage of time.

One of the staff cars and the lone remaining jeep rolled up, battered and dented. Spalko pointed out into the desert and gave her orders. The vehicles sped off across the sand, heading straight as the crow flies, following the smoky contrail left behind by the rocket sled.

Uncomfortable with uncertainty, she wanted to know the truth. Especially concerning Dr. Henry Jones Jr. She dared not leave Jones behind.

At least not alive.

INDY FELT THE WEIGHT of the world sitting on his chest. Or maybe two or three worlds. He still could not breathe. Accelerating g-force squeezed his vision narrow. The landscape blurred around him, turning reality into one long, rushing tunnel.

All the while, thrust stretched his face toward the back of his skull.

The sled covered miles in moments—then as abruptly as it had started, it ended.

The booster engine shut down. The rocket engine's brakes engaged, locking onto the rails and slowing their speed. The sled glided smoothly to the end of the tracks. It came to a gentle stop with the softest *thump* against a giant rubber bumper. A small dark shack marked the end of the line.

Freed, both men stumbled away from the blast shield. They fell off the railcar—but their war wasn't over. They immediately set upon each other, like punch-drunk fighters.

Indy swung a fist but missed his large target by a good foot.

Still, Dovchenko toppled backward as if KO'd by the errant

swing. The giant struck the sandy railbed, out cold. His larger body had not fared as well against the g-force. It was all a matter of mass and gravity.

Indy sat heavily on the railcar.

Across the desert he noted plumes of dust aiming in his direction. Certainly not a rescue crew. He wasn't *that* dazed. It had to be Spalko's men.

Indy climbed back to his feet. Turning away, he spotted the twinkle of lights through the dusk. A town? Out here? Regardless, surely someone could help him. He stumbled across the desert toward the only sign of habitation.

He had to raise the alarm.

The Russians were coming.

"Just leave it," Mac called over to Irina Spalko.

She didn't acknowledge him. She continued to drag the steel coffin down the aisle toward the crashed staff car. She refused to leave without it.

As she struggled with her obsession, Mac worried about the one thing dearest to his heart. *His own survival.* He had gotten the sedan's engine running, but the crumpled hood had been a problem. He had unbolted it and tugged it off, turning the staff car into what looked like a hot rod.

Across the giant hangar, the squeal of braking tires echoed from the open hangar door. The *real* US Marines had arrived, drawn by the firing of the rocket sled and subsequent alarms. There was no more time.

Mac hurried to the rear of the sedan and helped Spalko lift the coffin into the trunk—the same trunk he and Indy had been locked inside for most of the day. He shied away from the thought and slammed the trunk lid down. He stared off at the general trajectory of the flying rocket sled.

Sorry, Indiana.

But what was done was done. He had made his choice.

Mac climbed into the driver's seat, and Spalko settled on the passenger side. He gently hit the gas and edged the staff car toward the rear exit of the hangar. Behind them, orders were shouted across the expanse, echoing loudly.

Mac risked a little more speed.

As the marines entered the front of the hangar, they slipped out the back and into the deepening twilight. Mac raced across the desert.

"At least we got what we came for," Spalko mumbled.

But not what we deserve, Mac thought.

Dovchenko woke to stars.

Hands pulled him from the sand, dusted him off, and offered him tepid water. He scattered his men away with a sweep of his large arm. Enough. He stumbled a few steps and sucked in deep draughts of the night air. His head pounded, and his eyes burned like ground glass.

Off to the side, a staff car and jeep waited, engines idling.

Men waited, too. He searched among them.

There was no sign of Jones.

"Where is he?" he grumbled in Russian.

One of his men shook his head. "He was gone when we got here."

Lifting a corner of his lip in a silent growl, Dovchenko continued in a slow circle of the railcar. He discovered a set of boot prints in the sand and knelt beside them. The tracks headed off into the desert.

Jones.

Dovchenko narrowed his eyes and followed the path of the tracks. Across the rocky landscape, lights sparkled in the distance near the horizon. He stood up and grabbed one of his men by the collar. He pointed to the footprints, then to the distant lights.

"Find him," he ordered hoarsely in Russian. "Kill him and anyone he talks to."

With a nod, the man waved two more soldiers into the idling jeep. Motor growling, the jeep set off through the desert, casting up sand and heading toward the distant town.

Dovchenko watched for a few breaths, then scowled darkly and limped over to the staff car. He fell into the backseat. The driver turned the sedan around and headed in the opposite direction, back the way they'd come.

Dovchenko stared at the blasted landscape.

He'd had enough of the damn desert.

EIGHT

INDY HOBBLED INTO the small desert town. He could barely keep himself upright after the long walk. He crossed the main street, weaving in an unsteady course. Dark shops lined both sides of the street, closed at this hour. Streetlamps glowed merrily. Down the way, a gas station's neon sign slowly turned. Off in the distance he heard music drifting from some bar or diner that was still open.

He limped toward the sound, hopeful for a glass of water.

His throat was full of sand.

He jiggled his pockets. No money. He would have to hope for charity.

As he drifted down the center of the street, he kept an eye out for a police station or some other authority. The alarm needed to be raised. The Russians had to be stopped.

As he walked, Indy noted a few cars lining the street. He considered hotwiring one, but he had neither the strength nor the will. As much as he hated to admit it, he needed help.

Reaching the main crossroads in town, he stopped, unsure where to go. Then a rumble caused him to turn and look behind him. Off in the desert, a vehicle approached the town's edge. One headlamp shone brightly; the other was busted. He made out the vague shape of a jeep.

The Russians had followed him.

Indy slid around the corner and hid out of sight as the vehicle entered the town. It slowly crept down the main street, searching for him.

He swore and leaned on the wall for a breath, but he knew he had to keep moving.

Stifling a groan, he pushed off and hurried away from the intersection. The street had a row of tidy houses with manicured lawns, flowering window boxes, and picket fences. He hated to bring trouble down upon the peaceful residents, but he had no choice.

He also had to get off the road.

He cut between two houses and into a backyard. Focused on the street behind him, he plowed straight into somebody's laundry hanging on a line. He fought his way through it as if it were an Aboriginal pig net. Finally freed, he trampled the linen and headed toward the back door of the house.

Lights shone through the floral pattern of the window curtains.

He heard voices. And music.

Indy knocked softly, but there was no response. He dared not shout. He found the door unlocked and risked barging inside. He pushed into a tidy kitchen with a checkerboard-tiled floor and the latest appliances, including a heavy-duty King Cool refrigerator.

He glanced longingly at it, wanting to raid the icebox, to find something cold to drink.

But not yet.

"Hello? Anybody?" His voice was a scratched record. Even he barely heard it.

Desperate, he hurried into the living room, where the music grew louder. It rose from a TV set, airing *The Howdy Doody Show*. The theme song played as a family sat with their backs to him: mother, father, two kids. Again Indy felt a pang for destroying the perfect tableau here, especially as it was a life that would never be his.

But he had no choice.

He noted a phone on an entryway table. He grabbed the handset and started to dial. He called over to the father seated in an overstuffed wing chair. He fought his dry throat, parched tongue. He willed his voice to urgency.

"Russians! Spies! They broke into the military base and—" With the phone at his ear, he heard no dial tone. He clicked the receiver a few times. "Don't you have a phone that works?"

Nobody moved. Nobody answered. They just stared, transfixed, at the television set. On the screen, the freckled face of Howdy Doody chuckled and guffawed.

What's wrong with you people?

He limped to the father and grabbed the man's arm—but it came off in his hands. The man toppled out of his armchair, stiff, head at an impossible angle, a grin fixed on his waxen face.

Shock pushed Indy away.

A mannequin.

From the television, Buffalo Bob announced, "Why, Howdy, haven't you guessed yet? It's an *imaginary* place."

Indy glanced closer at the others.

All mannequins.

Dehydrated, exhausted, Indy could not process what was happening. He stood in place, frozen like the wax figures. He needed to get moving, but he couldn't.

Then as if trying to wake him, the blast of a siren wailed from the street outside. He turned his head toward the noise, something horrible coming together in his mind.

He recognized that klaxon.

An air-raid siren.

"Oh, that can't be good."

He rushed to the front door and shoved it open. He stumbled onto the covered porch, then down to the lawn. A mannequin mailman stood frozen by the mailbox, wax letters in hand. Across the street, a man walked a fake dog, forever in midstride. Up the street, a group of children were locked in a permanent game of kickball, while a passerby waved to them from his stalled Buick.

Indy noted a sign at the edge of the street. He noted the word WELCOME at the top. He swung closer to read it fully.

Welcome to Doom Town
U.S. Army Proving Ground
Civilians Forbidden!

Indy backed away. *That can't be good at all.*

The siren abruptly ended with a squelch, replaced by a deafening voice.

"ALL PERSONNEL TAKE FINAL POSITIONS. COUNT-DOWN TO DETONATION COMMENCING AT T-MINUS ONE MINUTE."

NINE

INDY DASHED down the street and back to the intersection, his pains forgotten in his panic. It was amazing how the threat of a fiery death could get one moving again, lubricating aching joints with raw terror.

As he rounded the bend, sparks suddenly flashed at his toes, and bees buzzed past his ear. Terrified, it took him an extra moment to realize he was being shot at. The threat seemed minor compared with what was coming.

Still, death was death.

In a diving roll, he ducked behind a mailbox. Risking a quick look, he spotted the Russian sniper as the man popped out of hiding behind a car and rushed his position. The sniper angled for a better vantage.

Indy had nowhere to go.

Then behind him, an engine roared. He twisted around as the battered army jeep careened around the corner a few blocks away, taking the turn on two wheels. It blasted straight at him. The soldier on the passenger side rose up and leveled his rifle over the windshield.

Ambush.

Little late, guys.

The loudspeaker confirmed it. "T-MINUS FORTY-FIVE SECONDS."

The sniper on the ground swung wide, looking for a clear shot. A round ricocheted off the metal mailbox like a gong.

Indy realized the impossibility of the situation and stood up, hands on his head. What did he have to lose?

"Wait!" he yelled. "Stop, you idiots! Don't you realize what *that* is?"

He pointed off into the distance, beyond the far end of Main Street. Perched on a hill overlooking the town stood a metal-framed tower festooned with speakers and sirens. Suspended from a platform in the middle hung a round metal ball, draped with wires and detonating cords.

It might as well have had BOMB written on its side.

In this particular case—*NUCLEAR* BOMB!

The Russian sniper's eyes went wide with recognition. Turning away, he ran out into the middle of the street and waved his rifle overhead. He screamed in Russian to his comrades in the jeep and pointed his rifle toward the hill.

The jeep shimmied as the realization struck the vehicle's driver. Then it steadied and sped toward the lone sniper. It slowed only long enough to allow the rifleman to leap headlong into the back—then sped off again.

Indy stumbled into the street after them, a forlorn arm in the air. "Sure! Don't wait for me!"

He ran a few steps in their direction, then realized how pointless it was.

The jeep left Main Street and shot out into the desert, casting up sand and cactus in its frantic wake.

"T-MINUS THIRTY SECONDS AND COUNTING."

Indy knew he had only one chance. He turned and ran—not *out* of town, but deeper into it. He headed back to the same little handsome street, to the same picture-perfect home. The front door of the house was still open. He crossed the yard, leaped the porch steps, and barreled through the living room.

He raced down the short hall, dogged by the inanely cheerful Howdy Doody theme music.

"T-MINUS FIFTEEN SECONDS AND COUNTING."

Indy burst into the kitchen and ran straight for the heavy-duty King Cool refrigerator. He threw open the door.

"T-MINUS TEN SECONDS AND COUNTING."

"C'mon, c'mon . . ."

Frantic, he hauled everything out of the fridge, shelves and all. He took a moment to pop an ice cube into his mouth for his parched throat. He sucked on the ice, savoring the cool water trickling down his throat. It might be his last chance.

"T-MINUS FIVE SECONDS AND COUNTING."

He crammed himself into the fridge and yanked hard on the door—

"FOUR."

—but the door bounced back open. His leather jacket had jammed it.

"THREE."

He tugged his jacket fully into the fridge and—

"TWO."

—slammed the door closed.

Just as the little interior light blinked off, Indy read the small steel plate affixed to the upper corner of the door. It read—

LEAD-LINED FOR SUPERIOR INSULATION!

"ONE."

A mile outside Doom Town the Russian sniper stared back toward the deadly steeple. His heart pounded as the jeep bounced and rattled. He never saw the brilliant burst of blazing white light. The world simply went black as the flash instantly blinded him, searing away his retinas.

The driver wasn't so lucky. The detonation lit up the desert for miles ahead, casting the world in an eerie brilliance. In his rearview mirror, he watched the world burst into flame. A massive blast wave of brimstone and hellfire rocketed across the flats, turning sand to glass in its wake.

He watched his doom sweep toward him.

In the instant before the blast wave vaporized them and melted the jeep into the sand, the Russian witnessed a strange sight:

A refrigerator flew through the air, riding the blast wave.

It shot overhead—then fire consumed the world.

Indy never remembered hitting the ground. In fact, he remembered nothing beyond waking in the dark, enclosed space. For a terrified moment he thought he'd been buried alive. For an archaeologist like him, it was a constant fear in ancient tunnels and tombs. Panicked, he punched and clawed in the darkness.

Then he remembered it all.

And his panic grew worse.

He fought, shouldered, and kicked at the refrigerator door. Finally the latch gave way, and the door fell open. The heat of a blast furnace swept over him as he fell out of the tight confinement. The refrigerator, half melted and blackened, lay buried amid a pile of smoking slag and debris.

Indy stumbled a few steps, struggling to find cool air.

He finally gave up and straightened, staring straight into the face of Hell.

A mile away, a massive mushroom cloud rose from the desert floor. It climbed in a swirling column of smoke and fire. For a moment, Indy imagined hollowed-out eye sockets and the gaping maw of a skull.

Human or demon.

At this moment, staring at what man had created, Indy doubted there was any difference.

HOURS LATER, Indy stood naked in a decontamination room on the military base. Four soldiers took sadistic pleasure in scrubbing him with bristled brushes, discovering creases and crevices he never knew were there. As they scoured his flesh raw, the soldiers continued an ongoing humiliating commentary on the state of his body. It was not flattering.

So he had a few scars. Who didn't? Each one told a story from a life lived at the shadowy edge of history. Over the past decades he'd traveled to every continent and most countries; he'd scaled high mountains and rooted through subterranean tombs; he'd survived in rainy jungles, sun-blasted deserts, and snowy tundras; he'd fought everyone from cannibals to Nazis—though of the two, he preferred the cannibals.

But today . . .

The bristled brushes scrubbed his skin as if trying to erase his past.

Hours earlier, a passing helicopter had discovered Indy wandering out of the atomic blast zone, nearly delirious in the desert. Upon coming here, he had been pumped with fluids, had pints of blood drawn, and had been forced to drink some salty-tasting slurry of potassium iodide to protect his internal organs.

Finally the brutal scrubbing ended, and a small doctor approached with a Geiger counter. He passed its wand up Indy's front side and down his back. There were, thankfully, only a few clicks.

"You have someone watching over you," the doctor said.

"Yeah. The good folks at King Cool. " Indy accepted a robe and slipped into it—gingerly. Every square inch of his skin burned; he felt as if he had been flayed alive.

Still, he should be grateful. He was alive.

Which didn't seem to please the two black-suited figures who had watched his humiliation silently from across the room.

They were two of a kind, cut from the same governmental mold, down to their polished patent-leather shoes and stern expressions. Indy had learned they were called Smith and Taylor. Apparently they didn't have first names. At least, not ones they cared to share.

As Indy crossed toward them, a soldier stepped through a side door into the room. He marched stiffly to Smith and passed him a slip of paper. The man read it and handed it to Taylor, who also read it, then neatly folded it into fourths and tucked it into the breast pocket of his suit.

Both their gazes settled on Indy.

Smith waved him to a chair next to a steel table. Though Indy would have liked to sit down, he remained standing. It was one of *those* sorts of situations.

Smith spoke first. "It appears your story checks out, Dr. Jones. But I'm still mystified as to why you were in the Russians' car in the first place."

Indy sighed. How many times did he have to go over this?

"First, I was in the *trunk*. As I already told you, I was captured, drugged, and kidnapped from a dig in Mexico."

"Along with your good friend, George McHale?"

Indy felt the wind knocked out of him. The sting of that betrayal would take years to fade. If it ever did.

He shook his head. "I had no reason to believe Mac was a spy. He was MI6 when I was in OSS. We must have gone on twenty to thirty missions together, both in Europe and the Pacific. We even—"

Taylor cut him off. "Don't wave your war record in our face, Colonel Jones. We *all* served."

"No kidding? Whose side were you on?"

Taylor glowered while Smith took over again. "I don't think you understand the gravity of your situation. You aided and abetted a KGB operative who broke into a top-secret military installation, right in the heart of the United States of America." He punched a thumb against his red-white-and-blue tie. "*My* country."

Indy refused to be baited. He changed the tack of the conversation. "So then what *was* in the steel box they took?"

Taylor leaned a fist on the table. "Why don't you tell us? You've seen it before."

Indy glanced between them. "You mean that air force fiasco in '47? They tossed me in a bus with blacked-out windows—along with twenty other people who I wasn't allowed to talk to—hauled me out to the middle of nowhere in the middle of the night for some urgent recovery project, and showed me . . . what? Some piece of wreckage and an intensely magnetic shroud wrapped around—" He shook his head, still unsure. "—mutilated remains? But none of us were ever given the whole picture, and you threatened us with treason if we ever talked about it. So *you* tell *me*—what was in that damn box?"

Taylor looked slightly shook up. "This process works best when *we* ask the questions, Dr. Jones."

Indy remembered the term Spalko had used. "Mummified remains," he said aloud.

It was Smith's turn to tighten his lips, then force them to relax. "Our records don't indicate anything of that nature was housed there," he recounted stiffly.

Taylor underlined the threat. "You must be confused, Dr. Jones." He stressed the word *confused* with all the weight of the US government, hinting at the threat of great bodily harm if he should be contradicted.

Smith nodded. "The only thing that facility stores is replacement parts for B-series aircraft. Nothing more."

Indy opened his mouth to argue—but he was saved as the door behind the two suits banged open. A barrel-chested man strode through. His face reminded Indy of a bulldog looking for a fight. He wore an army uniform with two bright stars adorning his epaulets. The general was a big man with a bigger voice.

"General Ross," Smith said, straightening swiftly.

The suit was ignored. The general crossed to Indy.

"Thank God, Indy! Don't you know how dangerous it is to climb inside a refrigerator? Those things are death traps!"

His words were followed by a belly laugh, ripe with good humor.

Indy grinned. It seemed like years since he had last smiled. Still, the expression quickly faded, weighed down by his exhaustion and his exasperation at the situation.

He shook the general's hand. "Good to see you, too, Bob."

"Sir—" Smith interrupted.

General Ross turned to the two suits. "At ease, boys. I'll vouch for Dr. Jones."

Indy finally sank into the offered chair. "Bob, what the hell's going on? KGB on US soil? Who was that woman?"

"What woman?" Taylor asked and flipped out a pad. "Describe her."

Indy glanced from Taylor to General Ross. His friend nodded. "Go ahead, Indy. What did she look like?"

"She was tall, thin, midthirties. She carried some kind of sword—a rapier, I think." He rubbed at his throat. "Knew how to use it, too."

Smith and Taylor shared a look—clearly, they recognized the description. With the barest nod from Smith, Taylor quickly exited the room.

General Ross swung to Smith, amazement in his voice. "Sounds like Irina Spalko."

Smith opened his briefcase on the table and produced a thick file. The topmost sheet was a surveillance photo. He slid it over to Indy. Though she was younger and wore a Russian uniform in the photo, it was the same cold woman.

"Yeah, that's her," Indy confirmed.

Through an observation window in back, Indy spotted Taylor in a neighboring office. The suit picked up a phone and turned away.

"You're sure she's here?" Smith asked, drawing Indy's attention back to the questioning.

"Here and gone, I imagine. Why? Who is she?"

Smith returned the photograph to his file, and the file to his briefcase. As answer, he snapped his case closed.

General Ross was not as reticent. "She was Stalin's fair-haired girl. His favorite scientist—if you can call psychic research *science.*"

Smith frowned. "General Ross," he said warningly.

"She's leading teams from the Kremlin all over the world, scooping up artifacts she thinks have paranormal military applications. She's—"

"General Ross . . . *sir*! I must insist."

A glare answered him, but this time Smith did not back down. "You can vouch for Dr. Jones, sir—but who can vouch for you?"

General Ross faced Smith. "Back off, Paul."

So Smith *did* have a first name.

The general continued, "Not everyone in the army is a Commie. And certainly not Indy."

Indy was familiar with the witch hunts being run across all levels of government and the military, led by a certain Wisconsin senator, Joseph McCarthy. Especially following the deaths of Julius and Ethel Rosenberg, executed for passing nuclear secrets to the Russians. Since then, hearings and trials had spread beyond Washington and crossed the country, reaching even Hollywood.

He sat straighter, understanding the tack of the accusations but not the details. "By the way, what exactly am I being charged with, other than surviving a nuclear bomb?"

Through the rear window, he noted that Taylor had hung up the phone. A moment later the suit returned to the room.

Smith answered Indy's question. "No charges yet, Dr. Jones. But frankly, your close association with George McHale calls into question all your activities, including those during the war."

General Ross's face turned a threatening shade of red. "Are you nuts? Do you know how many medals this son of a bitch won?"

"A great many, I'm sure. But does he deserve them?"

Taylor interrupted the start of another angry outburst from General Ross. "Dr. Jones, let's just say for now that you are a person of interest to the Bureau."

Smith nodded. "Of *great* interest."

Indy could not believe his loyalty was being questioned. Righteous indignation and cold disbelief warred inside him. How many of those freshly scrubbed scars had been earned protecting this country?

"Look," he said, sputtering, "you got any doubts about me, call Congressman Freleng. Or Abe Portman in army intel. Hell, ask anybody! I've got friends throughout Washington."

Taylor crossed his arms, his threat plain in his next words. "I think, Professor, you'll find you might be wrong about that."

ELEVEN

THREE HUNDRED MILES AWAY Irina Spalko stepped into the operating room at a private research facility. She wore blue hospital scrubs, and her face was half hidden by a surgical mask. Her hands were already gloved in latex.

The patient lay on a stainless-steel table. Her assistant, an expert in anatomy flown in from East Berlin, already waited there. A trio of bright lights, the size of garbage can lids, hovered over the surgical table.

The room was otherwise unoccupied.

No anesthesiologists or nurses were necessary.

Not for this patient.

The only other people in the room were three older men in suits, uniformly gray, uniformly stoic and stony-faced. They wore surgical masks and stood with their arms behind their backs.

Though they wore no name tags and their passports spoke of nationalities in France, Brazil, and Italy, Spalko knew them to be representatives of high-ranking members of the Soviet Politburo, known now as the Presidium. She knew they wielded the true power in Moscow.

With a nod to the men, she crossed to the table.

The New Mexico specimen recovered from the Nevada hangar had been carefully disinterred from the metal coffin. It lay on the table, wrapped in its metal cocoon. They had already attempted to x-ray it, but nothing had showed up.

"Are you ready?" the anatomist asked in German.

"Ja."

She had waited years for this chance.

The anatomist reached to a movie camera on a tall tripod and switched it on. Together the two carefully peeled and shed the outer layers of the metallic, silvery cocoon. The strange material fell away easily, but once discarded it returned to its original shape.

They carefully packed each sheet away for further study.

The last silvery layer was extracted with even more care. The movie camera buzzed behind Spalko, but the pounding of her heart drowned out almost everything else. She caught a whiff of something indefinable as the last layer was lifted. An organic mix of orange spice, licorice, and a deep musky earthiness. Yet she also caught a whiff of something electric, something metallic, like a fuse box that had short-circuited.

As they freed the last layer of wrapping, the shape slowly revealed itself.

Her fingers hovered over its small form, its spindly arms and swollen knees, its large ovoid eyes and smooth, pale grayish skin. The anatomist took countless measurements. Spalko concentrated on the head. She noted the elongated cranium, the small mouth and slitted nostrils.

After a full hour, the anatomist nodded to her and picked up a scalpel.

Spalko's body shuddered—not in revulsion, but in anticipation.

She picked up another scalpel.

Over the next six hours they performed a slow and meticulous dissection. With as much care as they had used peeling away the silvery wrappings, they dissected the body layer by layer. Measurements were taken, samples were collected; each discard was preserved in formaldehyde. Finally they were left with only the skeleton: skull, tiny rib cage, pelvis, arm and leg bones.

Spalko stepped back in awe.

The lights shone down upon the wondrous sight.

The entire skeleton was made of *crystal,* translucent and glowing in the bright surgical lights. The bones cast an iridescent rainbow of fractals and reflections. The strange light sang of places beyond this world, beyond normal comprehension.

Spalko circled the table, once, twice, three times.

She soaked it all in.

Motion behind her finally drew her eye.

She had all but forgotten the presence of the three Soviet representatives. They remained expressionless, if perhaps a bit brighter-eyed. Each spoke to her as they moved toward the exit, the matter settled in their minds.

"Do what must be done," the first one said.

"Let no one stop you," said the second.

The last man's words sounded like a threat. "Do not fail."

As they filed out, Spalko returned to the wonder on the table.

Her mind spun on the possibilities, the potentials—but she knew one certainty above all else.

She would not fail.

PART TWO
BACK TO
SCHOOL

TWELVE

Marshall College, three weeks later

INDY STRODE PAST THE BLACKBOARD, its surface chalked with Celtic glyphs and ciphers. The desk at the front of the classroom was piled with archaeological artifacts from Northern Europe, borrowed from both the university museum and his own personal collection: rune stones, crude hand axes, knives scrolled in Celtic symbols, a Viking shield, bits of silver jewelry, and larger pieces of pottery.

On the far side of the cluttered desk, rows of college sophomores tracked Indy's movements as if at a tennis match. Back and forth, he paced as he lectured, dressed in a tweed jacket, patches on the elbows, and sporting black-framed eyeglasses.

Gone native, as his old friend and former Marshall College dean, Marcus Brody, used to quip before he died. *Assuming full academic regalia to fit in with the local tenured tribe.*

But some things Indy couldn't mask so easily.

He limped his way to the other side of the room. He'd only been back three weeks. While the bruises on his face were mostly faded, he was far from recovered. He raised his pointer—hiding a wince from his strained shoulder—and tapped a series of photographs tacked up along the board. They depicted the Neolithic ruins of Skara Brae set among the rolling green hills of Orkney, against a backdrop of the Bay of Skaill.

"—along with the use of Grooved Ware and the beginnings of modern drainage, which we also see in Skara Brae, on the west coast of Scotland. Skara Brae dates back to 3100 BC and was occupied for about six hundred years until its apparent abandonment in 2500 BC. Like many lost civilizations, there's no solid evidence as to why—"

As he turned, Indy spotted a newcomer to the class. The older man—balding, gray-haired, with an air of dignity—had slipped silently into the room. He stood stiffly at the back of the class in a pressed herringbone suit that was currently about two decades out of fashion.

Dean Charles Stanforth.

Indy stumbled a bit at his presence. Something was wrong. Only dire circumstances drew the dean from his lofty mahogany-paneled tower.

With the barest nod, Stanforth acknowledged Indy. The man's eyes flicked toward the door in a silent request to interrupt the class and attend to a private talk out in the hall.

Indy laid his pointer on the lip of the chalkboard. "Let's stop there for a moment," he told his class. "Open up Michaelson, chapter four. We'll discuss emigration versus exodus when I get back."

Stanforth headed out into the hall. Amid a bit of grumbling from his students, Indy followed and joined the dean in the empty stone hallway. Arched windows on the far side framed a handsome campus: manicured lawns, ivy-covered gables, and a banner announcing the upcoming homecoming game.

Stanforth, ever formal, shook his hand as they met. "Henry."

It took Indy a moment to realize the dean was referring to him. To Stanforth, he was never *Indiana.* Stanforth always referred to Indy by the name stenciled on his office door: PROFESSOR HENRY JONES JR.

"I have some rather disturbing news," the dean continued. "The FBI showed up this morning. They ransacked your office, searched your files, and—"

"Wait!" Indy stepped back and lifted an arm. "What?" His voice was louder than he intended.

"They came with search warrants and federal identification."

"But you're the dean of the school. Why didn't you stop them? They had no right."

Stanforth lifted a sharp eyebrow. "They had every right. You know that. Besides, the college is not going to let itself get embroiled in that kind of controversy, not in this political climate."

Indy scowled. What a bunch of spineless bureaucrats. The old dean, Marcus Brody, would never have sat idle while a tenured professor's office was violated.

"And I'm afraid the news gets worse," Stanforth said.

Worse?

The dean cleared his throat. "The board of regents has also granted you a leave of absence."

"What?" Indy thought for half a second, then realized what that implied. "Are you telling me I'm fired?"

"No. A leave of absence." The dean shifted his eyeglasses and rubbed a finger along his brow line. "In this particular instance, an *indefinite* leave of absence—"

"So you *are* firing me!"

Stanforth held up a hand. "—during which time they have agreed to continue to pay your full salary."

Indy swung away. One hand balled into a fist, the other pressed to his forehead. "I don't want their money." He turned back, his voice rising. "In fact, you can tell them where they can deposit their damn money!"

"Please don't be foolish, Henry. You don't know what I had to go through to get that concession for you."

Indy clamped back stronger words. He stared at the dean with dismay. "What *you* went through? What exactly did *you* have to go through, Charlie?"

The dean stared him in the eyes, facing his anger. "Henry, I resigned."

The battered old suitcase landed on the bed in Indy's room, crinkling the threadbare comforter. Indy threw open the latches and swung the lid wide. He'd barely unpacked from his last trip. He crossed to his highboy dresser and began pulling out socks and shirts. He threw them at the case in no particular order. He would sort it all out when he got there.

"Where will you go, Henry?" Stanforth asked, seated in a chair at Indy's desk.

Indy straightened with an armful of shirts and a rumpled suit jacket. He shrugged and crammed them into the suitcase. He had many options.

Stanforth idled at Indy's cluttered desk, shifting a few objects, seeking to make some semblance of order out of the chaos. The desktop was crowded with artifacts: Maori masks, Inuit whalebone carvings, an Egyptian scarab beetle. A pile of dusty journals threatened to topple over, presently propped up by a bottle of red wine, already half empty, and it was only the middle of the afternoon.

"You should have a plan."

Indy had a plan, though it might be a tad rudimentary. "A train to New York," he explained. "Then overnight to London, for starters. Might end up teaching in Leipzig. Heinrich owes me a favor . . . a *big* favor, now that I think about it."

"I suppose there's nothing to keep you here." Stanforth swirled the wine in his glass and stared into its dark depths. "I barely recognize this country anymore. The government's got us seeing Communists in our soup." He sighed loudly. "When the hysteria reaches academia, I guess it's time to call quits to the career."

Indy slowed down, leaned a hand on the dresser, and faced the newly resigned dean of Marshall College. Indy could sometimes get too self-centered. Someone—several people, in fact—had been only too happy to inform him of this flaw. It had taken him until this age to begin to see it.

"How'd Deirdre take the news?" Indy asked.

Stanforth shrugged. "How does any wife take such things? The look on her face was a combination of pride and panic."

Indy read the same mix of emotions on the dean's face, along with regret. "I feel like a heel. I should never have doubted you for a second."

"You have good reasons to question your friends these days."

Indy sighed and sat on the bed. "It's been a brutal couple of years, Charlie. No doubt. First my dad, then Marcus . . ."

"Both great men." Stanforth lifted his glass in silent acknowledgment. "They'll be missed."

"And now Mac may as well be dead . . ."

Stanforth slowly nodded. "We seem to be at the age where life stops giving us things and starts taking them away."

A long moment of heavy silence stretched. Indy rubbed his sore knee. Stanforth continued to swirl the wine, seeking some answer in its depths. Both men snapped out of their melancholy at the same time.

Indy bolted up to resume his packing, and Stanforth reached for the bottle of wine. "Maybe just another half glass," the dean mumbled.

Indy rifled through the contents of a desk drawer. He collected a few papers, including his passport, and tossed them into the open suitcase.

Stanforth filled his wineglass to the rim and leaned back. "I wish you'd met someone like my Deirdre, to help you through times like this. Or if you'd realized it when you *did* meet her . . ."

Indy rolled his eyes. "Let's not tug on that thread right now, okay, pal?"

Stanforth held up his free hand in surrender—then noticed his wristwatch. "Good Lord, I've got to get home. Don and Maggie are driving *spousum et familia* up from the city for dinner. Emergency family council meeting."

"They're good kids," Indy reminded him.

Stanforth acknowledged the truth with a wry smile. "Healthy and employed. I'll settle for that." He stood up, swaying a bit from the wine. "And I believe I should walk home. It's a nice night."

Indy steadied him with a hand on his shoulder and squeezed his appreciation. "Thank you for what you did, my friend."

Stanforth nodded and shrugged. "I cut quite the dramatic figure. The regents were stunned into shamed silence. At least that's the way I'll tell it to the grandkids."

He headed toward the door under his own steam—then turned back with one last thought. "You know, when you're young you spend all your time thinking, *Who will I be*? And then for years you're busy shouting at the world, *This is who I am!*"

As Stanforth spoke, Indy opened the closet door. He found himself staring at a beat-up brown fedora hanging on a hook; his bullwhip was curled on the closet's top shelf. Both waited to be packed.

This is who I am, Indy thought.

Behind him, Stanforth continued, "But lately I've been wondering—after I'm gone, *Who will they say I was*?"

With a final wave, Stanforth shuffled off, but his words remained behind.

Indy stood in the closet, staring at the whip and fedora.

Who will they say I was?

The thought raised another question

Will there be anyone in my life even to ask that question?

Indy pictured the empty house behind him. Somewhere outside a mother called a child to supper. But inside all he could hear was the lonely ticking of his grandfather's antique Bavarian clock. This place had once been a home; now it was more like a museum, closed up, the curators gone.

What was he doing with his life?

Indy backed slowly out of the closet—fedora and whip untouched. Maybe with the suspension, it was time for a new path, a new direction.

With a click of the latch, he closed the door on his old life.

THIRTEEN

THE YOUNG BIKER throttled up and raced his Harley-Davidson motorcycle down the street. He was bent low over the bike, outfitted in a black leather jacket, his blue jeans rolled over polished boots. He sported dark sunglasses and leather gloves.

His target was in the backseat of a Yellow Cab. He'd missed him at the house and followed him across town. Ahead, the taxi pulled to the curb in front of the train station. The sharp blast of a train whistle pierced through the roar of the motorcycle's engine. His target climbed from the cab. He wore a tweed jacket and hauled a battered suitcase, bright with stickers from exotic locales. He was plainly heading out of town—far out of town. Now was the biker's only chance.

A second blast of a train whistle pierced the station's tumult.

The outbound 4:10 was readying to leave the station.

His target hurried, climbing two steps at a time.

The biker had almost missed him.

Maybe still would.

Taking no chances, he sped the cycle up to the station, turned sharply, and skidded sideways. He smoked his tires until they gripped. Then with a goose of the throttle, he shot forward, hopped the curb, and raced up the stairs.

Above, his target had vanished out onto the platform.

The biker followed, motor screaming. At the top of the stairs, he skirted out onto the platform and stood a bit on the cycle's foot pegs. The bike bobbled under him as he searched the crowd. The train steamed and smoked, already slowly rolling away.

Where was he?

Then he spotted him—the man with the suitcase. He was jumping into one of the closest cars as it was still moving.

Crap . . .

The biker dropped into his seat and gunned his engine. Platform attendants in red caps yelled at him. He swerved and bobbed through the crowd, drawing alongside the train car as it began to gain steam.

The biker whipped off his glasses, revealing the face of a young man barely out of his teens. He yelled toward the back of a tweed jacket. "Hey! Mister! Hey, buddy!"

Nothing.

He screamed louder, punctuating it with the whine of his cycle. "Hey, Professor!"

The man turned, frowning back at the sight of a motorcycle racing down the platform alongside the accelerating train.

"ARE YOU DR. JONES?"

A bewildered nod answered him. The man leaned out a bit and pointed to where the platform ended at a cement wall. "You're running out of track, kid!"

The young biker ignored the danger, racing even with the train. "YOU'RE A FRIEND OF DR. OXLEY, RIGHT?"

The professor stared harder at him. "Harold Oxley, the archaeologist?"

"YEAH!"

"What about him, kid?"

"THEY'RE GOING TO KILL HIM!"

That would have to do. He braked hard, squealing his tires, rising up on his front wheel. Then stopped—an inch from the wall.

The train roared past the platform and away, stirring a wake of smoke behind it.

He'd been too late.

The biker walked his motorcycle around as redcaps closed in on him. He hoped the professor had at least heard what he'd yelled at the end . . .

As the smoke cleared, he had his answer.

On the opposite platform, a man in a tweed jacket waited, suitcase in hand.

FOURTEEN

SEATED IN A BOOTH at Arnie's Diner, Indy studied the photograph on the Formica tabletop. Across the table, a platter of chili fries was efficiently being consumed by the young man. The kid pointed one of the fries toward the picture.

"That's Ox."

Indy recognized the bookish man in the photograph, buttoned-down and polished, in his midfifties. "Haven't spoken to him in twenty years," he mumbled.

And they hadn't parted well.

Indy also recognized the other person gracing the picture: dark hair, already slicked back, accompanied by a devil-may-care grin. He glanced up at the young man. The grin was gone, but his hair was oilier than ever. A comb rested next to the chili fries, ready to make sure every hair was in place.

Indy leaned back, stretched a kink from his spine, and surveyed the diner as the jukebox played "Glory of Love." The place was all neon signs, black-and-white tile, and U-shaped vinyl booths, set around a long curving counter. It smelled of frying grease and baking peach pie.

And it was packed with people.

The joint seemed equally divided between collegiate types in lettermen jackets with their arms around girls in pink sweaters—and a dozen or so harder-eyed toughs in leather jackets and slick hair. The former kept to the soda bar in front; the latter mostly kept to the back, drinking cheap local pilsner and looking for trouble.

Indy had no problem guessing on which side of the great divide the young man across the table fit. But what was his story? What was all this about?

"Oxley was a brilliant guy," he started, trying to draw the young man out. "One of the best."

"*The* best," the young man corrected.

"But he could get on tangents . . . talk you right to sleep sometimes."

This earned a small grin—not at Indy's pale joke but at some private memory. "When I was a kid, that's how I *did* get to sleep," the kid admitted. "The Ox was better than warm milk." The young man's arm slid across the table, hand out. "Name's Mutt . . . Mutt Williams."

"*Mutt?* What kind of name is that?"

The hand withdrew. "The one I picked. You got a problem with that?"

Indy held up a placating palm. "Take it easy." He slid back the photograph. "What was Oxley, your uncle or something?"

"Kind of. My dad died in the war, and the Ox helped my mom raise me."

The young man's fingers slipped to the comb. He mechanically drew it through his hair.

Indy checked his watch. "Listen, kid. I've got one last train I can catch. If you've got a story, tell it."

Mutt sighed, sounding much older all of a sudden. "Six months ago my mom got a letter from the Ox. He was down in Peru. He said he found some kind of crystal skull, like the one that guy Mitchell-Hedges found."

Indy frowned at the odd reference, though he was well familiar with the skull. In 1926 the famed archaeologist F. A. Mitchell-Hedges had discovered a strange crystal skull hidden beneath a collapsed Mayan altar inside a temple in British Honduras. It had been carved from a single block of clear quartz, with dimensions and details that matched a small human cranium, even down to an articulating jaw. The Mayan priests claimed the skull allowed the user to focus his thoughts to kill. Indy had been trying to get a peek at that skull for years. He'd been rebuffed.

But the Maya also told stories of another set of crystal skulls—a collection of ancient cursed skulls—hidden somewhere in the jungles of South America. They numbered an unlucky thirteen. It was said that if you could gather the thirteen together, they would speak and reveal the secrets of the universe.

As Indy wondered if Oxley truly had found one of these skulls, a waitress passed, drawing both their eyes. Mutt reached up and absently removed a bottle of beer from her tray without her noticing it.

Indy snatched the beer back from the young man and returned it to the waitress's tray. She remained none the wiser.

Frowning, Indy spoke. "About those skulls. Back in college, Ox and I were obsessed with the Mitchell-Hedges skull. How do you know anything about it?"

"You kidding? That obsession didn't end in college for Ox. He could talk about that thing till the cows came home. But what was that skull exactly, an idol or something?"

"More likely a deity carving. Meso-American. There're a few crystal skulls around the world. I saw one at the expo at the British Museum. Impressive craftsmanship, but that's about it."

"Then why was Ox going on and on about its psychic powers?"

Indy shook his head. So the kid had heard an earful of that, too. Oxley had been particularly fascinated by claims of the paranormal properties of the skulls.

"I know. Believe me," he said, having borne the brunt of Oxley's hypotheses during their college years. He did his best Bela Lugosi impersonation. *"Stare into its eyes, and it'll drive you mad."*

Mutt was not amused. "Laugh if you want, but Ox said he found one of those things. This one was real different, he said, and he was on his way to a place called Akator with it."

Akator . . .

Indy sat straighter and leaned forward. "Akator? He said that? Are you sure?"

Mutt's eyes widened at Indy's sudden intensity. "Yeah, I'm sure. What is that place?"

Indy settled back again. "A lost city in the Amazon. The conquistadores called it El Dorado. Supposedly a tribe, called the Ugha, was chosen by the gods seven thousand years ago to build a great city out of solid gold. They say it had aqueducts, paved roads, technology we wouldn't see for another five thousand years. Francisco de Orellana disappeared into the Amazon in 1546 looking for it. So did a British explorer, Colonel Percy Fawcett, in the 1920s. I almost died of typhus searching for it myself. I don't think it exists."

"But why would Ox want to take the skull there?"

"Because of a legend."

Now it was Mutt's turn to lean closer.

Indy went on. "It's said that a crystal skull was stolen from Akator sometime in the fifteenth or sixteenth century. They say whoever finds this skull and returns it to the city's temple will be given control over its power."

"What kind of power?"

"I don't know, kid," Indy snapped sourly. "It's just a story."

The young man nodded, as if expecting to hear this. "From his letter, my mom thought the Ox was going crazy." He tapped his head with his comb. "Smog in the noggin. She went down to find him. Only somebody had kidnapped him, and now they've got her, too. Ox hid the skull someplace, and if my mom doesn't come up with it, they're gonna kill 'em both. She said you'd help."

"Me?" That made no sense. "What's her name?"

"Mary Williams."

Indy struggled to place the name, but his file was long—with most entries brief, and a few anonymous. He didn't have enough to go on.

He sighed. "There were a lot of Mary Williamses, kid."

"Shut up, man. That's my *mother*!"

Indy raised a placating hand. Again. "Look, you don't have to get sore all the time just to show everybody how tough you are, okay?"

Mutt glowered back. "My mom said if anybody could find the skull, it's you. Like you're some kind of grave robber or something."

"I'm a *teacher*."

"Whatever. Look, she called me two weeks ago from South America, told me she'd escaped but they were after her. She said she'd just mailed me a letter from Ox, and I had to get it to you. Then the line went dead."

Indy opened his mouth, but he read the fear in the other's eyes—a boy's fear for his mother. He remained silent. It was a virtue after all.

Mutt pulled out an envelope from his jacket and passed it to Indy. Indy opened it and shook out a single sheet of yellowed paper. It was crammed with lines of script.

"Gibberish," Mutt mumbled. "Not even English."

"Be quiet," Indy said under his breath.

He feigned interest in the note while studying the two men at the counter. They were wearing suits too tight for their massive shoulders. Indy had been watching them since they'd come into the diner. After sitting down at the counter, they had kept a steady focus on their booth. Then as Mutt had pulled out the note, they'd suddenly shifted away from the diner's counter and stood up.

The men were making their move.

It had to be the letter.

From the moment the pair had stepped through the door, Indy knew something was up. They definitely didn't fit the normal clientele of Arnie's Diner, being neither college types nor greasers. And Indy was pretty sure he'd spotted the pair at the train station, too. Someone had been following him.

But why?

"See those two bricks leaving the counter?" Indy said softly to Mutt. He folded the strange letter and put it in his pocket. "They're not here for the milkshakes."

"Who are they?"

"I don't know. Maybe FBI."

The pair reached the table. The answer to Mutt's question came as soon as they spoke. They didn't even try to hide their thick Russian accents. That scared Indy more than anything.

The larger of the two, which meant gorilla-sized, spoke first. "Come quietly, Dr. Jones. Bring letter with you."

So it *was* about the letter.

"Letter? What letter?" he tried lamely.

"Letter Mr. Williams just give you."

"Me?" Mutt leaned on his elbows, his arms folded on the table in front of him. "Do I look like a mailman?"

The second Russian spoke. Though smaller in stature, there was something even more frightening in the fish-belly deadness to his eyes. "We don't ask again. Come now or—"

—SNICK—

A long thin blade popped out from behind Mutt's left elbow. The kid held a switchblade pointed at the closest man.

"—or what?" Mutt asked.

Indy admired the kid's moxie, but he had a lot to learn. These weren't local toughs who could be rumbled away so easily.

"Nice try, kid," he warned. "But I think you've brought a knife—"

The dead-eyed Russian cocked a pistol and lifted the weapon to the side of Indy's head.

"—to a gunfight."

FIFTEEN

MUTT ALLOWED HIS SWITCHBLADE to be plucked out of his fingers by the giant Russian. His face burned—half in anger, half in shame. The Russian closed the blade and slipped the weapon into his pocket.

"It's all right, kid," the professor said. "We all make mistakes."

The Russians stepped back.

"Outside," said the first, pointing.

"Now," added the second.

Mutt glanced to Dr. Jones, who nodded. Clearly they had no choice. Together they slid out of the booth. Jones carried his battered suitcase. They were forced to march ahead, trailed by the Russians, whose hands rested menacingly inside their coats.

Ahead, Mutt saw two other large figures enter the diner. They were wearing the same cheap suits. The newcomers nodded to their captors.

Great, more Russkies.

Mutt studied them with narrowed eyes.

Professor Jones nudged him with an elbow and drew his attention. He nodded over at a blond letterman who stood next to a redhead in a poodle skirt.

"Punch that guy," Jones mouthed.

"Wh-what?"

"Joe College. Hit him. Hard."

Mutt understood and took a step out of line. He bumped into the letterman's shoulder. "Hey, watch it, nosebleed!" Mutt called out.

Joe College whirled, his face already turning red and irritated. Then he spotted Mutt's black leather jacket. Irritation turned to territorial anger.

Before the letterman could react, Mutt took the offensive. He swung hard, from the shoulder, and smashed the guy square in the nose.

The letterman fell like an axed tree.

All around, his friends bellowed in rage. Girls screamed and pointed.

One footballer with a horse's face yelled, "Get that greaser!"

The Russian behind Mutt tried to grab the collar of his leather jacket, but three lettermen piled onto Mutt and knocked him away. Twisting around, Mutt ducked as a beer bottle was thrown from the rear of the diner. It struck one of the lettermen on the side of the head.

Freed, Mutt rolled away and saw the half dozen greasers in biker jackets coming to his support. Fists formed, and threats were shouted.

The song on the jukebox suddenly switched from "Glory of Love" to "Shake, Rattle and Roll." How appropriate . . .

Mutt swung around to see the tweed-jacketed professor punch a frat boy, then a Russian, then a greaser. He gaped at Professor Jones's sudden transformation. A hand grabbed Mutt's shoulder. Following the professor's lead, he lashed out blindly.

His fist ended up striking the largest Russian square in the Adam's apple. The man choked and dropped hard on his backside.

Jones grabbed Mutt's elbow. "C'mon, kid."

The professor hurled his suitcase at another of the Russians. Mutt held off long enough to bend down and grab his switchblade out of the gasping Russian's pocket.

Weapon in hand, Mutt dashed with the professor toward the front door.

The Russians fought to follow, but the diner was in full chaos.

The pair burst through the front door and sprinted toward the side alley, where Mutt had left his motorcycle. The red-and-black Harley had never looked better. Mutt dug into his pocket for his keys.

"What was that all about?" he forced out as he mounted the cycle.

The professor had plainly been pondering the same. From his expression, he had come to some disturbing realization. "Your mom didn't escape her kidnappers, kid! They must have let her go. They *wanted* her to mail that letter, for you to bring it here."

"For you to translate," Mutt finished.

"Smart kid."

Mutt felt a flush of satisfaction at the professor's faint praise.

But the roar of an engine interrupted. They both turned to the back of the alley. A black sedan barreled toward them, crashing through trash cans and debris.

Mutt slipped in the key, twisted, and kicked the motorcycle to life with a deep growl. He turned to the professor. "Get on, Clyde! Time to cut out!"

The professor eyed the cycle—plainly unsure, but he had no choice. He hopped on behind Mutt. "You know how to drive this thing, kid?"

In answer, Mutt twisted the throttle and goosed the engine hard.

The cycle roared and reared up on its back wheel, like a wild stallion. But Mutt had more than a single horse under him.

Hot rubber gripped cement, and the cycle rocketed out of the alley.

Tweed arms gripped tight around his waist.

A grin formed on Mutt's face.

Welcome to my world, Professor!

SIXTEEN

INDY HELD ON for his life as the motorcycle hit the street and skidded sharply into a hard turn, the pavement an inch from his knee. The kid straightened the bike and sped down the street, weaving between slower cars.

Indy risked a glance over his shoulder and saw the sedan burst out of the alley and give chase. But they had a good lead.

For once, they'd caught a break.

He should've known better.

As he swung around, a second black sedan, an exact match to the first, flew out of a cross-street and pulled up alongside them. Mutt shied away, but a speeding bus had the bike hemmed in.

The sedan squeezed closer, pinching tightly. Arms reached through the back window. Hands snagged Indy's suit jacket and dragged him toward the open window. He had to let go of Mutt or the kid would lose control of his bike and end up under the wheels of the bus.

With no choice, Indy allowed himself to be hauled through the window into the backseat of the sedan. The Russian in the rear clearly expected more resistance, so once inside the sedan, Indy obliged. Cocking an arm, he punched the Russian in the mouth and lunged over his body.

Through the rear window, Indy noted that Mutt had dropped back behind the sedan and gunned toward the other side of the car.

"Smart kid," he repeated.

Indy grabbed the window frame on that side and kicked the Russian square in the face, boosting himself through the window.

Mutt roared up next to the sedan. "Need a lift?"

"Funny, kid!"

Indy, half hanging out, snatched the chrome bar on the back of the cycle's seat. He lunged out—but missed his landing. Hanging tight, he was dragged behind the cycle. Asphalt burned through his shoes' leather. The heat scorched, and the rattling reached the fillings in his teeth.

Finally, Mutt tapped the brakes, and Indy flew forward. He struck Mutt's back and landed squarely in the seat behind the kid.

"What were you doing back there?" Mutt yelled.

"What was I doing?" Indy asked. He was indignant—until he sensed that devil-may-care grin behind the kid's words.

Mutt fed the bike more gas, and they shot forward.

With a squeal of tires, another sedan shot into the street a block ahead, cutting them off.

Mutt turned sharply, skinning Indy's knee on the pavement. He bumped over the curb and flew up a flight of steps in front of an ivy-covered brick building, stately with age. As the bike shuddered up the steps, Mutt read the sign over the doorway ahead.

Marshall College Library
Established 1856

At the top a stunned student held the door open for them. Mutt took advantage of the opportunity and shot through the library's vestibule and into the main reading room. Solemn mahogany bookshelves spread to either side, framing rows of desks. Overhead, leaded windows filtered dusty light. In the enclosed space, the motorcycle's roar was deafening.

Students leaped up from their desks as the Harley soared into their midst. A librarian dropped an armload of books when they shot past.

Mutt laughed wildly.

"Wall!" Indy shouted.

Mutt attempted a braking turn, but the polished floor betrayed him. Losing control, he laid the bike down and skidded across the floor. They stopped right in front of the checkout desk.

An elderly librarian sat at her station. With all the dignity of the century-old building, she raised a finger to her lips and warned them sternly, "Shh!"

"Sorry, ma'am." Mutt hauled his bike up.

Indy dusted himself off.

One of his sophomore students hurried over to them, recognizing the professor. "Dr. Jones, since you're here, I've got a quick question about Hargrove's normative culture models—"

Indy held up a hand. "Forget Hargrove. Read Vere Gordon Childe on diffusionism. He spent most of his life in the field."

Mutt kicked the bike's starter, and the cycle growled back to life. He turned to the librarian and mouthed *Sorry.* He slipped a comb from his pocket and ran it through his hair, fixing his appearance—apparently the kid had some respect for proper decorum in a library. Or maybe it was because of the coed giving him the eye up and down.

Indy backed away from the eager student and mounted the bike again. Still, he called back, wanting to pass on one last teaching tip. "If you wanna be a good archaeologist, you're gonna have to—"

Mutt throttled the bike and headed for the rear exit.

Indy twisted and shouted back, "—GET OUT OF THE LIBRARY!"

Mutt banged through the library's back door and burst out into the bright day. He shot into the street and searched around. Surely that shortcut had shaken their tail—then again maybe not.

From around the corner of the library, one of the sedans roared into view, having circled the building.

If anything, these guys were stubborn.

Mutt gunned his cycle's engine, smoking his rear tire, and shot toward the town's center. He heard music, voices. Turning a sharp corner, he discovered a demonstration under way. Folks crowded the streets. From the signs and banners, it appeared to be a political rally. Chants were shouted, hand-painted placards were waved, and leaders made speeches with bullhorns.

Mutt didn't slow. Heck, he didn't even vote.

Bobbing and weaving, he shot through the crowd. People shook fists at his rude passage. Someone threw an orange at him.

The sedan followed, but less nimbly.

One of the student demonstrators jumped out of the car's way. His placard went flying and landed on the windshield of the pursuing sedan.

Mutt caught a glimpse of its appropriate slogan: BETTER DEAD THAN RED.

Once clear of the demonstrators, Mutt throttled up and headed for the redbrick stadium at the end of the street. Distantly, the roar of the crowd reached him. This year's college homecoming game was already under way.

Mutt smiled.

He'd always wanted to go.

"Hike!"

The center snapped the ball to the quarterback.

The game was tied in the fourth quarter. They had seventy yards still to go. It would be up to him. He'd heard there were recruiters in the stands. He needed a shining moment, especially since he already pictured his face on a box of Wheaties.

The quarterback dropped back for an impossible forward pass.

Close by, two defensive linemen suddenly broke free and charged right for him. He was about to get sacked. Hard. His dreams of cereal boxes faded.

Then the massive linemen skidded to a stop, staring—but not at him.

Only then did he hear a strange screaming growl behind him.

He swung around—

—a motorcycle was aimed straight at him.

He zigged, and the cycle zagged. It shot past him and churned up the turf, heading downfield. Upfield, a dark car blasted through the rear fencing and raced past the goalpost, headed right for them.

The field cleared to either side.

The quarterback held his position as the sedan flew past him. He tracked it. With the field empty, he had the gridiron to himself.

He still needed a shining moment.

For the recruiters. For himself.

Stepping back, he cocked his arm and pitched the ball.

It sailed high and far.

A perfect pass.

Indy urged Mutt faster.

"I'm trying!" the kid yelled back.

But the bike had become mired in the muddy turf. Twisted in his seat, Indy watched the sedan close the distance.

Intently focused, he noted motion in the air. It drew his eye.

A football came sailing out of the sky.

Instinctively, he put his hands up. The pass landed squarely between his palms as the sedan pulled even with him.

The stadium erupted into a wild cheer.

Indy shifted and snapped the ball in a hard spiral—straight through the sedan's window and smack into the side of the driver's head.

The sedan swerved off.

The motorcycle finally found traction and shot through the end zone. Mutt aimed for the exit tunnel, chased by the sedan, which was now weaving erratically. Still the vehicle bore down upon them. Mutt shot into the tunnel, the roar of the cycle thunderous in the enclosed space. The sedan gained speed behind them, closing in on the motorcycle's back tire by the time they reached the exit.

Directly in their path rose a commemorative statue of a seated figure, bronze hands resting on the knees, the face wryly smiling. Indy knew that smile. It was a memorial to his friend and former dean of students, Marcus Brody.

Mutt veered to the side, skidding. He cleared the statue, missing a collision by inches.

The sedan was not so lucky.

The vehicle struck the statue's base. The bronze figure toppled over. Marcus's head smashed through the windshield, only too happy to offer the Russians that wry smile of his.

Mutt sped away.

But Indy stared behind him, grateful.

Even in death, his friend had his back.

Thanks, Marcus.

SEVENTEEN

UNDER THE COVER OF NIGHT, Indy led Mutt up the front steps of his house. He had dared come no sooner. They had lain low in the town's outskirts, in the woods. He unlocked the door as silently as possible and listened. A few crickets chirped, but the house remained dead-quiet.

Satisfied, Indy waved Mutt through and followed him inside.

"Keep the lights off," Indy warned.

He closed the door, went to all the windows and pulled the shades. Only then did he cross to a table lamp and switch it on. Shadows warmed away and revealed a brick fireplace and walls of books, along with shelved artifacts from around the world. A ladder leaned against one set of shelves. The place smelled of old wood smoke and yellowed parchment.

Home.

Mutt collapsed onto a sofa and kicked his boots up on the coffee table.

Indy passed him with a deep frown.

Mutt dropped his feet to the floor, but he stayed slouched.

"This is where you live?" Mutt asked. "It's the first place they'll look for us. We gotta get out of here."

"In a minute."

Mutt didn't argue. In fact, he looked ready to settle in.

Indy pulled Oxley's letter from his pocket and studied it. He ran a finger along the line of strange script. *If I'm right . . .*

He crossed to one of the bookshelves and pulled down a thick book. Heyerdahl's treatise on Mesoamerican languages. Opening it, he stepped backward and sat in a seat. There was one other chair in the room. A leather wingback, as weathered as Indy's jacket. It rested beside the hearth. It had been his father's. *Henry Jones Sr.* And though it had been two years since his father had died, Indy still couldn't get himself to sit in it.

It was still too full of the old man.

Indy settled with the book on his lap and compared the symbols found inside with Oxley's letter. He tapped the open page.

"I thought so. Koihoma."

Mutt stirred. His eyes had drifted closed. "What's that?"

"An extinct Latin American language. Pre-Columbian syllabary system. See these diagonal stresses on the ideograms? Definitely Koihoma."

"So what? Do you speak it?"

"Nobody *speaks* it; hasn't been heard out loud in three thousand years." Indy shrugged. "Might be able to read a little."

He flipped to another page, farther in the book. It was also covered in ancient symbols.

Indy muttered to himself, comparing the two pages and scribbling on a pad of paper on a side table. "—if I walk it through Mayan first."

He squinted at the squiggles and glyphs. They began to blurrily run together. Indy wished it was just because he was tired. He rubbed at his eyes and finally surrendered to the passage of time.

Reaching into a pocket, he pulled out a set of bifocals and slipped them on.

Mutt noticed. "You know, for an old man, you ain't bad in a fight."

"Thanks a lot," Indy said sourly.

"So what are you, like, eighty?"

Indy didn't look up. "Hard livin', kid. I don't recommend it." He lifted up the page he'd translated. *"Follow the lines in the earth only gods can read to Orellana's cradle, guarded by the living dead."*

He was beginning to understand. He stood up. "*Only gods can read*," he repeated. "That must refer to the Nazca lines."

"The what?" Mutt asked.

Indy crossed and shifted the library ladder, then climbed and retrieved a dusty book, *Mirror of the Gods: Ancient Astronomy and Celestial Navigation.* He jumped down with a wince at his hip. He flipped through the tome, searching for a certain page.

"Geoglyphs," he explained. "Giant ancient carvings, scratched into the desert floor in Peru. From the ground, they don't look like anything, but from the air—ah!"

Finding what he wanted, he joined Mutt on the couch and showed him the open section of the book. Two whole pages were devoted to aerial photographs of beautiful carvings in the Peruvian desert. One looked like a monkey, another like a giant spider. The last depicted a large-headed humanoid figure.

"Only gods can read the Nazca lines, because gods—" Indy pointed to the sky. "—live up there. Oxley's telling us the skull is in Nazca, Peru. And it's a good bet the Russians are the ones who've got him. The Kremlin must think the skull is some kind of weapon. That's why they're after it."

"If it gets my mom back, they can have it." Mutt stood up. "Let's go . . . and try not to slow me down."

Mutt headed toward the door, but Indy didn't move. Instead, he continued to flip through the book until he found the page he was looking for. It showed an elaborate sketch of an ancient city, carved atop a jungle plateau.

He spoke as he studied its fine detail. He had to squint even with his bifocals. "Akator. Where Oxley was taking the skull. If it exists, it would be the find of a lifetime. Make a reputation even politicians can't touch."

He pictured the faces of Smith and Taylor.

Indy ripped the page from the book, along with another near the front, covered with Mayan symbols. He folded them both into a pocket and finally stood.

"So, old man, are you ready to go or not?"

"Not."

Indy headed to his bedroom. He crossed to the closet door and yanked it open. His fedora still rested on the hook where he had left it, and his bullwhip lay curled on the top shelf.

Stanforth's previous words still echoed: *Who will they say I was?*

Indy knew the answer.

Reaching inside, he snatched the hat and crammed it on his head.

His other hand settled on the whip's worn handle. He gave it one strong pull with a skilled flip of his wrist.

KUH-RACK!

PART THREE

LINES IN THE SAND

EIGHTEEN

Nazca, Peru

DIDN'T THE KID ever sleep?

Traveling at twenty thousand feet, Indy drowsed to the thrum of the aircraft engines. They had changed planes in Mexico City, switching from a DC-3 to an Antonov An-2, and were now flying over Peru. It had been a long trip, but they were due to land in another hour.

Indy had the brim of his fedora pulled over his eyes, discouraging conversation with the passenger seated next to him. He wanted to get as much sleep as possible. Once they were wheels-down in Peru, he didn't want any delays.

"Are those what I think they are?" Mutt asked.

Indy groaned. "More clouds?"

"No, no, not this time."

Indy pushed back his hat and turned to see what the kid was yammering about. Mutt pointed down from the window. Indy had to shift higher to see. The wing of the An-2 partially blocked his view. Propellers spun in a blur.

"On the ground," Mutt said. "Over there. Are those the Nazca lines you talked about?"

Below the airplane, a vast desert plain filled the world. Sunlight glared off it, but Indy saw what had excited the kid. Etched across its surface was the stylized figure of a giant monkey with a spiraling tail. The artwork stretched over nine hundred feet long. Hundreds of other figures, flowers, and geometric shapes crisscrossed the landscape like so much graffiti.

"How did they do that?" Mutt asked.

Indy sighed. At least the kid was curious. He motioned down to the ground and up to the sky. "The Nazca Indians used crude surveying equipment and celestial measurements to map out their drawings. Then they formed the lines by digging through the desert surface, which is coated with dark iron oxides, down to the lighter ground beneath."

"But why did the Nazca people go to all that trouble? You can't see the drawings on the ground . . . only up here."

Indy shrugged. "Lots of theories, kid. Religious symbols, celestial sky charts, road maps to underground rivers. But no one really knows. It's still a mystery."

He settled back into his seat as Mutt continued his vigil on the passing scenery.

"You should get some sleep," Indy said.

"I can sleep anytime."

Indy rolled his eyes and yanked the brim of his hat back over his eyes. He offered a final warning. "Once we land, kid, we're not going to be just sitting around."

This is why I traveled thirty-two hours?

Mutt sat in an outdoor cantina in the center of the town of Nazca. The sun blazed in a merciless, cloudless sky. He wiped the sweat from his brow with a perspiring glass bottle of soda. More empty bottles were piled in front of him like a stack of bowling pins.

He had been waiting *that* long.

Off in the distance, red-baked mountains stitched a jagged line across the horizon like fangs. Closer at hand, metal hitching posts outside the cantina were tied up with a horse, a mule, and a llama—the last of which had the nasty habit of spitting, showing its distaste for its surroundings.

Right with you, brother.

At the last post, chained securely, stood Mutt's Harley-Davidson, ferried all the way from the East Coast of the United States.

Mutt kept it constantly in sight.

Beyond the cantina's railing stretched a maze of adobe buildings, blindingly white under the blistering sun. Local Peruvians in rainbow ponchos and wide-brimmed hats crammed the streets or hawked trinkets from wooden stalls. Llamas, loaded high, ambled down the packed-dirt road amid carts of every size, some pulled by mules, others by people. Shadier figures haunted crooked alleyways, selling and luring and watching.

You had to always *watch* here. It was that sort of place.

Teeming, dangerous . . . a regular Casablanca. At any moment, Mutt expected to see Bogie wander around the next corner.

It wasn't all grim. Children with round, bronzed faces danced through the chaos, laughing brightly, calling to one another, oblivious to the chaos.

Still, even they had to be *watched.*

A small girl in a dusty sundress relieved an oblivious German tourist of his wallet and darted away.

Bored, Mutt had taken to counting the number of languages he had heard: Dutch, French, Italian, Chinese, Portuguese, and a thousand different dialects of Spanish.

But, thank God, not *Russian.*

At least not yet.

He had half an ear tuned to the professor, who was involved in an animated discussion with a few locals, a conversation that consisted of some strange language and much gesturing. Mutt barely recognized his traveling companion now. The tweed had been replaced with a scarred leather jacket, a crumpled fedora, and a bullwhip over one shoulder. His clean-shaven face had grizzled into darker shadows.

At last, Jones patted each man on the shoulder and turned away. He strode over to Mutt's table. His eyes shone brightly.

It had to be good news.

Finally.

"Someone saw Ox," Jones confirmed. "He came staggering into town a few months ago, ranting like a wild man."

"What?" Mutt shifted to his feet with concern. He pictured the man who had all but raised him, always dapper with a perfectly knotted tie, precisely combed hair, and a briefcase as organized as a file cabinet. Mutt could not balance the description—*ranting like a wild man*—with the professor he'd known all his life.

Jones continued and motioned him to follow. "The police locked him up in a sanatorium on the outskirts of town. It's this way."

Jones headed out into the blazing sun. Mutt followed, matching him stride for stride.

"Back there," Mutt said, thumbing toward the cantina. "That language you were speaking. I took Spanish, but I couldn't make out a word of that. What was it?"

"Quechua. Local Incan dialect."

"Where'd you learn that one?"

"Long story, kid." The professor removed a street urchin's small hand from his back pocket and continued down the street, but not before flipping a coin toward the boy.

"I got time," Mutt said. He couldn't explain why he wanted to know more about this man's life—but he did.

Indy shrugged. "I rode with Pancho Villa."

Mutt stumbled a step. "Bull—*shit*!"

"You asked. And watch your language."

"Pancho Villa. The Mexican revolutionary general."

"Okay. Technically I was kidnapped."

"That seems to happen to you a lot."

"Comes with the territory, kid."

Mutt shook his head. "So Pancho Villa really kidnapped you?"

"It was during the fight against Victoriano Huerta." The professor spit to the side, as if mentioning the name *Huerta* required clearing his throat.

"Wait a sec. That woulda been, what, nineteen years—how *old* were you, man?"

"'Bout your age."

"Crazy. Your parents must've had a cow."

Jones shrugged. "Worked out okay. Things were—a little tense at home."

Mutt snorted his understanding. "Yeah, my mom and I aren't exactly on the best of terms right now, either."

"Treat her right, kid," Jones grumbled. "You only get one. And sometimes not for long."

Mutt heard something catch in the professor's voice, and he stayed silent for a few steps. But he still needed to get something off his chest. "It ain't my problem. It's hers. She got pissed 'cause I quit school, like I'm a goof or somethin'."

The professor glanced over at him. "You quit school?"

"Sure . . . lots of 'em. Fancy prep schools. Where they teach you chess, debate, fencing." He fingered the switchblade in the pocket of his jeans. "I can handle a blade like nobody's business, school's a waste of time."

"You never finished?"

"Nah, it's all useless skills and the wrong books. I mean—don't get me wrong—I like books. The Ox made me read everything under the sun when I was a kid. Even one of *your* books."

"Really?" There was surprise in the professor's voice, along with a twinge of pride.

Mutt had grown to suspect that some bad blood had passed between Jones and the Ox. "But now I pick my own books, you get me?"

"So then what do you do for scratch . . . for money?"

"Fix motorcycles. I know my way around most engines."

"Plan on doing that forever?"

A twinge of irritation spiked through Mutt. "Maybe I *do,* man. Is there something wrong with that?"

"Not a thing, kid. If that's what you love doing, don't let anybody tell you any different."

The professor led Mutt around a corner and pointed to the end of the next street. Up a slight rise hulked a massive adobe building. It squatted atop the hill, baking under the sun, looking less than hospitable. Adding to the effect, most of its windows were barred in iron.

The sanatorium.

As they approached its looming façade, Mutt read the words carved over the door. "Saint Anthony de Padua."

The professor grunted under his breath, darkly amused.

"What?" Mutt asked as they climbed the steps.

"Anthony de Padua. He was the patron saint of *lost* things."

Mutt studied the carved name again. "Then we've come to the right place."

Down the street, a figure stepped out from behind a fruit stand. He watched the boy and the man shove through the heavy wooden doors of the sanatorium.

He removed his wide-brimmed hat and wiped his brow with a handkerchief, then replaced the hat with a shake of his head.

"Indy . . . you just couldn't stay away, damn you." The man's voice had a distinct British accent.

NINETEEN

INDY FOLLOWED THE NUN down the sterile white corridor lined by closed steel doors with barred windows in them. The nun's steps echoed on the red adobe tile. The kid lagged behind, looking ill at ease.

The nun held her hands folded in front of her. A heavy key hung from a chain dangling between her palms. She fingered it nervously, like a rosary, as she continued her story in Spanish. "I remember him. He was here a couple of months ago. And then men with guns . . . bad men. They came and stole him away." She glanced over at Indy. "He was a nice man."

One of the inmates beckoned to them through the barred window. His hair was wild, standing up. His teeth were crooked—all three of them. He babbled at them in a furious blur of words, unintelligible, as if he were speaking in tongues.

Mutt drifted closer. "I think I can make out a few words. Something about an *arqueólogo.* An archaeologist."

The inmate lunged out with both arms and grabbed Mutt by the collar of his leather jacket, by his hair. The kid yelped as he was hauled toward the cell door.

Indy reached over, snagged Mutt by the belt, and yanked him free. He dragged the kid a step along with him. "No speaking with the locals."

With a shake of his head, Indy resumed following the nun.

Mutt stuck closer to his heels now, his eyes wide. "What is going on?"

The professor nodded to their guide. "She says Oxley was deranged. Obsessed. He drew pictures all over the walls of his cell."

As a sullen-eyed janitor slowly passed with his squeaking cart, Indy pulled out Oxley's letter. He read it again out loud.

"*. . . the lines that only the gods can read . . . Orellana's cradle . . .*" He folded the note. "That makes no sense. *Cradle.* Orellana wasn't born in Peru. He was a conquistador, born in Spain. He came looking for gold. Disappeared along with six others. Their bodies were never found."

Ahead, the nun stopped at a door. She pulled up her thick key and unlocked the door. "This is where your friend was kept. We keep it locked. It disturbs the others."

She looked back along the corridor. As soon as the key had freed the tumblers, the chatter and calls of the deranged men and women in the other rooms went deathly silent. With a nervous look over her shoulder, she stepped away from the door. "I'll give you some privacy."

The nun tapped her way back down the passage, sticking to the center of the hallway. The inmates remained silent.

Indy entered first.

The room was twenty feet square. It held only a cot with a neatly folded blanket at the foot and a small white sink. Two small windows, barred, were high up on the wall. The walls and floor were plastered stone.

Mutt followed Indy inside. "Oh. My. God."

Indy knew the nun's diagnosis was correct.

Deranged obsession.

Across every surface of all four walls, as high as a man could reach, were scrawled hundreds of pictures. Different sizes, altered angles, some detailed to a lifelike realism, others more abstract. But the subject matter was all the same.

The crystal skull.

Indy was drawn to the back wall. It was filled with a single image of the skull. The room's two small windows were its eyes, aglow with the blaze of the sun.

Mutt slowly turned in the center of the room. "Ox, man, what happened to you?"

Indy turned to the kid, recognizing the depth of the emotion. He thought he should say something, offer some consolation. But Mutt turned away, embarrassed. Indy took a step in the kid's direction—then realized he didn't know what to say. What was there to say?

Indy did the only thing he knew how to do well. He returned his attention to the walls. He made a slow circuit, examining each surface, searching for some clue. When he was done, he stretched a kink from his back. He had come to one realization.

"This skull—" He approached the most detailed drawing on one wall. "It isn't anything like the Mitchell-Hedges skull. Look at the cranium—how it's elongated at the back."

Mutt drew closer. He hugged his arms around him, but he seemed more in control again. "Why's it like that?"

"There's a tradition among the Nazca Indians. Head binding. The Indians used to bind the heads of royal infants so their skulls would distort like that."

Indy studied the drawing of the elongated skull. The scientific term for the procedure was *plagiocephaly.* It was accomplished by tying boards to an infant's skull, deforming the natural growth. The practice was not limited to the Nazca. It could be found throughout early civilizations: ancient Egyptians, Aborigines of Australia, even the Chinookan and Choctaw tribes of North America.

"That's nuts," Mutt said. "Why would they do that?"

"To honor the gods."

"God's head ain't like *that.*" Mutt pointed to the skull.

Indy studied the charcoal etching. "Depends who your god is," he mumbled. His attention caught on a word written below the skull. The word was repeated throughout the chaos of artwork, buried among the skulls—the same word translated into a hundred languages.

Mutt leaned closer and read the word under this skull. It was Spanish. *"Vuelta."* He glanced at Indy and translated. " 'Return.' Return where?"

"Or return *what.*"

Indy glanced at the giant skull with blazing eyes.

"You think Ox meant the skull?" Mutt asked.

Indy waved to encompass the four walls. "Seemed to be on his mind, kid."

"But where was he supposed to return it?"

Indy tugged out Oxley's letter. He read it fully, stopping again at the phrase *Orellana's cradle.* He glanced to the hundreds of translations for the word *return.*

"Cradle," he mused. "It also has more than one meaning. In Mayan it means 'resting place.' "

Indy felt his heart skip a beat.

Of course.

He searched the room again, frantic with his certainty. "C'mon, Ox, you had to have left another clue."

"What's wrong?" Mutt asked.

Indy's mind spun.

Orellana's *cradle* . . . Orellana's *resting place.*

"Ox was talking about the conquistador's *grave,*" Indy said.

He stared down at his toes. And where did someone find a grave?

In the ground.

With his attention focused on the skulls, Indy hadn't seen it. Dirt and dust half hid most of it. He dropped to his knees and swept his hand across the stone floor. He felt the lines more than saw them. It was one last drawing by Oxley, scratched into the stone floor itself.

Indy leaped to his feet and dashed out the door.

"Where you going?" Mutt called after him.

Indy returned a moment later with a broom he had borrowed from the janitor. He tossed it at the kid. "Sweep!"

"What?"

Indy pantomimed how to use a broom and waved to encompass the entire cell. "All of it."

As Mutt set to work, Indy crossed to the far wall and used the bed to climb up to one of the windows. He hauled himself up onto the ledge of the windowsill and crouched there. He turned back toward the room, as if staring through the eyes of the blazing skull.

As the sun baked his back, Indy waited, concentrating, thinking back to his years in college with Oxley. Even back then, the man put the *p* in pomposity. He could hold an overflowing discourse on any bit of obscurity, whether the audience was interested or not. He would never leave the dormitory without every button secured, every hair in place. He was equal parts aggravation and obstinacy.

But the man was also brilliant, with a dazzling ingenuity.

Even back then.

Some part of *that* Oxley had to still exist.

Even here.

Below, Mutt continued to work. With each sweep of the broom, a vast etching was revealed across the stone floor, Oxley's masterpiece. It was the professor's own version of the Nazca lines, visible only from above by the gods.

Or Indy.

It was an elaborate rendering—but not of a skull this time. Indy stared down as Mutt swept. Lines of jagged peaks appeared, along with painstakingly rendered burial temples and funeral monuments.

And a slew of grave stones.

It was a cemetery.

"Where Orellana is buried," Indy realized aloud.

Mutt glanced to Indy, then down to the floor. "I thought you said that the conquistadores all vanished. That their bodies were never found."

Indy stared down at the etched lines.

. . . a dazzling ingenuity.

"Looks like Oxley found them after all."

LIGHTNING SPLIT THE NIGHT SKY, illuminating the landscape ahead, etching the view in silver. Thunderclouds rolled low over the desert highlands and rumbled as if warning off any intruders. The heat remained trapped in the sand, but a cooling breeze swept over the broken landscape.

Mutt perched his Harley at the top of the rise as another burst of chain lightning shattered through the jagged peaks. It had taken the entire day and most of the night to climb up into the mountains above Nazca.

The lightning revealed another valley ahead.

"There!" Jones said, seated behind him on the motorcycle. The professor pointed across the valley to a ridgeline on the far side.

Mutt had seen it, too. Perched atop the next cliff was a jumble of stone crosses, crumbling statues, and squared-off mausoleums. A handful of windswept thorn-pines stood silhouetted against the sky, tortured into twisted shapes by centuries of storms.

"Chauchilla Cemetery," the professor said. "Just like Oxley's drawing."

They had copied what was scratched in the floor of the sanatorium and shown it to a few locals. Someone finally recognized it and warned them against going there. *Maldecido* was how he described the place. *Cursed.* It had taken a few pesos to convince the half-blind man to sketch out a map of the mountains and the cemetery's location.

Even with the map, Mutt had almost given up, convinced the man had been lying.

But here it was.

Mutt understood why they'd been warned off. The cliff where the cemetery perched had eroded away beneath it. Now the old graveyard sat atop a crumbling promontory that jutted out over the open desert. Even some of the tree roots hung exposed along the underside of the promontory in mossy drapes and tangled vines, looking like a hoary beard.

Another flash of lightning revealed what lay on the desert flats hundreds of feet below: *the famous Nazca lines.*

With each burst of lightning, the mile-wide drawings raced with silver fire. Mutt spotted a crooked-legged spider and a tall man with a bowl-like head. They seemed to be staring straight at him. He shivered. Then they vanished again into the darkness.

"Let's go," Dr. Jones urged, impatient, his eyes on the cemetery.

Mutt remained for another breath. He hoped the professor didn't notice his trembling. He had never liked cemeteries . . . even in bright daylight. But his mom's life depended on finding Ox's crystal skull.

So he edged the cycle over the lip of the ridge. A switchbacked trail led across a ridgeline and toward the precariously perched cemetery. It took another half hour to reach the wrought-iron gateway that led into the cemetery proper. By that time the winds had begun to kick up, causing a hand-painted sign to teeter. It read:

Mataremos a Los Huaqueros

Mutt parked under the sign as the professor hopped off and crossed to a dark, ramshackle caretaker's house, plainly long abandoned. The adobe bricks were cracked and covered in lichen. The roof timbers sagged. It looked like another strong wind would blow the whole place down.

Jones kicked in the door and disappeared inside. Mutt heard some rustling, then the professor returned with a lantern in hand. He fired it to a feeble brightness, preserving what little kerosene remained.

"Shovels," the professor said and lifted the lamp.

They found two leaning just inside the gate.

Mutt pointed toward the swinging sign overhead and translated it aloud. *"Grave robbers will be shot."*

Indy headed into the cemetery. "Good thing we're not grave robbers."

The path passed between two of the scrabbled, twisted pines. The gusting winds stirred the branches, knocking them together, sounding like the rattle of bones. Mutt looked up.

He really, really hated cemeteries.

As he stared, something stirred up in the branches, a shift of shadows. He tried to see what it was, but it vanished. He stood for a moment longer, then hurried forward, running square into the professor's back.

"Watch it, kid!"

Jones had stopped at the edge of the graveyard. He was staring out at the spread of tombstones and crypts.

"Grave robbing," he mumbled sourly. "Looks like we're late to the party."

Mutt stepped to the side and searched ahead. Statues, crosses, tiny mausoleums spread all the way to the cliff's edge. The place had seen better times. Half the graves had been strip-mined, pillaged, emptied, and left open. Any valuables had long since been stolen. Only the occupants of the graves had been left behind. Skeletons were strewn everywhere, sprawled, propped, toppled, trampled.

The graveyard had become a boneyard.

The professor lifted his lantern higher. The growing winds kicked up dirt and sand into swirling eddies, like the ghosts of the dead.

Now, that wasn't a good thought.

"Wh-what are we looking for?" Mutt forced out.

"I don't know yet. Something that isn't obvious. Maybe an antechamber to one of these open barrows."

The professor pointed and headed out, thought better of it, and turned in a new direction.

Mutt shook his head and followed.

At this rate, they would be here all night.

Off to the left, shadows suddenly jumped and shifted. Mutt flinched and whirled, striking Dr. Jones in the arm. The professor almost dropped the lantern.

"What's wrong, kid?" he asked angrily.

"Thought I saw something."

"Quit jumping at shadows. There's nothing here but a bunch of dead—"

One of those shadows *jumped* from behind a gravestone and knocked Indy flat. Another dropped from a tree limb and pounded Mutt to the dirt. Mutt flailed wildly at whatever had struck him—but nothing was there. Jones yelled and kicked—but he had no opponent, either.

Ghosts.

Mutt scrambled to his feet in a panic. He backed against one of the grave markers. His heel crunched through the arm bones of a skeleton. He shuddered away—bumping into another skeleton propped up against the neighboring gravestone.

The skeleton's skull turned and looked up at him.

Mutt choked out a scream of horror as it leaped at him, bony arms reaching, clawing. He threw it off of him with a strength born of terror. But it just bounced back to its feet and crouched.

Mutt finally realized it wasn't a living skeleton—but a wiry, feral man, covered in black mud and dressed in a carapace of bones.

Shock kept him frozen for too long.

The madman leaped at Mutt again. But as he lunged, a shovel swung and clocked him flat in the face. The man fell back as his bony mask shattered, revealing a human face behind the skull.

Still, as he struck the ground, he immediately rolled away with preternatural speed and vanished back into the dark.

Mutt joined the professor, shoulder-to-shoulder. They brandished their shovels like weapons.

"Man, that was *not dead*!" he yelled at Jones.

"Oxley's letter," the professor gasped out. "He mentioned something about the *living dead.* He wasn't kidding. He—"

—thwack, thwack—

Two blow darts bloomed along the wooden handle of the professor's shovel, their tiny feathers quivering. The professor dropped flat.

Mutt moved too slowly.

Two shadows leaped over the professor's back and struck Mutt in the chest. He stumbled, then fell backward—into an open grave.

He landed on his back in the hard-packed dirt, the wind knocked out of him. As he wheezed for air, one of the skeletal shadows appeared at the lip of the grave, blowgun ready, pointed toward Mutt.

No escape.

Mutt dug into his pocket and whipped out his switchblade, thumbed it open, and hurled it at the warrior. Silver flashed and grazed the man's forearm, enough to throw off his aim.

The blowgun fell from his fingers—only to be snatched up by a second warrior, who raised it to his lips and pointed it down into the open grave.

Mutt had no other weapon.

He winced, knowing what was coming.

He was wrong.

A hand shot out, grabbed the blowgun, and tugged it away. Leaning close, the professor brought the wrong end of the pipe to his lips and blew hard into it.

The warrior gasped and fell back, dropping the blowgun. One hand clutched at his throat; the other dug into his mouth. The poisoned dart had lodged deep. In another heartbeat, he fell over dead.

On the other side of the grave, the first warrior leaped to his feet, his arm bleeding. He held Mutt's switchblade in his fingers, his arm already cocked back, ready to return the blade to its owner.

—KUH-RACK—

Mutt jumped.

Overhead, Jones's bullwhip had snagged the warrior's wrist. With a jerk, the switchblade tumbled out of the attacker's grip. It flew high, then plummeted—straight for Mutt.

He scrambled back, doing a split. The blade impaled itself into the dirt between his legs.

Close call . . . too close.

"Sorry, kid," the professor called down, but he had his own problems.

The warrior had freed his arm and was preparing to lunge at Jones.

The professor raised his other arm and revealed a black pistol. He cocked it loudly and pointed it at the warrior's bony chest.

The attacker eyed the gun, the man, and the whip—and ran off in the opposite direction. Mutt grabbed his switchblade and stood up. He watched other *shadows* flowing away in all directions.

Smart shadows.

Lightning shattered overhead, limning the professor, bullwhip in one hand, pistol in the other.

"You're a teacher?" Mutt asked.

Indy reached down to pull him out of the open grave. "Part-time."

TWENTY-ONE

INDY HOLSTERED HIS PISTOL and helped haul Mutt out of the grave. Back on his feet, Mutt wiped the blood from the handle of his knife onto his jeans. Indy noted the slightly sick turn to the kid's lips.

It was tough to grow up.

"I . . . I never really used it before," the kid said, staring down at the blade. "Except as a bottle opener."

Indy clapped him on the shoulder. "You did all right, kid."

He crossed to the poisoned warrior, propped him up on a grave, then borrowed a hat and serape from one of the skeletons. He wrapped the dead man in the poncho and planted the hat atop his head.

"That oughta keep him for a couple hundred years."

Mutt stood with his arms hugged around his chest. He studied the dead body. Indy imagined it was the first corpse the kid had ever seen. He had to give the kid credit. He didn't shy away.

"Who were those things?" Mutt finally asked.

"The Nazca. Or maybe their descendants."

Indy contemplated the implication. The Nazca had come to the region more than two thousand years ago. They flourished for a millennium, developing farming methods and complicated irrigation systems. They were great artisans in pottery and weaving. Then they were wiped out. So what was a secret tribe of them still doing out here?

Indy stared across the boneyard.

"Whoever they are," he said, "they don't like us poking around here. Which begs the question: What are they protecting?"

Off to the left, something caught Indy's attention. A stone wall near the back of the cemetery. There was something odd about it. He led Mutt toward it. The surface was riddled with niches, crammed with bones and skulls—most of it covered with spiderwebs.

He fingered the silk.

"*Lasiodorides striatus,*" he mumbled.

Mutt leaned closer. "What's that?"

Indy straightened. "Peruvian giant stripe-knee."

Mutt still looked confused.

Indy moved along the wall. "Giant tarantulas."

"How *giant*?" The kid looked over his shoulder.

"Come see this," the professor said. He ran his fingers down the face of the rock wall. "The stonework's from two different eras. One ruin built atop another. Civilizations do that all the time, layering one atop the other."

As Indy followed the wall, he discovered footprints in the sand: one set heading toward the wall, another away.

He searched that section more closely, his nose an inch from the wall. He examined each niche, gently pulling aside the webs.

"Careful of the tarantulas," Mutt warned.

Indy ignored him. All he discovered were more funerary bones. He came to a skull in another niche, in the more ancient section of the stonework. As he reached to clear the sticky webs for a better view, the silk moved away from his fingers—then back out again.

As if the skull were breathing.

"Air circulation," he muttered.

"What?"

"Sign of a subterranean passageway or cavern."

He reached and pulled the skull from its niche by its eye sockets. A fat tarantula scurried across his hand. Mutt gasped, but Indy ignored the spider. It scampered back to the wall and dove into another niche.

With the skull out of the way, Indy searched the back of the space. His fingers discovered a loop of rope. Leaning back, he hauled on the rope, and the section of wall creaked open with a grinding of stone.

A narrow crawlway stretched into an inky darkness.

Mutt bent down with Indy, shoulder-to-shoulder, and leaned a hand on the jamb of the secret door.

Indy motioned him back. "I wouldn't touch—"

Too late.

A dozen black scorpions streamed out along Mutt's arm.

"GAAH!"

The kid shot backward, shaking his arm. Scorpions rained down and scattered.

"Relax," Indy said. "They're only scorpions."

Mutt suddenly cried out and smacked his forearm. "One . . . one of 'em bit me." He stared over at Indy, his eyes huge. "Am I going to die?"

"Kid, we all die. That's life." His words failed to comfort Mutt in the slightest. He sighed. "Listen, how big was the scorpion?"

"HUGE!"

"Oh, good."

"Good?"

"With scorpions, the bigger the better." Indy turned his attention back to the tunnel, then thought of something and swung back around. "But if you get stung by a small one, kid, don't keep it to yourself. Okay?"

With this sage advice, he retrieved his lantern and crawled off into the tunnel.

Mutt watched Jones vanish down the tunnel. He glanced behind him toward the dark cemetery. A few raindrops pelted from the sky. Lightning flashed and stripped the cemetery of all its shadows. Skeletons and open graves all seemed to be staring back at him, angry at his trespass.

Mutt shuddered.

Cemetery or scorpions?

As darkness fell back over the cemetery, Mutt made his decision.

He pulled out his switchblade, flipped it open, and headed after the professor.

When he ducked inside the crawlway, he saw that Jones was already a good distance down the tunnel. Mutt hurried to catch up, scrabbling on hands and knees. The place smelled moldy and earthy. Cobwebs tickled the back of his neck. Ants and roaches skittered over his hands. Finally he reached Jones. Relief swelled through him—until the ground buckled beneath his knees.

The lower half of his body plunged into a hole. He clawed for a grip on the side of the rocky dirt floor, but more and more of his world crumbled. He fell deeper, sliding.

A hand gripped the collar of his jacket and yanked him back up. He beached onto a solid section of the tunnel. He lay flat, gasping.

"We're on a promontory. This whole cliff is eroded underneath. Be careful."

Jones set out again and quickly vanished around a corner in the passageway. He took the light with him. Mutt caught his breath and called out after him, "Thanks for the advice!"

With no choice, Mutt set off after him. The light was the only thing keeping the scorpions and his terrors at bay. He followed after the professor, balanced between wanting to keep up and fearful of the ground under his hands and knees. He tested each section of the floor cautiously.

As he edged around the corner, he glanced up to see how far the professor had gone—and came face-to-face with three skeletal figures.

A scream escaped him before he could stop it.

The figures crouched upright in niches, their arms and legs bound to their chests. Skeletal eyes stared back at him. Mouths hung open in their own silent screams.

The professor called back to him, "Keep it down, will ya, kid!"

Mutt tried to force his heart to stop pounding. "Their skulls, man! Did you see their skulls?"

Jones returned reluctantly. He held the lantern up to illuminate one of the skeletons. Its skull was misshapen. He reached out and gently turned it. The back of the cranium was elongated into an egg shape.

"Just like Oxley's drawings in his cell," he said. "We're getting close."

He headed out. Mutt stuck close to his backside. "Who or what are they?"

"Human," Jones said. "Most likely Nazca royalty."

Mutt remembered Jones's story of how the tribes used to bind the skulls of royal infants to mimic the gods. "Maybe this is what those skeletal warriors outside were guarding," he offered.

"And maybe something more," Jones said cryptically. "Come see."

Ahead, the professor jumped down into an open space. The roof was high enough to allow them to stand upright. The chamber was as large as a two-car garage. It smelled less moldy, more dry and heavy, weighted with a strange expectancy.

Mutt climbed down and joined Jones. He began to step forward, but the professor blocked him with an arm.

"Don't touch anything."

Remembering the scorpions, Mutt obeyed.

"This is incredible," Jones whispered under his breath.

He lifted his lantern, revealing footprints crossing the dusty floor.

"Somebody else was here. Recently." He leaned down to study the prints. There were two complete sets. "Two people."

Mutt knelt and measured both sets with an outstretched hand. "Same size." He craned up at Jones. "Could have been the same person . . . came here twice."

"Not bad, kid."

The professor raised his lantern higher, stretching the light. Mutt could just make out more niches and corpses in the back wall, about the same size as the Nazca royalty out in the tunnel. But the shapes were indistinct and covered with dust and sand.

"Stick with me," Jones warned and set off across the chamber. "Step where I step."

Mutt noted that the professor was carefully matching his stride to the dusty footprints on the floor. Mutt did the same. One behind the other, they crossed the floor and safely reached the other side.

Mutt stepped out next to the professor. He studied the closest niche. It definitely seemed to hold a body, but it was hard to make out, as each niche's figure was wrapped in something like a cocoon. Through the dust, Mutt noted a glint of silver. There was a strange bite of electricity in the air. He could taste it on his tongue. Curious, he took a step closer, but Jones placed a restraining hand on his shoulder.

Jones counted the niches, pointing his lantern toward each. " . . . five . . . six . . . seven." He set the lantern on the floor. "It must be Orellana and his men."

"Only one way to find out," Mutt said.

TWENTY-TWO

INDY APPROACHED the nearest niche. Reaching carefully, he pinched and fingered the burial shrouds. He shook the material. Sand and dust fell away, revealing pure silver underneath. Definitely not cloth, but not metal either. Indy recognized the material: It was identical to the shroud that had wrapped the mummified remains found inside the coffin stolen from Hangar 51.

But what lay hidden here?

Indy peeled back the layer only to discover another one beneath.

"Like unwrapping a Christmas present," Mutt said, breathless with anticipation.

Indy parted another layer, then another. He found himself holding his breath. The small hairs on his arms stood on end, not with fear, but from some strange emanation that crackled from the shroud as he parted each layer.

At last, Indy reached the heart of the cocoon. He saw what the layers of burial shroud hid and stepped back. It was indeed a body, but one perfectly preserved, as if the figure had just fallen asleep. A man sat with his arms crossed, his legs pulled to his chest. His head tilted, eyes closed, as if in slumber. The skin looked soft, the beard full. Even the frill of cloth around the neck looked worn but free of any decay.

Indy ran a finger along a breastplate of armor inscribed with the Spanish Cross. The body also wore an ornate scabbard and a tall, conical helmet.

"The conquistadores," Indy said. "It truly is them."

Mutt leaned closer. "It looks like they died yesterday."

"But it's been over four hundred years." Indy touched the silver shroud, sensing again the strange energies. "The wrappings must have preserved them."

Studying the conquistador, Indy noted that the figure clutched a solid gold dagger with a ruby-and-emerald-encrusted pommel. With great care, he slipped it from the man's dry fingers. Turning, he edged the dagger more fully into the lantern light, admiring it. He noted the filigreed inscription in Spanish, perhaps the owner's name. He wondered about the dead man. Who had he been? What sort of life had he lived? How had he come to be buried here?

Lowering the dagger, Indy began to slip the artifact into his satchel.

Mutt cleared his throat. "I thought we weren't grave robbers."

Indy realized what he'd been about to do: standing knee-deep in a grave, holding a dead man's riches. "I was going to put it back."

"Uh-huh."

Indy turned back to the conquistador. But the man's body had disintegrated. Everything organic, even the clothes, had withered to dust in the space of ten seconds. All that was left were the bones.

"Ick," Mutt commented.

Indy knelt down and pulled up a section of the metallic cloth. "I've seen this kind of stuff before," he mentioned. "Ten years ago at some kind of crash site."

And again a few weeks ago in Nevada.

He grabbed a section of the soft metal and crumpled it into a ball, then tossed it back down. It unfolded all by itself and returned to its original shape.

"Whoa!" Mutt edged nearer. He pointed his switchblade, but it was torn from his fingers and snapped up against the wrapping. "Double whoa!"

"Whatever it is, it's highly magnetized."

"Ya think?" It took some effort, but Mutt pulled his knife free and stuck it in his boot for safety.

"Wherever these conquistadores stole the skull from, they must have taken this wrapping along with them."

"But that's not all they took," Mutt said and pointed near the corpse's feet.

A small chest lay open, overflowing with jewels and gold coins. Indy dropped to a knee and picked up a handful of coins. He examined them as they sifted through his fingers. There appeared to be some from all over the globe. He spotted a bust of Athena on one, a Corinthian helmet, an Eye of Horus.

"Greek, Macedonian, Egyptian," he mumbled. "What are they all doing here? From so many eras? So many corners of the world?"

"Were they also stolen from Akator?" Mutt asked.

Indy straightened. "I don't know."

He moved to the next niche and quickly unwrapped the cocoon there. He found the same thing: a perfectly preserved body of a four-hundred-year-dead Spanish explorer, who immediately decomposed to dust and bone upon air contact.

Mutt had moved a few niches away and called out, "This one's already been opened!"

Indy joined him. "What did I say about sticking to my side?"

"Man, lighten up." Mutt pointed to the floor. "I followed the footsteps like you did."

Indy frowned. "Well, at least you're learning . . ."

He turned his attention to Mutt's discovery. The kid was right. The mummy had already been opened. He parted the loosened layers of shroud to reveal a skeletal figure decked out in full armor—chest plate, helmet, even a death mask. But here the armor had been crafted of solid gold.

"It's Orellana himself."

"How do you know?" Mutt asked.

"All the gold. They called Orellana the Gilded Man. Everything he wore was made of gold, even—" Indy stopped himself and furrowed his brow.

"What's wrong?"

"Something's not right." Indy pointed to the golden mask. "Spaniards didn't wear burial masks."

He reached up and ran his hand along the edges of the mask.

"Careful," Mutt warned.

Indy glanced back and gave him an *I-know-what-I'm-doing* look, then closed his fingers around the mask and pulled it slowly. Behind it was the skull of Orellana, frozen in a horrible death shriek. Though it was only bone, the shape screamed terror and pain. There was a wrongness that disturbed.

"Put it back, put it back," Mutt said.

Indy considered doing just that—until he noted a brilliant gleam that reflected the lantern light. It came from behind Orellana's skull, framing it in a halo of brilliance.

Crouching, Indy grabbed the body by its golden shoulders. He pulled the torso and head forward and passed them to Mutt. "Here. Hold this."

Mutt obeyed, wearing a sickened expression, nose-to-nose with Orellana's corpse.

Behind the body, hidden in a niche not unlike those in the cemetery wall, rested a large skull, twice the size of an ordinary man's. And unlike any real skull, this one had been sculpted of brilliant clear-blue crystal. It captured every bit of lantern light and reflected it back with a beauty a thousandfold richer.

Indy reached for it, but his fingers hesitated. He remembered all the tales Oxley used to tell of these strange skulls, of killing curses and paranormal powers. Forcing down these superstitious fears, he studied the skull more closely. It appeared to be cut from a single piece of pure crystal, perfectly transparent, yet multifaceted.

Curiosity finally overcame caution. Indy's fingers touched the skull's polished surface, and the light dimmed fractionally. Scooping it out, he carefully lifted it free of the niche.

Mutt shouldered Orellana's body back into its niche with a shudder of revulsion.

Indy lifted the lantern and held the skull in front of it. The fiery light cast a prism through its crystalline surfaces and concentrated it back out through its oversized eyes, like a laser beam. It hurt his head to look into that gaze, like staring into an eclipsing sun. He turned the crystal skull in his fingers and discovered the cranium to be egg-shaped, like the corpses outside.

"No tool marks," he murmured to himself. "No evidence of a lapidary wheel. Unbelievable."

He brought the skull closer to his nose. *What's that . . . ?*

Deep within the cranium there appeared to be a *second* crystal, embedded in the brain cavity, opal in color, shimmering through a prismatic series of hues, almost seeming to flow like liquid.

Turning it again, he examined its every surface.

"A seamless piece of quartz, cut against the grain. That's not possible, not even with today's technology. The stone would shatter."

Mutt joined him, studying the skull at his shoulder. "You think it's the one from Akator?"

"Maybe. The conquistadores must have looted the rest of this stuff along with it, then headed for their ships on the coast. Got this far before they died or were killed. The locals must have wrapped 'em in the stolen shrouds and buried 'em."

Indy finally lowered the skull and returned his attention to the dusty floor and its footprints. He knelt at the edge. He pointed to the footsteps, tracking them.

"Then a few hundred years later, Oxley finds the skull, takes it away . . . maybe to Akator, maybe he found that place, too—but then he returned it here."

Mutt stirred. "*Return.* Like he wrote on the wall."

"Makes no sense," Indy mumbled. "He hid the skull right back where he found it. Why?"

Mutt suddenly grabbed his arm, squeezing hard. "*L . . . look!*"

Indy glanced over and watched Orellana's skeletal arm rising, reaching for the skull. A surge of superstitious fear flooded through him, but he calmed himself. He slowly raised and lowered the skull. The arm tracked his movements.

Ah . . .

"It's alive, man!" Mutt said, dancing back. "Give it back the skull!"

Indy reached forward and tapped the golden armor still strapped to the skeletal arm, the vambrace and rerebrace. He pointed to all the gilded surfaces and fastenings.

"It's the metal in the armor," he explained. "It's just being attracted to the skull."

"But crystal ain't magnetic, man."

"Neither is gold," Indy conceded. He studied the skull with a frown and lifted it again before him. *What is this thing?*

He found himself gazing into those eyes again. Though it still hurt his head, he kept looking, wanting answers, needing to know its secrets. The light blazed out of the skull's eyes and into Indy's. It felt like a searchlight burning into his skull. Deep in that brilliance, Indy sensed . . . something . . . something he could almost grasp.

"*Hey—*" Mutt said behind him.

Indy barely heard him. It sounded as if the kid were calling to him from down a deep well.

"*—something's hap—*"

Close . . . so close. All he needed was a moment longer . . .

"*—pening, man. Ground's trembling. We must—*"

Fire burned into his skull. Almost there . . .

"*—get the hell out of here! NOW!*"

TWENTY-THREE

MUTT GRABBED the professor's elbow and yanked his arm down. The skull tumbled from Jones's fingers and landed in a pile of soft sand, its crystalline eyes blazing toward the ceiling.

Jones swung around. "What do you think—?"

Mutt fell back from him. The professor's eyes glowed in the darkness, shining with their own inner fire. Frightened, Mutt bumped into Orellana's body behind him.

Jones blinked and pressed his fingertips against his forehead as if warding away a fierce headache. The light in his eyes faded as he glanced around, but his eyes also grew huge. "Shaking . . . ground's shaking!"

"Man, what do you think I've been trying to tell you?"

Across the floor, sand vibrated and small pebbles bounced. Larger rocks rattled against one another. The bones of the skeletons shook as if frightened.

Jones twisted toward the exit and pointed. "Out! Now!"

Mutt stepped to obey—but the floor gave way under him. His legs were swallowed into a widening fissure. With a sharp holler, he slid, plummeting within a cascade of sand and rock. His hands scrambled for some purchase. His fingers found something hard and clamped to it.

Still, his body continued to fall. Blinded and choked by dirt and sand, he coughed and spit. Then his plunge stopped. He jarred to a halt, hanging by one hand, his fingers still tight on whatever he'd grabbed. A last slide of rock and dust washed past around him and away.

Mutt looked down—and gasped.

He was dangling five hundred feet above the desert floor. A flash of lightning ignited the Nazca lines below: a spider, a monkey, a lizard.

Mutt tore his eyes away and stared up.

A shrieking skull looked back down at him. Orellana. Mutt had grabbed the conquistador's ankle—or rather, the lower end of his armor. Lantern light showed Jones clutching the gold plates of the skeleton's arms. The professor must have caught the corpse as Mutt dragged it with him through the hole.

Mutt tried to pull himself up.

Bits of Orellana's skeleton shook out of its armor and spun down toward the desert floor to shatter far below: femur, ankle bones, ribs. The armor was hollowing out.

"Stop wiggling already!" Jones yelled down at him.

Mutt's motion and weight were beginning to widen the hole in the burial chamber's floor. Rocks and sand fell, along with more bones. He stared overhead. The entire promontory was fissuring and cracking. Large sections fell away, tumbled, and exploded upon impact with the desert floor.

Desperate, his heart hammering, Mutt met the professor's eyes.

"Stay calm, kid! I'm going to pull you up!"

Stay calm?

More stones fell as another section of the hole's lip collapsed. Amid the new rockfall, a spark of brilliance flashed from out of the wash of sand and stone, reflecting the lantern light above.

The skull . . .

Mutt swung his lower body, heaving into a swing, and reached out his free arm. Rocks pelted him, but his hand caught the falling skull. He dragged it to him and hugged it to his chest like a football.

"What don't you understand about *stop wiggling*?" Jones called down to him.

Mutt showed him the cradled skull. "Thought you might still want this!"

That shut him up.

Piece by armored piece, Jones hauled Mutt up. More skeletal bits rained down, but the gold suit of armor held. At last, with a final grunting heave, the professor dragged Mutt back into the burial chamber. The crystal skull rolled out of his grip and across the floor. Gasping and sweating, the professor grabbed it and shoved it into his satchel. He pointed to the exit.

"Go! Hurry!"

They scrambled to their feet. Jones dove first into the crawlway. As if he'd done this many times before, the professor moved swiftly through the tunnel. Shimmying inside after him, Mutt felt a great shudder in the mountain—then a massive thunderclap erupted behind him. He turned in time to see the entire burial chamber crack and fall away.

"Quit gawking, kid!" Jones said.

Mutt scurried down the crawlway as fast as he could move. More and more of the promontory broke away behind them, trying to drag them down, too. Mutt chased after the professor, who urged him to move faster and faster. With the world falling away at his heels, Mutt needed no additional encouragement.

At last they reached the tunnel's end and piled out into a frantic heap.

The professor helped Mutt to his feet. They stumbled a few steps from the cliff's edge onto solid ground. Behind them, the promontory stabilized, though some sand still seeped and a few rocks fell. Beyond the cliff, dawn finally approached, turning the dark skies into a mix of pinks and oranges.

"We made it," Mutt said.

"Yes, you did," said a voice.

They both turned as a trio of figures stepped around the corner of a crumbling mausoleum. Two were in uniform, carrying rifles. The Russians again. The center figure wore a khaki suit and wide-brimmed Panama hat. He faced the professor with a welcoming smile.

"Hello, Indy."

"Mac . . ."

Indy shouldn't have been surprised, but he was.

Before they could extend their greetings, Indy heard the crunch of boots on rock. He turned to see Colonel Dovchenko step behind Mutt. The Russian swung a blackjack and clubbed the kid in the back of the skull. Mutt dropped like a brick.

"You bastard," Indy growled.

Sneering, Dovchenko kicked Indy to the ground and swung a glancing blow to his skull with the same weapon. Stars danced across Indy's vision as he fell hard to the sandy dirt. As he struck, the crystal skull rolled from his satchel and landed eye-to-eye with him.

A shadow fell across him.

Dovchenko.

The Russian had picked up a gravestone and hoisted it over Indy's head.

"No!" Mac called. "She said she needs him alive!"

Dovchenko smiled at Indy and heaved the stone straight down.

Indy winced, but the chunk of gravestone only struck the ground beside his head. Dovchenko strode away, grumbling in Russian. Indy didn't understand it, but it sounded like a cross between a threat and a promise.

As the man left, Indy found himself focused on the crystal skull again. The sun rose behind it, shining the first rays of the new day through the crystal. The eyes blazed at Indy. Somewhere deep in the skull, Indy sensed something stirring . . . reaching out for him.

He opened his own eyes wider.

Fire filled him.

Then a hand reached down. He caught a glimpse of a syringe and felt a stinging stab into his neck. A plunger pushed and filled him with darkness, extinguishing the skull's fire, too.

He had one last thought.

Not again.

PART FOUR

EYES OF FIRE

TWENTY-FOUR

Iquitos, Peru

THE SCREECH of a monkey woke him.

Sensations returned piecemeal: an ache in the shoulders, a scent of wet loam and cinnamon, a pasty thickness of the tongue, a mosquito's buzz, a dense moistness to the air. Vision blurred and steadied, then blurred again. A camp cot. A tent pole. A hanging lantern.

He felt his head pulled back by the hair. Liquid fire burned down his throat. He fought, but his head was as heavy as a cannonball. He spotted a bottle with Cyrillic lettering. Vodka. *Cheap* vodka. The fire hit his stomach and exploded outward along his limbs.

He struggled and realized he was seated in a chair, tied to it. He tugged at the ropes that bound his wrists, rubbed raw. How many days? He vaguely recalled a steam locomotive, piled with cargo, flashes of jungle, a river ride.

Where was he?

Indy lifted his head. He sat in a sparsely furnished camp tent; it was square-cornered, with walls in green-and-black camouflage. The place had *military* written all over it. Through the mesh windows, it was pitch dark. Nighttime. Somewhere to the left a bonfire crackled and glowed through the tent walls. Shadows shifted in front of it. He heard singing, carousing. From the hop and twirl of shapes, they were even dancing. The boisterous songs revealed the celebrants' nationality.

Russian.

A figure stepped into his sight line. He carried a chair in one hand and the vodka in the other. Dressed in khaki, bare-headed and red-faced, he dropped the chair and sat down in it. He rested the vodka bottle on his knee and smoothed down his mustache as he contemplated his prisoner.

"Mac . . ." Indy spat with a scowl. He pictured the man ambushing him at the Chauchilla Cemetery. He stared curses at the traitor.

"Lucky for you I showed up when I did, Indy. Dovchenko wanted to smash your head in back in that cemetery. That's the third time I saved your life."

"Untie me, and I'll say thanks."

Mac leaned back and tilted the chair up on its back legs. He swigged from the bottle with a wince, then sighed. He held up a finger. "Let's keep track. The first time, you had a Luger pointed at the base of your skull. In fact, that's how we first met, wasn't it?"

"I had the situation under control."

A second finger rose. "Then there was Jakarta. Remember the amnesia darts I pulled out of your neck?"

"Amnesia darts?" Indy crinkled his brow.

"See, you don't remember!" Mac shook his head. "And maybe just as well. Take my word for it, you owe me. Owe me big!"

Indy leaned forward as far as the ropes would allow him, his face hard. "After the war, when you turned traitor—how many names did you give the Reds? How many good men died because of you? What do you owe *them*?"

Mac sighed. "I don't think you see the big picture, mate."

"Eventually these ropes are coming off, comrade. And when they do I'm going to break your nose."

"*Comrade?* You actually think I care about flags? Uniforms? Lines on a map? Those all change."

"But money doesn't."

"No, even money does, Indy. But *gold.* That's forever." Mac glanced nervously to a reel-to-reel tape deck. It was slowly turning, recording their every word. He lowered his voice and spoke more conspiratorially.

"And not just gold. A gigantic pile of gold. Forget what the Russians are paying me. It's nothing compared to what's at Akator. You know the legends. An entire city of gold. It's what those bloody conquistadores were after, for God's sake. We'll be richer than Howard Hughes."

Indy sneered. "Blood money. Every nickel of it."

Mac leaned even closer, his voice dropping to a whisper. "I need you to see the angle here, Indy. Be smart and play it right. Remember, just like in—"

The lantern light flickered as the tent flap behind Indy was pulled back. A night breeze swept through the stifling tent. Someone pushed inside behind him.

Mac leaned to his ear. "*—like in Berlin.* Get me?"

The traitor stood up, a welcoming smile blooming on his face.

Beyond the tent, Indy heard the coughing call of a hunting jaguar. *Panthera onca.* On the fresh breeze, he caught the sweet scent of *Victoria amazonia,* the night-blooming giant lily pad. He noted the flutter of a bright yellow moth with a long tail—drawn inside by the lantern's light. A comet moth.

In his head, Indy cross-referenced the flora and fauna, ranges and locations, trying to calculate where he had been taken.

Deep Peruvian rain forest.

If he wasn't mistaken, he had to be somewhere along the Ucayali River, which meant they were perched at the edge of the darkest part of the forest, where few men ever ventured, and even fewer ever returned. Why were they here?

The breeze suddenly died as the tent flap dropped. The mysterious visitor stepped into view on Indy's right. She had changed out of her US Army uniform and into another: gray with black boots and a squared-off cap. A *Russian* uniform. Showing her true colors at last.

She did, however, retain one part of her old uniform: the belted scabbard at her side, slung low on her hip.

Irina Spalko.

Mac bowed his head slightly. "*Dobroi nochi,* Colonel Doctor," he said. "I'll leave you to your interrogation."

She barely noted his acknowledgment as he slipped past her, but Indy caught Mac's worried glance. Once Mac had left, Spalko stepped forward with her hand on her rapier's pommel.

"Dr. Jones, you survive to be of service once again."

Indy kept his voice flat. "You know me. Anything I can do to help."

Her eyes narrowed. "*Now I am become Death, the Destroyer of worlds.* You recognize these words, *da*? It was your own Dr. Oppenheimer . . . after he created the atomic bomb."

Indy flashed back to the mushroom cloud in the Nevada desert. "He was quoting the Hindu Bible."

"It was nuclear intimidation. But no longer. Now this next level of weapon is *ours* to have—yours to fear."

"Weapon? What weapon?"

"A *mind* weapon. A new frontier of psychic warfare. It will bring about Stalin's dream for this world."

Indy glowered at her madness. "Now I see why Oxley put the skull back where he found it. He must have known you were after it."

Spalko settled into Mac's former seat. She picked up Mac's vodka bottle and poured herself a drink.

"You may scoff, Dr. Jones, but that skull is no mere deity carving. Surely you knew it the moment you laid your eyes on it—it was not made by human hands."

"Then who do you think made it?"

Spalko lifted one eyebrow, as if to say, *Isn't it obvious?*

"C'mon, sister."

She leaned over and removed a blanket from the neighboring camp cot. It had been thrown over a familiar object: the steel coffin from Hangar 51. Its surface glowed with reflected light from the lantern.

"That body your government found in New Mexico," Spalko continued, "it wasn't the first. We'd already dissected two others from similar crash sites in the Soviet Union. Perhaps you remember the Tunguska explosion?"

Indy sat straighter. He did. In 1908 some mysterious object had crashed to earth near the Tunguska River in Siberia. It had flattened two thousand square miles of trees, with the force of one thousand atomic bombs. The Russians had said it was a meteoric event. Apparently that wasn't exactly the truth.

Spalko noted the widening of his eyes and smiled thinly. "The legends about Akator are true, Dr. Jones. From descriptions in the historical texts of the Maya and the Nazca, early man couldn't have conceived such a city, much less built it. It was a city of supreme beings with technologies beyond our current comprehension . . . and paranormal abilities beyond anything on this planet."

"You gotta be kidding me."

Indy wanted to scoff more strongly, but a seed of worry settled into him. He remembered his own short study of the skull. Even in such a brief examination, he knew he held something amazing. The artifact had been cut against the natural planes of the crystal, yet polished so smooth that it felt almost watery to the touch. And then there were the finely crafted details. Indy had to admit it: The skull *had* to have been carved with a skill beyond modern tools.

Still, Spalko read the lingering doubt in his face. "Why do you stubbornly choose not to believe your eyes? The New Mexico specimen gave us hope. We dissected it."

Indy glanced sharply at her. They had done what?

She continued, "Unlike the others we'd found, the New Mexico specimen's skeleton was pure crystal. Including its skull. Though it was much smaller. Perhaps the New Mexico specimen is a distant cousin of the larger skull you found? Maybe the smaller ones were sent to *find* Akator. Perhaps we're all searching for the same thing. There's no other explanation."

Indy shook his head. There was no hesitation in his next words. "There's *always* another explanation."

She refused to listen. Adamancy entered her voice, along with a shine of fervor. "The skull was stolen from Akator in the sixteenth century. By the conquistadores. Whoever returns it—"

"*—to the city's temple gets control over its power,*" Indy finished. "I've heard that bedtime story, too, sister. But you're forgetting one detail."

"What's that?"

"What if Akator doesn't exist?"

She shrugged. "That is a good question, Dr. Jones. One we've been trying to answer with the help of your friend—Dr. Harold Oxley."

"Ox? He's here?" Indy sat up straighter.

She nodded. "But there's a bit of a problem."

TWENTY-FIVE

INDY RUBBED HIS SORE WRISTS as he ducked out of the tent. Two Russian guards in gray uniforms flanked the exit and kept rifles leveled at him. Spalko followed at his back, a Makarova semiautomatic pistol in hand, pointed at his spine.

They were taking no chances.

At the door to the tent, Indy stood for a moment, gaining his bearings, chasing the last of the cobwebs out of his head by taking several deep breaths of the fresh breeze. The jungle encircled the camp, its canopy leaning over the clearing. The scent of night flowers and damp loam was carried in the wind as it whispered through the forest like some shadowy hunter. Insects whirred in a constant chorus. A few frogs croaked in counterpoint. The jungle loomed, ancient, forever brooding.

Unlike what lay ahead of Indy.

A giant bonfire blazed in the center of the Russian encampment. Flames crackled high, churning smoke toward the dense jungle canopy overhead. Firelight danced shadows all around, warding back the rain forest and its darkly primeval heart. A rutted track led to the campsite, which was crowded with jeeps, trucks, and a giant machine fronted by a pair of horizontal saw blades twice as large as manhole covers.

Indy eyed the number of Russian forces. Not good. There had to be more than fifty soldiers: cleaning weapons, smoking, carousing with one another. Many were crowded around the blaze, singing in Russian and clapping along.

A regular Boy Scouts of the Soviet Union jamboree.

"This way," Spalko said.

She led him toward the fire. The two guards fell into step behind them.

Indy continued his surveillance, looking for some way out of this mess. Ahead, the path cleared for Spalko. Men backed away, voices died down, and cigarettes were ground underfoot. Indy noted the fear with which the soldiers viewed their leader. She had them firmly under her thumb.

She crossed the camp to the bonfire.

The singing faltered with Spalko's arrival. Those who hadn't seen her started another chorus. A path opened toward the flames. She led Indy to the clearing around the firepit.

A single figure still danced around its roaring flames. Barefoot, he hopped and twirled, twisted and cavorted. The man's hair was tangled, greasy, and long. His beard reached his collarbone. He wore a ragged striped poncho that flapped and flared. His pants were muddy and shredded.

He circled the fire, nearing Indy, spinning to face him—then away again. His cheeks were sunken, his body skeletal, his limbs emaciated. Still, Indy recognized him.

"Ox?"

It couldn't be.

Dr. Harold Oxley.

Deaf to his name, the man danced away, even though the clapping and singing had ended. Indy followed along behind Oxley, trailing him. He tried to reconcile this scrawny, wild man with the prim, buttoned-down professor he had known, a man who had always been as stiff as his starched shirts.

Indy closed the distance to the professor and stepped in front of him. "Ox! It's me, Indy, remember?"

Oxley moved to spin past him. His right arm bounced and twitched in the air as if he were conducting his own orchestra. His eyes darted everywhere, never stopping. His head lolled as if listening to some faraway voice only he could hear.

Indy grabbed his friend by his thin shoulders and pulled him closer, whispering urgently, "You're faking it, right, pal? Tell me you're pulling a fast one on the Reds."

The professor shuddered and shivered in his grip, barely constrained. Indy cupped the man's chin and noted, distantly, that Oxley's skin burned, even through his scrabbled beard. Indy forced Oxley to face him. The man's pupils were dilated, despite the bright blaze of firelight. His gaze rolled over Indy with no spark of recognition.

Words babbled from Oxley's lips. "*Through eyes that last I saw in tears . . .*"

Indy shook him gently. "Listen to me. Your name is Harold Oxley. You were born in Leeds, and you were never . . . never . . ." He looked the professor up and down. "Never this interesting. We went to school together at the University of Chicago. We had pizza together every Tuesday at Gino's. I'm Indiana—"

Indy sighed and winced. Seeking another path through to the man, he spoke a name he hoped would jar Oxley's memory. "Ox! It's me! *Henry Jones Junior.*"

Oxley twisted free of his grip and flung himself away. His arm thrust out, and he began conducting his ghostly orchestra again.

Indy turned toward Spalko.

Mac had joined her, standing with his arms crossed. He wore a concerned expression. But was Mac worried about Oxley or just about his lost City of Gold?

Indy confronted Spalko. "What did you do to him?"

Spalko shook her head.

Mac answered, "We didn't do a thing. Truly. It was the bloody skull."

Spalko kept her voice clinical, detached. "Your friend is a divining rod that will lead us to Akator. But we need someone to interpret him for us. His mind, it seems—" She shrugged. "—is quite weak."

A hand dropped to Indy's shoulder. From the size of the mitt, Indy didn't have to glance back. It had to be Dovchenko. The Russian squeezed hard, bruising down to the bone.

Spalko turned on a heel. "Let's hope yours is stronger, Dr. Jones."

She strode away toward the opposite side of the camp. Dovchenko shoved Indy after her. Two soldiers followed with weapons ready.

The group ended up outside the camp's largest tent, which was aglow with lantern light.

Spalko ducked inside without a word. Indy was half dragged, half pushed to follow. Straightening, he frowned at what he found inside. At first he thought it was a first-aid tent. Banks of medical equipment lined one side; a desk sat on the other. But instead of a hospital cot in the center, a single straight-backed chair stood in front of the central tent pole.

Leather straps hung from its arms and legs.

Oh, great . . .

Dovchenko forced Indy into the chair. He tried to resist, but his limbs were still weak from the days he had spent drugged. Still, it took another two soldiers to strap him to the chair. He tugged and thrashed at the bindings for another breath—then gave up.

Another soldier, dressed in a laboratory smock, came forward dragging a tangle of electrical wires. He bore down on Indy with clear intent.

"If you think I'm telling you anything . . . ," Indy spat, anticipating some type of electrocution-as-torture.

Spalko had crossed to the back of the tent, out of view. "Calm down, Dr. Jones. They are only leads for an EEG."

Electroencephalogram? Why would they need to check his brain?

Indy tried to twist to see her, but another soldier pinned his head while the technician taped electrodes to his temples, behind his ears, and across his forehead. The wires trailed to a piece of medical equipment. The technician flipped a switch, and a small needle began tracing a line of black ink across graph paper.

Spalko returned with a wooden box and placed it on the nearby desk.

Indy turned, dragging the wires that draped his head.

She opened the box and lifted out an object wrapped in silver. She peeled off the strange metallic cloth and revealed the large crystal skull. The lantern's flames fluttered slightly as if the room's light were momentarily sucked into the crystal. The skull glowed brighter with the stolen fiery light.

Spalko spoke, her back to Indy. "As best we can determine, the skull's crystal stimulates an undeveloped part of the human brain, opening a psychic channel."

Turning, she dropped the silver wrappings to the desktop. Paper clips and a penknife slid across the surface and clung to the wrapping. Spalko barked in Russian to two soldiers, who dashed out of the tent.

She turned her attention back to Indy. "Professor Oxley went mad by staring too long into its eyes. Perhaps you can get through to the professor after you've done the same."

Indy recalled staring into the skull's eyes, back at the cemetery. He remembered the blaze of light burning into him. One part of him shuddered at the thought of meeting that crystalline gaze again—but another part *craved* it. He couldn't dismiss the desire. Twice he'd been interrupted. He'd been close to something . . . some understanding.

"And what if I won't cooperate?" he asked.

The tent flap tore open in front of him. Two soldiers returned, wheeling a .30-caliber machine gun into the tent. The muzzle pointed at Indy's nose.

Well, that was one way of getting him to obey.

But instead, the soldiers pulled the gun from its mount and headed out with it, leaving behind the weapon's stand. Spalko crossed to the gun mount, placed the skull atop it, and wheeled the skull square in front of him.

Its inner fire glowed brighter.

The eyes blazed, waiting.

Indy kept his gaze averted. "You know, if you're so anxious to talk to Ox, why don't *you* look at it?"

"I've tried," Spalko said with disappointment in her voice. "And failed. Many have."

She snapped a finger and a soldier positioned a chair next to Indy's. She sank down into it. She reached to Indy's face and moved a few leads out of the way. The back of her hand brushed his cheek.

Off to the side, Indy sensed the skull beckoning to him. He felt its gaze like a sunburn on his cheek.

"You're not afraid, are you, Dr. Jones? You've spent your entire life searching for answers . . ."

Answers, the skull seemed to echo with secret promises.

" . . . think of the truth behind those eyes."

Indy's head slowly turned, unbidden. He could not help himself. A part of him didn't want to stop. His eyes swung and faced that blaze. Despite the brilliance of the skull, he could feel his pupils widening, making his eyeballs ache, drawing in more of the refracted light.

The skull filled his vision.

Spalko whispered at his ear. "There could be hundreds of these skulls at Akator, maybe *thousands.* Whoever finds them will control the greatest natural force the world has ever seen. Power over the mind of man."

Dazed by the brilliance, Indy muttered back, "Be careful. You might get exactly what you ask for."

"I usually do, Dr. Jones."

More and more light blazed into him. In the background, he could hear the technician who operated the EEG voice concern. Indy heard the machine's needle rattling up and down, scratching across the graph paper.

"Imagine that power," Spalko said. "The power to peer across the world and know your enemy's secrets. To place our thoughts in the minds of your leaders, to command your soldiers to attack on *our* orders."

Indy barely heard her. In the spaces between her words, there was only light. Somewhere far away, a needle scratched faster and faster across paper.

He felt Spalko's breath at his ear. "We will be everywhere at once, as powerful as a whisper, invading your dreams, thinking your thoughts for you while you sleep."

Fire burned away all vision. It filled his skull, building pressure. The world became brilliance. And in that brilliance—something stirred, shifted toward him.

Far, far away, someone cried a warning.

A woman nattered like a gnat in his ear. "And the best part? You won't even know it's happening."

He was only light. He no longer had a name.

From deep inside him, a single word bubbled forth, intoned from his core. It was all that mattered. It was his entire vocabulary.

Return . . .

It grew in his head.

It became his name, his purpose.

His lips moved, though he was deaf to it.

RETURN . . .

But someone else heard.

TWENTY-SIX

MAC CIRCLED THE BONFIRE, a bottle of vodka hanging from his left hand. The Russian soldiers had abandoned their earlier festivities. The quiet of the jungle pressed back down over the camp. The shadows grew darker beyond the firelight. Unseen eyes seemed to stare back at him out of the forest.

Or maybe it was just Mac's own conscience.

He marched in a slow parade around the campfire, following the dancing scarecrow. Though no one had ordered him to, he kept a vigil on Harold Oxley, becoming the man's babysitter.

It was better than being in that tent with Spalko. He had no desire to see what was happening in there. He knew what she intended to do to Indy. Mac had only to watch Harold Oxley cavort around the fire, mindless and maddened, to know Indy faced a similar fate.

Completing another circle of the bonfire, Mac glanced toward the large tent. He rubbed at his mustache, a nervous gesture. *Indy, why couldn't you just have minded your own business?*

Distracted as he stared, Mac ran into Oxley's back. The professor had halted dead in his tracks. For the first time this entire evening, he had stopped.

Must've finally run out of steam . . .

The professor swung toward the large tent, his head slightly cocked as if listening. His lips moved. *"Return . . ."*

"Oxley? What's wrong, ol' chap?"

The man ignored him. The blankness of the professor's face crumpled to confusion. The dullness left his eyes, and the slack features tightened. Lips parted, and the mad professor's voice cracked on a single name.

"Henry . . . ?"

The vodka bottle slipped from Mac's finger and hit the dirt.

Oh God . . .

Mac grabbed the professor, guided him to a log, and made him sit. Oxley folded, compliant, and rubbed his eyes, as if struggling to fully wake up.

"Hang on, mate."

Mac ran across the camp, breathless with fear. When he reached the large tent, a guard tried to stop him, barking in Russian, but Mac ignored him. He had no time to argue. He jammed straight through the flap and burst inside. He was ready to shout about Oxley—then he spotted Indy.

His old friend was strapped to a chair, nose-to-nose with that damn skull. His face glowed a fiery red, his temples visibly throbbed, and sweat poured down his face. But most disturbing of all, bloody tears flowed from both of his eyes.

"Enough!" Mac shouted.

Faces turned to him.

Mac pointed out toward the bonfire. "Indy's broken through to Oxley!"

Spalko stepped forward. She and a technician had been studying a needle racing up and down across graph paper, so fast that the tracing it was leaving was solid black. Mac knew the machine was an EEG. He noted that the leads ran to Indy and gaped at the needle blurring over the paper. What was going on in Indy's brain?

Mac pointed at Indiana. "Stop! It's enough. We'll never reach Akator if he dies, for God's sake."

Spalko hesitated. She glanced from the EEG to the prisoner, her eyes bright with the desire to continue—but then she waved an arm to one of the soldiers. He dashed forward and threw a hood over the skull.

Indy jerked back as if jolted by electricity. A gasp burst from his throat as if he were surfacing out of deep black water. His head wobbled, rubber-necked, his cheeks bloody. Off to the side, the fluttering needle slowed.

Spalko picked up the printout, excited. "His theta waves are off the chart. A full hypnagogic state!"

Mac ignored her and went to Indy's side. *Is he all right?* He took Indy's chin to steady his head and studied his old friend's face. The whites of his eyes were bloodshot, almost bruised. The pupils had grown huge, making it impossible even to tell the color of his irises. Trembling, Mac wiped the trail of blood from Indiana's cheeks. At least the bloody tears had stopped.

He stared blankly up at Mac.

"Indiana?"

Spalko joined Mac. "Dr. Jones?"

Indy's gaze twitched in her direction.

"He needs medical attention," Mac said.

Spalko backed up and motioned to Dovchenko. The Russian colonel came forward and began unhooking the leather bindings. Dovchenko freed an arm.

Mac stayed with Indy, leaned close. "You're going to be—"

A fist slammed square into Mac's face. As pain exploded in his nose, he fell and landed hard on his backside. Stars danced across his vision.

Still half strapped in the chair, Indy shook his freed hand and glared down at Mac. The blank expression had been replaced by fury.

Mac tasted blood on his lips. He fingered his face and felt an agonizing crunch of bone. "You broke my nose!"

"Told you I would."

Dovchenko held Indy down in his seat, but the Russian giant's eyes danced with dark amusement.

Spalko was not as amused. "Enough." She pointed out the tent. "Dr. Jones, you will speak to Professor Oxley and convince him to lead us to Akator. Yes?"

Indy turned his glare toward her. *"Nyet."*

She sighed, as if she expected nothing different from her captive. "So be it. It looks like you will need convincing, Dr. Jones." She headed out of the tent with a final sharp order for Dovchenko. "Bring him!"

TWENTY-SEVEN

Indy wobbled on his feet as he was shoved through the tent flap and back out into the firelit camp. His head pounded as if his brain were trying to push out of his ears. The firelight stung his eyes, and he had trouble focusing.

The cooler air outside the tent helped steady him. He took deep breaths and rubbed a knuckle into each temple.

The rubber in his legs slowly firmed.

Ahead, Dovchenko disappeared into a neighboring tent, then returned dragging a wriggling, protesting figure.

Indy dropped his arms as a familiar young man in a black leather jacket was shoved toward Spalko and Mac. *It was Mutt Williams!* Red-faced, the kid rubbed his wrists and glared at the tall Russian. The kid's clothes were rumpled, and his oiled hair stuck up in a cowlick and behind his ears.

Indy struggled to comprehend Mutt's appearance here. He'd thought the Russians had left the kid unconscious in the Chauchilla Cemetery. Why had they brought him here? Indy glared over at

Mac—*The boy has nothing to do with this.* The traitor had the decency to glance down to his boots.

Indy took a step toward Mutt, but Dovchenko blocked him with a thick arm.

"You okay, kid?" Indy called over.

Mutt's voice rang with outrage. "They left my bike in that cemetery."

Indy frowned. "But are *you* okay?"

Mutt still wore a deeply wounded expression. "They left my *bike*, man! How could they?"

A soldier approached. He cradled in his arms an antique, polished rosewood case, two feet wide and four feet long, covered in ornate Byzantine gilt scrollwork. Spalko crossed to the box and opened it. The interior was molded velvet, formfitted to secure its contents: three handsome swords. Spalko drew her rapier from the scabbard at her waist and gently secured it into an empty slot in the box.

She studied the other weapons, fingering each one lovingly, contemplating, then selected the thinnest and meanest-looking silver blade. The sword was the least ornate but appeared the most deadly, a weapon hammered for only one purpose.

To draw blood.

With a deft flick of her wrist, she turned to face Mutt. "Dr. Jones, I'll have to teach you a lesson about cooperation."

The kid eyed the blade and backed away, one palm raised. "Hey, wait! Don't! Don't!"

Indy heard the panic in his voice—but instead of begging further, Mutt simply freed a comb from a back pocket. He quickly ran it through his hair, patting every strand in place, then straightened, chest out.

"Okay, now go ahead," Mutt said. His eyes flicked to Indy. "Don't give these pigs a thing."

Indy had to smile. What else could he do? The kid had moxie.

He turned to Spalko and shrugged. "You heard him."

Spalko sighed her exasperation and lowered her sword. "Clearly I've chosen the wrong pressure point. Perhaps I can discover a more sensitive one."

Her sword swung toward George McHale. Indy's smile widened.

Not this time, sister! Do with that bastard what you want!

But she kept turning and barked to two guards outside a small dark tent. *"Privedite zhenshchinu!"*

They ducked inside and Indy heard a fierce struggle. A voice shouted out in English, furious, fearless . . . *and damned familiar.*

"GET YOUR HANDS OFF ME, YOU ROTTEN RUSSKIE SON OF A—"

Indy felt his stomach sink. It couldn't be. Impossible.

From the tent, a woman was dragged into the firelight, carried between two soldiers, her legs kicking at them. She was planted on her feet between Spalko and Mac. She shook off her guards and straightened her khaki vest over a powder-blue long-sleeved shirt. Though older—in her late forties—there was no mistaking her: her dark auburn hair, a dusting of sun freckles, her deep blue eyes.

Those eyes . . .

Indy still pictured her eyes when they'd first met, when she'd been a young woman, staring at him with such fire and amusement from the back row of his graduate class. It had been those eyes from the start . . . and always would be.

Marion Ravenwood.

Indy's knees weakened under him—though this time it had nothing to do with the crystal skull. Memories tangled: her mischievous smile as she pulled him into a closet at the university library for the first time . . . the smoky scent of her hair outside the burned-out Raven Saloon in Nepal . . . the taste of her lips when they'd first kissed . . . and at the end the angry, wounded disappointment in her eyes after what was to be their final fight.

During their brief but fiery time together, Marion had proved to be equal parts passion and fury, brilliance and frustration. She was all soft curves and hard corners.

No wonder he loved her.

No wonder they hadn't lasted.

Steps away, her eyes sparked with a familiar fire—until she spotted Indy. Then it flamed even higher. " 'Bout time you showed up, Jones!"

Mutt also turned to her. His eyes widened in surprise. "Mom!"

Marion turned to the kid. "Sweetheart! What are you doing here?"

Indy stared between the kid and Marion. He felt gut-punched. One word encompassed all his confusion. *"Mom?"*

No one heard him. Mutt tried to reach Marion's side, but Dovchenko held him back by the collar. "Forget about me, Mom!" the kid yelled. "Are you all right?"

Indy shook his head, rattling his already bruised brain. "*Marion* is your mother?"

He was still ignored. Marion pointed an accusing finger at Mutt. "Young man, I *specifically* told you not to come down here yourself."

Indy had to state it once more aloud. "*Marion Ravenwood* is your mother?"

Marion glanced over to him, exasperated. "For God's sake, Indy, it's not that hard."

"I just, I never . . . I mean I didn't think you'd—"

"Have a life after you left? Guess again, buster."

Indy raised a hand. "That's not what I—"

"And it was a pretty good life, I might add."

"That's great, I just—"

"Pretty *damn* good life," she added, punctuated with a sharp nod.

Indy felt his blood rising. "Well, so have I, Marion!"

She leaned on one hip. "Yeah? Still leaving that trail of human wreckage . . . or are you retired?"

"Why, are you looking for a date, sister?"

Marion took a threatening step toward him, but a guard grabbed her elbow. Off to the side, Mac was smiling broadly at her.

Indy glared at him. "What're you looking at, bub?"

Marion fought the guard holding her. "Will you let go of me so I can punch that son of a—"

Indy turned to her. "What are you mad at me for?"

"How much time you got?" Further words died as one of the soldiers pressed the barrel of a pistol against her head.

"Enough," Spalko snapped. "Dr. Jones. You will help us."

She waved for the soldier to lower his pistol and raised her sword. She held it dead-steady toward Marion. An inch from her left eye.

"A simple yes will do, Dr. Jones."

Indy sighed, frowning. "Aw, Marion. You had to go and get yourself kidnapped."

"Not like you did any better!"

They simply stared at each other.

Just like old times.

TWENTY-EIGHT

LED AT GUNPOINT, Indy marched toward the camp's bonfire. Mutt came with him, but Marion was kept under guard back at the tents, ensuring his cooperation. He had a thousand questions for the kid, wanted all the details of Marion's life, but Dovchenko slapped Mutt in the back of the head every time he tried to speak.

Spalko kept her rapier at Indy's back.

Still, an inexplicable lightness filled him, a surge of hope.

Marion Ravenwood was *here*. He had not spoken to her in years. Yet as soon as Indy had laid eyes on her, it was as if no time had passed at all. He felt younger already, drawn back to their earlier time together. Even now his heart thudded stronger, his hip ached less, and the bruising wasn't as tender.

But Indy also recognized the danger they all faced.

Marion's life depended on what he could learn from Oxley. Spalko would punish Marion for any failure. And Indy could not let that happen.

Ahead, lit by the fire, Indy spotted Ox seated on a log. The professor stared at the flames. If anything, he looked even thinner, sagging within his poncho, a frail shade of the man he'd once been.

Mutt noted the professor's sorry state, too. The kid's face screwed up with fear and worry. "Man, what happened to him?"

This earned another cracking slap from Dovchenko.

"The crystal skull," Indy answered. He glared at the giant Russian. That was Marion's kid he was hitting!

Indy reached the log and sat down next to Ox. At least his friend appeared calmer. Oxley had even donned a khaki hat, decorated with several bright feathers. The odd choice of apparel concerned Indy. The Oxley he knew preferred bowlers, checkered caps, even top hats for formal occasions. The tips of the feathers bobbed as a slight tremor shook the professor's body. Oxley's right hand trembled and jumped on his knee, some form of residual palsy.

Still, Oxley glanced over to Indy. His bleary eyes widened with recognition. "Henry Jones Junior!"

"That's right, Ox!"

A surge of relief flowed into Indy. Mac had been right. Ox was back! Indy had to hand it to the Russian ice queen. Spalko had been right about how to free his friend. He felt a measure of hope that all would work out fine.

Off to the side, two soldiers hauled up a reel-to-reel tape, ready to record everything. Clearly, Spalko did not want to miss anything crucial. Or maybe it was some form of record for her, a personal diary of her accomplishments here.

Behind Indy, Mac spoke to another soldier. "Just so you know, I'm giving three to one odds that the Yank figures out where the City of Gold lies."

Ignoring him, Indy focused his full attention on Ox. Despite recognizing Indy, his friend still looked addled around the edges. "Now listen, we need—"

The professor grabbed Indy and said intently, "Henry Jones *Junior*!"

Uh-oh.

Indy glanced to Mutt, then back to the professor. The boy's eyes also narrowed with worry and suspicion.

Oxley's fingers clutched harder at Indy. "Henry *Jones* Junior!"

"We've established that, Ox."

Indy studied Oxley's face. Something was wrong. The professor was back, just not *all the way* back. Indy read the frustration in his friend's eyes, teetering at the edge of insanity, trying to find a bridge across.

Words flowed out of Oxley's mouth. *"To lay their just hands on that Golden Key . . . that ope's the Palace of Eternity."*

Indy tried to make sense. "The palace of—?"

Spalko interrupted, standing stiff at his shoulder. "He's quoting from Milton. He's said it before." Disappointment rang in her voice . . . along with something more menacing. "What does it mean?"

Indy took a deep, shuddering breath. He didn't know. And Marion's life depended on answering that question. He needed more information.

"Harold, listen to me. I need you to tell me how to get to Akator . . . *Ak-a-tor.* Do you understand me? You must tell us or they're going to kill Marion."

"Through eyes that last I saw in tears . . . here in death's dream kingdom."

Oxley's palsy grew worse. His right hand jerked and bounced. How much longer until he was bounding around the campfire again?

Indy grabbed his wrist, trying to keep that from happening. "They're going to kill Abner's little girl, Ox. You remember Abner . . . and his daughter Marion, don't you?"

Oxley's brows furrowed with his frustration. *"Eyes! That last I saw in—"*

Indy squeezed the man's quivering wrist. "How do we get there, Ox? You've got to be specific."

The palsy in the professor's trapped hand only grew more intense. It drew Indy's attention. Restraining Oxley's wrist, Indy noted how the professor's fingers were held pinched together, as if he were holding something. Indy remembered Ox dancing around the fire, his scrawny arm up in the air as if conducting an orchestra. His fingers had been pinched then, too.

Indy stared down.

He wasn't trying to conduct an orchestra.

He was *scribbling* in the air . . . and now on his knee.

Indy swung to Spalko. "Get me paper and pen!"

She yelled, and in seconds someone ran up with a notebook and a pen.

One-handed, Indy flipped open the notebook to a blank page and stuck it under Oxley's scribbling hand. He jammed the pen between the professor's clenched fingers.

Instantly ink flowed across the page as Oxley wrote. A crude picture formed on the blank sheet. Yet the professor seemed mindless of what he was doing. He wasn't even looking down at the paper. His gaze remained fixed on Indy.

"Henry Jones Junior."

"That's right, Ox."

The professor leaned closer, his voice lowering conspiratorially. *"Three times it drops. The way down."*

"I'm sure it does," Indy said, focused on what Oxley was scribbling.

The professor finished one drawing—*waves, or the ocean.* Indy flipped to a new blank page, and the drawing continued. *A pair of closed eyes.*

Spalko leaned closer. She glanced with grudging admiration toward Indy, then back to the sketching. "He's auto-writing! Of course, I should have seen this."

Oxley's scribbling began to speed up, completing three more sketches:

The sun with an arc across the sky.

A snake with a flickering tongue.

A horizon over mountains.

Then the palsy slowed, and the pen fell from his fingertips.

Spalko studied the scattered sheets. "What are they?" she asked. "Pictographs of some sort?"

"No!"

Indy shifted on his log and reached into a pocket of his jacket. His fingers discovered crinkled papers inside. They were still there, the pages he'd torn from the book at his home library. Pulling them out, he flattened them on his knee. He compared Oxley's drawings with what was on those pages.

A dictionary of Mayan symbols.

Indy worked quickly. In his element, he bent over the pages and became lost to his surroundings. "They're ideograms! Bits of Mayan language. I think I may be able to translate them."

TWENTY-NINE

MARION SAT with her arms folded atop a camp table. Two guards flanked her, pistols in hand. The weapons weren't necessary. She wasn't going anywhere, not without her son.

She stared toward the flames of the bonfire.

He shouldn't have come.

She meant Mutt, but her eyes were on another.

Even from here, Marion made out his shape, limned against the firelight, a battered fedora in place. Her eyes traced his shoulders, the crook of his head in deep concentration. She remembered all the late nights. She would be in bed, and he would be at his desk, poring over a thick book or studying some bit of antiquity by candlelight. She would wait for him to come to bed, no matter how long it took. He would eventually blow out the candle, slip from his clothes, and slide under the covers beside her.

She would turn and kiss him, reminding him that life was more than history, that there was also a *present* waiting for him, too.

And she *had* waited.

Each night.

But one night he never came home.

Then another.

Still she waited.

Eventually, there was nothing but an empty side of the bed.

She knew the truth then . . . as she knew now.

The man had only one love.

And it wasn't her.

So she had stopped waiting and turned her back. She found a good man, a home, a family. They had married. It had been a happy time: birthday candles, scabbed knees, Christmas trees, long green summers, and even longer winter nights with someone in her arms.

Then a war stole that life away, too, snuffed it out like one of those midnight-burning candles, leaving her dark and empty.

Only her son was left, a bright spark in the night.

As she gazed at the bonfire, its flames ignited a bitter ember in her chest. Now he was here again. After so many years.

As she stared toward the fire, she recognized a painful truth.

Though she had moved on with her life, a small part of her—buried deep in her heart—had never truly stopped waiting for him.

She recognized both this reality and the delusion that lay beneath it.

She looked over at Mutt. She was no longer the carefree young woman who would drink men under the table on a wager. She was a mother, tempered by responsibility and life into something far greater. It was time to set aside such girlish fantasies.

Still, her gaze drifted back to Jones.

Her heart burned—not with *passion,* only anger.

At Jones, at herself.

She was done waiting.

Mutt sat on the log as Jones worked on his pages. Off to the east, the skies had begun to brighten with the approach of dawn.

He stared into Ox's face. This couldn't be the same man. The one who had taught him how to ride a bike, who had helped him pick out his prom tux, who had listened to him late in the night when he couldn't deal with his mother. He'd been like a second father.

Mutt reached out and tried to hold the professor's shaking hand—but Oxley just jerked it out of his grip. Mutt leaned forward, trying to make eye contact.

"Ox?"

The man's red-rimmed eyes stared off into nowhere, seemingly blind to the boy whom he had helped raise.

"C'mon, Ox," Mutt begged. "Look at me, man."

Mutt had lost one father to a war. He couldn't lose another.

But there was no response, no recognition, nothing.

Mutt wiped at his eyes. "Please, Ox . . . I need you, man. I . . . I love you."

Mutt had never said that to Oxley, the man who had filled the void in his home and heart after his father died. Wasn't love supposed to heal all?

Oxley continued to stare into the firelight.

Apparently not.

"I think I got it!"

Indy straightened and sifted through the papers. He brought up each sketch, one after the other.

"*Wave lines,* that was water. *A closed eye* meant sleep. *The sun with the arc across the sky* stood for a span of time. The *horizon* and the *snake* represent vastness and a river."

Spalko shook her head, not comprehending.

Indy slowly put it all together, like working a jigsaw puzzle. "Water and sleep. A span of time. A vast river." He swung to Spalko and shook the papers at her. "Don't you see? These are *directions.*"

Her eyes grew larger.

Indy sprang to his feet. "I need a map!"

"Over this way," Spalko said.

She waved them to their feet. All of them, including Oxley and Mutt. Dovchenko and the guards did not leave any choice in the matter.

The group shifted across the camp to where Marion was being held at gunpoint. She sat slumped in a chair before a table. Indy moved toward her, but Marion glanced up at him. He read the fiery look in her eyes and shied away, but her gaze mellowed into something warmer as she spotted her son.

Mutt went to her side, hugged her, then took a guarding position over her. The kid clearly was not going to let anyone hurt her. And from the way Mutt glared in his direction, that included Indy.

A soldier ducked into a nearby tent and returned with a rolled-up map. He unfurled it across the table and weighted the corners down with rocks.

"Planning a vacation, Jones?" Marion asked.

"Just looking for somewhere well off the beaten path."

"I've heard *Hell* is nice this time of year. You should try it."

"Already been there, sweetheart. Remember that year we spent together?"

Marion's eyes narrowed slightly, wounded. Indy regretted his words, but it was too late to take them back. Her features hardened. He silently cursed himself. What was he doing?

Spalko interrupted them by slapping a hand on the map. "Where do we go, Dr. Jones?"

Indy returned his attention to the task at hand and smoothed his palms over the map, leaning in close to read. *Damn fine print.* The letters were just blurry shapes. If he was going to solve this puzzle, he needed to see every detail. He gave in, reached to his pocket, and donned his reading glasses.

"Priceless," Marion muttered, staring at his bifocals.

His face heated up, so he focused on the map. "The vast river must be the Amazon," he said and traced a finger along the twisting, curving river. It did look like a snake. "But I'm not sure what *water* and *sleep* mean . . ."

Spalko leaned next to him, her shoulder touching his. She tapped the map. "Here. The Sono. It's the Portuguese word for 'sleep.' It's a smaller waterway. It joins the Amazon here."

Indy nodded, excited. "That's got to be it!"

Off to the side, Marion scoffed, "I knew you two would hit it off."

Indy ignored her, lost in the riddle. "He wants us to follow this curve of the Sono River—for a span of time—all the way until it hooks up with the Amazon to the southeast. After that, I'm not sure."

Indy leaned back and ran through the sketches in his head. What was he missing? Maybe something from the verses that Oxley had quoted. But what?

Through eyes that last I saw in tears . . .

Death's dream kingdom . . .

Indy returned his attention to the map. "This route has to be right. It heads off into a completely unexplored part of the jungle. See, the mapmaker only sketched in a few rough—"

Suddenly the table crashed up and struck both Indy and Spalko in the face. He fell back but kept his footing. Spalko tripped over Dovchenko, and they both went down.

Mutt grinned proudly on the other side of the table. "Run!" he yelled and plucked Marion out of her chair.

Before any of the guards could react, mother and son fled between two tents and headed for the jungle beyond.

Indy had no choice.

He swung, swooped up Oxley around the waist, and sprinted after Mutt and Marion. Gunfire erupted behind him, shredding foliage and chasing him into the dark forest.

He cursed Mutt's rash action.

Leaping without thinking.

Like mother, like son.

MUTT FLED down the narrow animal trail, leading the others. Wet leaves slapped and tangling vines snagged. He fought a path through the dense jungle. Rifle blasts chased them; soldiers called out in Russian. Some creature howled up in the canopy like a strangled kitten, protesting their passage. Something stung his neck. He ran, panting. The air grew thicker under the canopy, heavy, almost too thick to breathe.

Still, he kept going.

He had spotted the narrow path earlier. He didn't know where it led, but as long as it was *away* from here, he was happy to follow it. He kept a grip on his mother's hand.

Behind him, something heavy crashed after him, cursing loudly and in a steady stream. Mutt risked a glance over a shoulder. He spotted Jones, sweaty, frantic. The man clutched his fedora to his head and dragged Oxley with his other arm.

"Harold!" Jones hollered. "For God's sake, keep up!"

Mud grew heavier underfoot as Mutt slogged ahead. It slowed him down. He struggled harder, but the muck fought him.

Jones caught up with them, half carrying Ox. His face burned red, but not just from exertion. He drew even with Mutt and stomped along beside him.

His voice was hard and unforgiving. "Kid! What the hell was that? What were you thinking?"

"They were going to kill us!"

"Well, *maybe*!"

"Boys," his mom said and tried to step between them. "Maybe we'd better—"

Mutt refused to back down. "Somebody had to do something!"

"Something *else* would have been good!"

"At least I *got* a plan!"

A bullet blasted between them, burning through the dense jungle.

"Like I was saying," his mother said more sharply, "maybe we'd better get off this path."

With a tug on Mutt's arm, his mother dragged him off the trail and down a steep, narrow cut. Jones and Oxley skidded after them. They slipped and scooted to the bottom. The ravine emptied into a dense copse of giant trees with a clearing in the middle.

Jones pointed.

They hurried toward the clearing. His mother and Jones, Oxley still in tow, ducked behind some tall thorny bushes and hid.

Mutt hung back and returned a few steps higher, so he could spy on the upper trail through the jungle. He sheltered behind the bole of a giant tree. Shouts, threats, and an occasional rifle blast echoed to them. A moment later a squad of Russian soldiers trampled into view. Mutt froze. The soldiers slowed—then continued past and away. After half a minute the voices faded, smothered by the thick jungle.

Sighing with relief, Mutt turned and headed back to the clearing. He kept his voice low. "I think we lost—"

But no one was there, only a thick wall of underbrush.

He hurried down. "Mom?" he called in a low voice and pushed into the clearing.

Oxley had settled to the ground and was picking thorns off the bushes. Beyond him stood his mother and Jones in the middle of the clearing, but they were sunk into the sandy floor up to their knees, arms out as if unbalanced.

It made no sense.

He took a step toward them.

"Stop!" Jones growled.

"Keep back!" his mother warned.

As he watched, Jones and his mother sank farther into the sand, now up to their thighs.

Jones spoke between clenched teeth, whispering urgently. "Don't move, Marion. The motion makes space, and space makes you sink."

Mutt hovered at the edge, not sure what to do.

His mother scowled at their predicament. "I think I can get out if I just—" She tried to pull one leg up but only managed to sink deeper.

"Stop it already!" Jones warned. "You're pulling against a vacuum. It's like trying to lift a car. Just stay calm."

"Don't move, Mom!" Mutt called to her.

She stood still, arms out, motionless. She barely moved her lips. "Okay. I'm calm." She slipped deeper. "I'm calm, and I'm still sinking."

Mutt searched around. "What is it? Quicksand?"

Jones answered, exasperated. "What are they teaching you in school nowadays?" He waved his hands over the sucking sand. "This is a dry sandpit. Quicksand is viscous mud, clay, and water, and because of its fluidity, it's not as dangerous as you might—"

Marion shoved him in the shoulder. "Jones! For pete's sake, we're not in school here!"

"Just stay still, Marion. There's nothing to worry about, unless there's a—"

A geyser of sand exploded between them, showering Mutt at the bank of the pit. He spit sand and cleared his eyes. His mother and Jones had now sunk almost to their chests.

"—void collapse," Jones explained sourly. "A pocket of space in the sand."

Mutt could stand it no longer. He thought quickly and knew the pair had only one chance of getting out of that trap alive. He hated leaving his mother, but he had no choice. "Hold tight! I'll find something to pull you out with!"

He tore off into the shadowy jungle.

"Kid!" Indy called out. "Get back here!"

But Mutt vanished through the foliage. Indy heard his stomping, ripping passage fade away. What was the kid thinking? Besides the Russians, there were a hundred ways to get yourself killed out there. Even experienced explorers could get lost in the dense jungle, turned around, confused. And the kid didn't have a compass.

Indy mumbled under his breath and glanced to the woman trapped at his side. "He's definitely *your* son, Marion. Always flying off half-cocked."

He didn't give Marion a chance for a retort. Instead, he called over to Oxley, who stood at the edge of the sandpit chewing on a thorn, staring off blissfully. "Ox, for God's sake, don't just stand there! We need *help*!"

The professor's bleary gaze focused back on them. He tugged his feathered hat more firmly on his head. "Help?"

That's right, Ox . . . you understand.

"Harold, I need you to—"

Without another word, Oxley turned, shoved straight through the thorn bush, and disappeared.

Great.

Indy heard him stomp and rip his way through the jungle, heading off in the opposite direction from the kid. He shook his head as he slipped another inch into the sand. Why wouldn't people listen to him?

"Okay," Marion said, drawing back his attention. She wore a

slightly guilty expression and waved in the direction that the kid had vanished. "I'll admit, Mutt can be a little impetuous."

She turned more fully to face Indy and arched an eyebrow toward him. "Maybe like someone else I know."

He straightened the fedora on his head. "Well, I guess it's not the worst quality in the world," he admitted. "He could—"

Another geyser erupted, shattering sand into a coughing flume. Indy coughed and choked. As it cleared, he saw that they were now buried up to their armpits. The sand squeezed hard around his chest, making it difficult to breathe. From Marion's strained expression, she was suffering the same. Her eyes teared from all the stinging sand.

Indy didn't know what to do, what to tell her. He gasped out what reassurance he could amid the crush of the pit. "Keep your arms . . . above the surface . . . the kid comes back, grab on . . ."

She turned to him. He saw something in her expression, a tenderness. He suddenly realized the tears were not from the sting of sand in her eyes. "Indy, Mutt's—"

"—not a bad kid, Marion . . . I know . . . you should get off his back about school . . ."

" . . . what I meant . . . Mutt, he's . . ."

"It's okay, Marion . . . not everybody's cut out for school . . ."

The tenderness in her eyes flashed into annoyance. "Indy!" she snapped, gaining his full attention. "Mutt's name . . . it's *Henry.*"

Indy forced his neck to crane around to view her fully. "Henry?"

"He's your son, Indy."

He felt a sinking sensation that had nothing to do with the sand pit. "*My* son?"

"Henry Jones the third."

Indy looked away. He felt a fury build in his chest. He couldn't stop it. Now was not the time to lash out, especially about this, but there was no stopping it.

He turned back to her. "Why the *HELL* didn't you make him finish school?"

Before she could answer, something long, brown, and heavy landed between them. The impact sent fresh sand up into Indy's face. Coughing and spitting, he struggled to get the sand out of his burning eyes. He could barely keep his eyelids open. Tears streamed, blurring his vision.

Did a tree branch crash down from the canopy?

"Grab on!" a voice yelled from the edge of the pit.

He recognized the kid's voice . . . his son's voice. He'd made it back! Then again, he shouldn't be so surprised. Mutt *was* his kid, a chip off the old block.

Marion had already grabbed onto the blurry tree limb, hugging tightly to it. Indy struggled to lift his arms high enough to reach the limb. His hands reached for it—when the limb's end reared up and hissed in his face.

He yanked his arms back. "Ack!"

Not a tree limb.

A giant snake!

"Are you crazy!" he hollered toward Mutt.

Panic cleared his vision. The massive snake was as thick around as his forearm. It undulated and slowly writhed in front of him. It extended all the way across the pit to Mutt. Black eyes stared back at Indy with all the menace of its entire genus. A long venom-red tongue flickered a full foot from its scaly maw.

Marion hugged it farther along its coils. "Indy, just grab on!"

"It's a *SNAKE*!"

Mutt heard him. "Don't worry! It's just a rat snake!"

Indy tried to point at it, but he didn't dare get any closer. "Rat snakes aren't that huge!"

"Well, this one is! You should've seen the size of some ants I saw; big as my hand."

Giant ants? The kid was full of wild stories.

"Besides, it's not even poisonous!" Mutt assured him.

Indy kept his arms well away from the snake. "Go get something else!"

"Like *what*?"

"I don't know . . . some rope or something!"

"Man, this ain't no Sears and Roebuck. *Just grab ahold!*"

Indy tried to move his leg. "Maybe I can touch bottom."

Marion shifted and stared back at him as if he were crazy. "There is no bottom. Now do what Mutt says . . . *and grab it!*"

"I think I can feel it with my toe."

Marion and Mutt both screamed at him. *"JONES!"*

THIRTY-ONE

MUTT WATCHED the man's face scrunch up with distaste. Jones reached out toward the brown rat snake, closing his eyes and turning his head away.

Mutt still had his end of the snake slung over his shoulder. He crouched with his legs braced against a tree trunk. He remembered the professor's description of the sand's vacuum hold.

Like trying to lift a car.

He might not be able to drag them out, but he could keep them from sinking deeper. In the center of the pit, Jones gave one final cringe and snatched the snake into his arms. It coiled around his forearms. He visibly shuddered.

Now all Mutt could do—

—Ka-phooom!

Another massive geyser, bigger than the others, erupted out of the pit with a plume of sand as high as the canopy.

Void collapse.

In that instant Mutt remembered another lesson from the professor. A void was a *pocket* in the sand.

A gap.

Mutt took advantage of it. As sand rained down, he shot out with his legs and yanked hard on the snake's body. His shoulders burned with strain, his knees shook—then suddenly the resistance gave way. He backpedaled using rocks and trees for footing.

As the sand cleared, he saw his mother and Jones beached up on the bank of the pit, limbs entangled. Mutt dropped the snake and rushed up to their side.

His mother sat up and patted the snake's scaly trunk. Jones opened his eyes and jerked away from it. He rubbed his hands vigorously on his pants, his face screwed up with horror and revulsion.

The snake, freed now, rolled and writhed its way toward the jungle, vanishing back into the undergrowth.

Mutt stood over Jones. "You have no problems with tarantulas and scorpions . . . but one little snake . . ."

Jones pointed a trembling arm toward the vanished serpent. "That was no *little* snake, kid."

Mutt shook his head. "You are a crazy old man."

A sudden snap of branches froze them all.

Oxley burst through the thorn bushes, wearing a big grin.

"Ox!" Mutt said.

Then behind the professor, soldiers appeared, bristling with rifles. The soldiers parted to allow Spalko and the guy with the British accent and broken nose to step forward.

Snuffling around his broken nose, the man straightened his Panama hat and asked, "Why do you wanna do everything the hard way, Indy?"

Oxley matched the man's pose a bit proudly, adjusting his own feathered cap. *"Help!"*

Jones eyed Oxley. "Yeah, that's great, Harold."

Spalko stared over them all with a dispassionate expression. She waved the soldiers to drag them to their feet. "Enough delays," she said and pointed back toward the encampment. "We must get going. We will now see if your suppositions about the map were correct, Dr. Jones."

Jones scowled back at her.

Spalko eyed first Mutt, then his mother. "And for their sakes, you'd best pray that they are."

As the convoy was being organized for their departure into the jungle, Colonel Dovchenko watched the woman practice with her sword.

Irina Spalko stood apart from everyone else, stripped to a tight-fitting shirt and loose pants. She had cleared an area behind her tent, where she thought she had full privacy. But Dovchenko had a good vantage point from the side, shadowed by the forest fringe. He leaned an arm on the trunk of a tree. The heat here was oppressive, the forest too dense—nothing like the birch forests and frost of his Siberian home—but at the moment, Dovchenko wished to be nowhere else.

Spalko lifted the rapier to her nose in a silent salute, hips angled parallel to the attack line, square with her shoulders. She danced a step forward and lunged out with the sword in a flash of steel. It was so rapid that the blade became more mirage than real. Without stopping even for a beat, she darted, turned, leaped, and slashed. She had the grace and balance of the finest Russian ballerina, and the fierceness and cunning of an experienced warrior.

Dovchenko held his breath, both frightened by and drawn to her.

She sparred for a full ten minutes, never stopping, changing sequences, flowing from one to another. Dovchenko knew little about fencing. She had attempted to instruct him once, to train him as a dueling partner, but he had given up. He could not tell a *coup d'arrêt* from a *moulinet.*

Still, at the moment, he did appreciate the sport.

Truly appreciated it.

Sweat soaked her shirt tight, gave her skin a molten sheen. It outlined every curve and swell. Her lean muscles rippled and shivered.

She continued sparring, fighting empty air.

But Dovchenko knew the space was not truly empty. It was full of ghosts from her past. He saw it in the fiery set to her eyes. Dovchenko also knew she challenged a shadow of herself, expending her frustration, needing to prove something to herself. It was motion and purpose given physical form.

Ultimately, he knew what she was doing.

She was readying herself for what was to come.

Dovchenko turned away and stared across the breadth of the convoy to the dark jungle beyond. It would be a difficult trek.

And they had their orders.

They must not fail.

PART FIVE

INTO THE FOREST PRIMEVAL

THIRTY-TWO

Deep in the Amazon

Irina Spalko sat in the front passenger seat of the lead jeep as it rocked and bumped through the jungle. The driver was a young Ukrainian, dark-haired, dark-eyed, and not much older than she'd been when she had fled her small mountain village home.

The entire Russian convoy trailed behind her. It consisted of a dozen vehicles and sixty men. The only vehicle in front of hers was the jungle-cutter, nicknamed the mulcher. Trundling forward on tank treads, it went ahead of them all, its two massive horizontal saw blades screaming and smoking as they cleaved a path through the rain forest, cutting through underbrush and trees, choking up clouds of diesel smoke. Its operator sat high in a cab at the rear.

A trail of fallen trees and trampled mud was left behind in the convoy's wake, but in the jungle, any trace of the convoy's passage would be erased within the space of a couple of seasons. The jungle was a living thing, consuming all within its dark heart, swallowing the footsteps of human intruders.

Or at least that was what Irina hoped.

Somewhere out there, buried under vine and leaf, must lie the fabled city of Akator. It was the convoy's goal but—more importantly—it was her own.

As they moved slowly forward, Spalko returned her attention to the burlap sack in her lap. She had retrieved it from a lockbox secured in the bed of the jeep. Though it was safer under lock and key, she could not leave it there. She wanted it close to her at all times. She undid the ties and opened the sack. With great reverence, she freed the crystal skull and cradled it between her palms.

In the dappled light the crystal sparked with brilliance, an electrical storm under glass. She raised it high enough to stare into its eyes. She remembered the EEG readings done on Dr. Jones: a neural stimulation of incalculable strength. She also recalled the flow of bloody tears down his cheeks.

Still, she felt no fear. Both Oxley and Jones had untrained, unsophisticated minds. To handle that power, to open the gateway to vast knowledge, would require a supremely disciplined and orderly mind.

An arm reached from the backseat and over her shoulder, straining for the skull. She knocked the hand away. Dr. Harold Oxley sat in the back with George McHale. Like her, Dr. Oxley was drawn to the skull's power. But unlike her, he had been broken by it—overwhelmed.

Lifting the skull before her eyes, she stared deeply into it again, trying to tap into that power. She tuned out the revving engines, the squealing brakes, the popping gears, and the constant scream of the jungle-cutter. She sank into a half trance. She had attempted every meditative state, every cognitive exercise. She had studied with master yogis, trained with the best parapsychologists. But when she stared into the skull's eyes, all she saw was translucent crystal and flickering fractal patterns of light.

Why won't you speak to me?

The truck hit a stump and bumped high. The crystal skull bobbled in her fingers, and she almost dropped it. She clutched it to her belly, her heart thudding. She quickly slipped it back into the burlap sack and snugged the ties, cursing her foolishness. The skull must not be damaged. Not when they were so close. It had been imprudent to handle it now—but the skull's mystery nagged at her, whispered to her.

Even now she wanted to open the sack again.

A voice spoke behind her, at her shoulder. "Skull's got a mind of its own, eh?"

She turned to face George McHale. The Brit had scooted forward on the jeep's backseat. Behind him, a short flatbed extended, crowded with soldiers.

McHale nodded to the burlap sack in her lap. "It's bloody choosy about who it talks to, isn't it?"

"Apparently not *that* choosy." Spalko glanced at the pitiful skeleton of the professor next to him. Dr. Harold Oxley seemed to have lost interest in the skull and now craned upward, watching the dance of morning sunlight through the canopy.

She clenched a fist in frustration. So much power. She stared at the half-demented professor. Why choose him? All the skull needed was someone stronger, someone with a trained mind.

So why not her?

Spalko knew she must not fail—not so much for the Soviet Union as for herself. Raised in a superstitious Ukrainian village, she had been shunned for her gifts. *Witch* was the least of the insults cast her way. Villagers ostracized her family. And when she began dissecting small animals in a childlike attempt to understand life and biology, even her mother grew fearful of her. As soon as she was old enough, she fled the mountains and the village. She knew answers would not be found among such closed-minded people. So she headed out into the broader world.

All her life, she had sought to find some reason for *who* she was, *what* she was, *why* she was.

And here in a jungle in South America, she was finally nearing an answer.

She would not let anyone stop her.

Settling back in her seat, she faced forward. Ahead, the mulcher continued to burrow into the heart of the dark jungle. A massive tree crashed into the forest, scattering birds and monkeys.

But McHale was not done. He leaned forward between Spalko and the driver, pointing to the burlap sack.

"That skull. C'mon, it's all a crock, right? People stare into that thing, work themselves up into a state—self-hypnosis or something maybe. But ESP? Not bloody likely."

"Why not?" she asked. "Telepathy already exists in man, though in a less developed form."

"Are you kidding? You actually think you're psychic?"

"Have you never picked up the phone to find the person you were about to call is already on the line? Is this coincidence? Or some other form of transmission . . . bio-transmission?"

"It's called luck. Trust me, I know all about it. Mine's usually bad."

"Then what about the bond between mother and child? We sent a submarine under the surface with a mother rabbit's new litter onboard. She remained onshore while one by one, the young rabbits were killed."

"Lady, you need another hobby."

She waved away his response. Science was not for the squeamish. "As each young rabbit was slain, the mother's EEG readings showed reaction at the *very instant of death*." She glanced back to him. "There is an organic mind–body link shared by all living creatures. If we could control that collective mind—"

"A'right!" He held up a hand. "Let's put your money where your mouth is. For double or nothing on my fee, what am I thinking right now?"

He leaned in closer, eye-to-eye with her.

She lifted an eyebrow at his slightly leering expression. "I don't need psychic powers to surmise that, Mr. McHale."

"Other than that! C'mon, amuse me. I'm thinking of a question. What's the answer?"

She stared at him, deep into his eyes. She noted the perspiration on his brow, the slight dilation of his pupils. Lust, worry, anxiety. The constant state of man. She looked deeper. Slowly, the smirk on his face shifted. She pushed into him. He began to shift away, an animal's response to danger.

She snatched out and held him by the back of the neck. She pulled him closer, while probing deeper. She spoke, her lips almost touching his.

"The answer to your question is: *If I feel the slightest need.*"

She enjoyed the momentary terror in his eyes. She released him, and he fell back. He mumbled something and retreated into his seat.

The driver glanced to her, his hands clutching the wheel. He spoke in a thick Ukrainian accent. "What was his question, Colonel Doctor?"

Spalko answered, "He wanted to know if I plan to cut his throat once we reach Akator."

The driver's fingers tightened on the wheel. He turned away, but she saw his lips move silently, forming a single word in Russian.

Witch.

THIRTY-THREE

"YOU GOTTA BE KIDDING ME!" Mutt shouted.

Marion had known it would come as a shock to her son, but he had to be told. And since Mutt was tied up across from his father—and neither of them could run off—it had seemed like an opportune moment, especially considering their dire situation.

She glanced sidelong at their surroundings.

The three of them were imprisoned in the back of the last truck of the convoy, a canvas-topped personnel carrier. They were seated on benches, and each had been tied to one of the truck's steel frame supports. They shared the bed of the truck with several crates stamped with Cyrillic lettering—and one large Russian colonel named Dovchenko, who rested a Kalashnikov rifle across his lap.

Marion sat next to Indy, who looked pained and uncomfortable. Mutt looked little better on the other side.

Father and son.

Here they all were, a happy little family.

Mutt still blustered. "My father was British. An RAF pilot. A war hero." He glared at Indy. "Not some *school*teacher."

Marion waited for her son to take a breath. "No, sweetie. Colin was your stepfather. We started dating when you were three months old. He was a good man, but he wasn't your father."

Indy straightened next to her and turned. "Wait a minute. *Colin* as in Colin Williams? You *married* him? I introduced you!"

Next to Mutt, Dovchenko rolled his eyes at the family melodrama.

Marion didn't care. "You know, Indy, I think you gave up your vote on who I marry when you decided to break it off a week before our wedding."

Indy's voice lost an edge of its high timbre. "It wasn't going to work, Marion. We both knew that. Who wants to be married to somebody who's gone half the time?"

"I did!" Marion's voice cracked a little, and she hated herself for it. He hadn't earned that emotion from her. He plainly had no idea how much heartache he'd caused her. "And you would've known that if you'd asked me."

Dovchenko lifted his rifle and pounded the butt on the seat boards. "Shut in hell up!"

Everyone looked at him, paused—then turned back to one another.

Indy continued, "Asked you what? To spend most of your life alone?"

"Did you ever think I might've liked the peace and quiet?"

"You?"

"Yes, me. You didn't know. Why didn't you ever just talk to me?"

"Because we never had an argument that I won."

"So that's your excuse, Indy? It's not my fault that you can't keep up."

Indy leaned back, accidentally bumping his fedora over his eyes. He shook his hat back in place. "I was trying *not* to hurt you, Marion."

"You damn well failed. Didn't you wonder years ago why Ox stopped talking to you? He hated that you ran away."

Mutt stamped his boot on the floor. "Would you two stop it?"

Dovchenko seconded this with a nod.

Indy scowled and swung his chin toward Mutt. "Yeah, Marion, don't make him listen to Mom and Dad fight."

Mutt strained at his bonds. "You're *not my dad*, okay?"

"You bet I am, kid. And I've got news for you—you're going back to school!"

Mutt's eyes widened with shock. "What! What happened to *there's not a damn thing wrong with it and don't let anybody tell you any different*?"

"I wasn't your father then." Indy frowned at Marion again. "And you should have told me about the kid. I had a right to know."

"If you recall, you vanished after we broke up."

"I wrote."

"A *year* later. By then Mutt was born and I was married."

"So then why'd you bother telling me now?"

"Because I *thought* we were dying."

Dovchenko shoved up to his feet and cursed a scathing streak in Russian. Though Marion didn't know the words, her ears still burned. He slapped his rifle down, crossed to a pile of rags, and began balling them up, plainly preparing to gag them.

Indy spoke fast, trying to get in the last word. "Don't worry, Marion. There's still time. We may die yet."

Dovchenko turned with a fistful of rags. He crossed to Marion first, ever the gentleman, and bent over her—

Which gave Indy the perfect angle to pitch back in his seat and kick him square in the face with both boots.

Dovchenko spun with a groan and toppled toward Mutt on the other side.

Who was ready as planned.

Mutt struck Dovchenko the same way Indy had, kicking like a kangaroo. Both biker boots smacked him square on the chin. "All yours," Mutt called over as Dovchenko fell the other way again.

Indy popped the Russian again, coldcocking him with both feet.

"The bigger they are—" Indy mumbled.

"—the harder they fall," Mutt finished.

Dovchenko toppled and fell flat on the floorboards, unconscious.

Indy called over to Mutt. "Still got that switchblade you stuffed in your boot back at the cemetery?"

Mutt grinned.

Indy matched his expression. "Now, there's a good boy."

Indy leaned over Marion, the switchblade in his hands. To get to the ropes, he had to reach behind her. The blade was awkward; the ties were oily and stubborn. He sawed at the ropes, cheek-to-cheek with her.

God, she still smelled great.

Vanilla and spice.

She spoke, her breath tickling his ear. "You know, I wasn't the only one who moved on."

"What do you mean?"

"I heard stories about you, Jones. Plenty of women over the years."

He strained against the ropes. "A few. But they all had the same problem."

"Yeah, what's that?"

With a final tug, the rope broke, freeing her wrists. He leaned back and saw no reason to lie, not now. He was nose-to-nose with her.

"They weren't you, honey."

Across from him, Marion's eyes sparked, and her expression shifted ever so subtly, sexily, into a shadow of a grin. Freed at last, she leaned closer, their lips almost touching—

—then out of the corner of his eye, Indy spotted a crate with a familiar military stencil on the outside.

Perfect!

He jerked to his feet and stepped away. To the side, Mutt stood guard over Dovchenko, who still lay sprawled on the floorboards. Indy pushed past the kid toward the crate.

"Jones?" Marion asked.

The box was long. He lifted the lid, praying it wasn't empty.

It wasn't.

He stared down at the length of black military steel packed into the straw. As he weighed his options, his fingers traced the weapon's surface. A moment later, a crooked grin formed on his lips. This would do. But he needed a better vantage point.

He stared up at the canvas roof of the transport carrier.

Good enough.

The switchblade snicked open in his fingers.

Time to get to work.

THIRTY-FOUR

MUTT STEADIED the stack of crates under Jones. "Careful, old man!"

Jones crouched, perched atop the pile as the truck bounced and rattled. He carefully stood up. "Don't worry about me."

"I wasn't. I meant be careful with my switchblade."

Jones frowned down at him, then reached up to the canvas roof of the personnel carrier. He grabbed a support strut with one hand and stabbed upward with the knife in the other. The blade popped through the truck's canvas roof. Holding steady to the strut, he dragged the knife and cut a long ragged slice through the thick material. It sounded like a zipper being tugged down. Once done, he snapped the blade closed and tossed the knife down to Mutt.

"Good as new, kid."

"Better be."

Jones ignored him, stretched up, and chinned himself through the hole. As Jones shimmied to the roof, Mutt leaned over to stare at his mother, who was shouldering the other side of the stack of crates.

"Him?" he asked.

She shrugged guiltily. "You warm up to him, you'll see."

He sighed. "You could've told me, Mom."

"I should've, sweetheart. I'm sorry."

Mutt went over and joined his mother. She put her arm around him and they stared up at the roof together. The man's shadow crawled across the canvas roof, heading toward the cab.

Jones.

His father.

Mutt shook his head.

Together they stepped over the Russian giant's slack body and tracked Jones's shadow. A steel door blocked the bed of the truck from the cab in front. They had dared not use the guard's rifle. Any shots would have drawn unwanted attention to their escape.

Overhead, Jones's shadow teetered at the top edge of the rear compartment—then vanished.

A ripping crash followed.

Through a tiny window in the steel door, Mutt spied Jones dropping straight down through the canvas roof and landing square atop the driver.

"He did it—" Mutt said.

The truck lurched to the side, throwing them flying to the left.

"Hold on!" his mother yelled at him.

Hold on? He was still in midair!

Suddenly the truck crashed to a stop with a grind of metal and splintering of wood. Tangled together, he and his mother went tumbling forward as the steel door ahead popped open. They fell straight through it and into the cab.

Mutt hit the dashboard; his mother landed in the passenger seat.

Nose to the windshield, Mutt saw they'd smashed into a tree. Jones kicked open the driver's-side door and booted out the unconscious man, then dropped into the vacant seat, ground the gear into reverse, and hit the gas. The truck bucked backward. Jones tore the wheel around, popped the gears, and they were moving forward, chasing the convoy.

Mutt pushed himself upright.

To his left, Jones wore a fierce and determined expression.

On his right, his mother grinned back at Jones. "That was a good one."

Jones shrugged. "Not out of this yet, sweetheart."

Mutt stared between the two, gaping in horror.

These were his parents?

THIRTY-FIVE

INDY SHIFTED into third gear and sent the truck bounding after the convoy. The line of Russian vehicles stretched in a long arc through the jungle, led by the massive machine that chewed and sawed through the rain forest. As Indy neared the rear of the convoy, he studied his adversaries.

He had to hand it to the Russians. They were prepared for every contingency that the forest might throw at them. Amid the jeeps and transport carriers were a couple of odd-looking vehicles. Their chassis were shaped like heavy outboard boats but with wheels beneath them. Clearly they had been engineered as amphibious vehicles and were to be used for river crossings. *Ducks* was what Mac had called them, but these fowl had teeth. A machine gun had been mounted to the prow of each vehicle.

Still, Indy kept his focus on the smoking, screaming lead vehicle of the convoy.

The jungle-cutter.

The massive machine's two horizontal blades ripped and sawed a wide path through the jungle, large enough for the convoy to follow. The path had originally been a raw, overgrown trail, suitable for horses or someone on foot. It ran alongside a wide river. Without the jungle-cutter, passage would have been impossible for the convoy.

Which gave Indy an idea.

His eyes narrowed on that lead vehicle.

"What's the plan, Jones?" Marion asked from the passenger seat.

He leaned over the wheel, concentrating, calculating. His plan was simple as he explained it: "Get Oxley back, get the skull, and get to Akator before they do."

A familiar sarcasm filled Marion's voice. "Oh, is that all?"

Up ahead, the convoy approached an oxbow in the river, a U-shaped turn of the water's raging course. The line of vehicles began to stretch along the curve.

That should do, but he had to hurry.

Indy shifted up to his feet. "Marion, take the wheel!"

She slipped over and grabbed the steering wheel. Turning around, he slid past Mutt, who dropped into the passenger seat. Indy headed into the rear of the truck. The vehicle bobbled under his feet, but Marion steadied it as best she could over the rutted road.

Mutt called to Marion, "What's he going to do now?"

"Honey, I don't think he plans that far ahead."

Ignoring them, Indy dashed into the rear and crossed back to the crate he'd noted earlier. Off to the side, Dovchenko was still out cold on the floor, sprawled on his chest, snoring through a bloody nose.

Indy parted the straw in the crate and extracted the four-foot tube of black steel. The heavy weapon drew a grim smile from him. Its weight instilled a measure of hope. A Soviet hammer-and-sickle had been stamped onto the side of the bazooka. An explosive sixty-millimeter head had already been loaded in one end.

He hauled it up and carried it like a battering ram back toward the cab. When he pushed his way in with it, Mutt's eyes grew huge.

Indy motioned with the weapon's explosive head. "Scooch back a little, will ya, son?"

"Don't call me that!" But the kid flattened against the seat.

With a little maneuvering, Indy got the unwieldy length pointed out the passenger window. The other end waved in front of Marion's nose.

Balancing the bazooka on his shoulder, Indy studied the terrain and possible trajectories. The convoy continued around the oxbow, slowly and cautiously rounding the U-shaped bend. Their vehicle—at the end of the convoy—was the last to enter the oxbow, while up at the front the jungle-cutter had made it all the way around.

So at the moment, the two vehicles stood at opposite horns of the U.

Which meant the jungle-cutter lay directly across from Indy.

He lined up his target. He had one plan, one hope, one shot. If the jungle-cutter were taken out of commission, the convoy would be mired in the forest. With that goal in mind, Indy waited as the massive vehicle trundled into his crosshairs. He would have to be certain of his aim. He wouldn't get a second shot.

Indy spoke as he aimed. "You might want to close your—"

His finger accidentally twitched. The explosive blast cut off his last word. The windshield cracked. Smoke blasted out the rear of the bazooka, and the missile screamed across the bend in the river, sailing straight as an arrow.

Indy, his ears ringing, cursed the premature firing. Then again, maybe it was just as well . . .

As he watched, the rocket blasted across the river's bend and slammed straight into the jungle-cutter. The vehicle detonated with a great explosion of flame, dirt, and smoking debris. The wreckage shot high into the air in a wicked cartwheel.

Behind it, the convoy ground to a halt as vehicles smashed into one another in a chain-reaction pileup. Searching through the smoke, Indy spotted the vehicle that had been traveling directly behind the jungle-cutter. It was Spalko's jeep. In the back, he could see Oxley.

"Indy!" Marion screamed in terror.

Irina Spalko gaped as the cutter exploded in front of her.

One second, it had been cleaving around the river bend—the next it blasted upward amid flames and mud. Its two saw blades ripped away. One sailed ahead, struck a boulder with the ringing note of a great bell, and vanished into the jungle. The other flew straight at their jeep.

With a gasp of fear, she and the driver flattened, but the whizzing giant disk sailed past overhead, missing their jeep by inches.

Twisting around, she followed its deadly trajectory toward the rear of the convoy. Back there, she spotted something suspicious. Smoke was pouring out of the cab of the very last truck. A thin contrail of rocket exhaust led back to the same vehicle. She clenched a fist in frustration. The truck had to be the source of the surprise missile attack. And if so, there could only be one explanation.

Dr. Jones.

White-hot fury flared through her. Then, just as quickly, it mellowed into amused satisfaction when she noted how the flying saw blade banked and angled around the river. It aimed straight for—

"Duck!" Marion screamed and yanked Indy and Mutt down.

She caught one last glimpse of the silver disk as it arced along the curve of the river and flew straight at them. She dove on top of Indy and her son, protecting them while covering her head with her arms.

The impact shook the massive truck, accompanied by a shrieking rending of tortured steel. Canvas shredded into confetti, showering down over them.

A second later, it was over.

Waving debris from her face, Marion sat up in the driver's seat. She stared at the sight around her. The bright sunlight was blinding. The entire upper half of the truck had been buzz-sawed away.

"I'll be damned," Indy said.

"We may be, Jones," Marion muttered.

THIRTY-SIX

Spalko kept her face passive as the jungle-cutter's saw blade cleaved off the roof of Dr. Jones's truck. A moment later figures straightened into view in the front cab. She spotted Jones, the woman, and the boy.

They were still alive.

Clenching her fingers on the pommel of her sword, Spalko stood in her seat. "Go!" she ordered her jeep's driver and pointed her arm toward the raw jungle trail beyond the smoldering wreckage of the cutter. "Keep heading down the trail!"

As the jeep revved with a growl that echoed how she felt, Spalko vaulted over the front seat and into the back. She landed between McHale and Dr. Oxley.

"Guard that skull!" she shouted to McHale as she continued past them and climbed into the jeep's rear bed. "Your life depends on it!"

Soldiers in the back moved out of her way.

With a two-step running start, she flew out of the back of the jeep—and landed on the hood of the jeep trailing behind hers. She landed in a crouch like some jungle panther. The driver of the jeep gaped at her.

She hurdled the windshield, grabbed the assault rifle leaning on the front seat, and hopped into the back. With murderous intent, she lifted the rifle to her shoulder. Nothing would stop her. She would not let anyone have the skull.

As the jeep slowed under her, she screamed to the driver, "Keep going! Follow the lead jeep!"

"Keep going!" Indy shouted to Marion as she wrestled the stalled truck into gear.

With smoke from the rocket exhaust still choking the cab, the troop transport lurched forward. Marion pounded the gas, and the truck bucked and rolled toward the pileup of vehicles. Indy climbed up into the passenger seat and shoved back a flapping piece of the shorn roof. He studied the remains of the crashed convoy. At the opposite end of the wreckage, he spotted two jeeps crawling around the remains of the jungle-cutter and striking off into the jungle by themselves.

Spalko was trying to escape with Oxley and the skull.

Indy recognized another problem. The pileup of trucks blocked the way ahead. Their large troop transport would never make it through the mess. Some of the smaller vehicles were already skirting and grinding around other stalled trucks, trying to continue after the lead jeeps.

It gave him an idea.

Their truck bumped and rattled toward one of the odd-shaped amphibious vehicles as it fought its way free. Indy eyed the machine gun mounted at its front end.

He yelled over to Marion and pointed down to the boat-like vehicle. "Pull up alongside that!"

She nodded and gunned the engine. The noise drew the attention of the duck's driver and passenger as they drew up next to them.

The driver shouted and pounded a fist on his steering wheel. The other soldier squatted up and swung around with a rifle.

No you don't, buster.

As the truck pulled up alongside, Indy used the edge of the roof to swing through the open passenger-side window and fly across the gap. He crashed between the startled driver and the soldier.

Grabbing the business end of the soldier's rifle, Indy yanked it sharply—then battered it back, slamming the wooden butt straight into the Russian's nose.

The soldier's finger caught on the trigger, and a spat of automatic fire blasted from the rifle. The rounds burned past Indy's ear and pinged against the flank of the truck.

Concerned, Indy glanced to the troop transport. He need not have worried. Mutt hung out the side window of the roofless cab. Holding a length of wood in his hands, Mutt swung from the shoulders and clubbed the driver.

"Not bad, kid!" Indy called up to him.

Shots startled him awake.

Dovchenko groaned and sat up in the back of the bumping truck. He shoved a tumbled crate off his legs. Overhead, tree branches whisked past; sunlight shone down. It made no sense. It took him a full dazed breath to realize the roof of the transport was gone.

He swore in Russian. Though he didn't know what had happened, he knew who to blame.

Jones.

Dovchenko shoved to his feet, wobbled a bit, then stumbled over to a torn section of canvas on the truck's side. Through the flap, he spotted the American in one of the Russian ducks. Jones tossed the limp driver out the side and waved to the truck.

Dovchenko struggled for comprehension.

Then a figure leaped from the cab of the truck and into the duck.

Dovchenko recognized the boy.

Swinging around, he stalked toward the front. Through the loose steel door as it swung open and shut, he caught a stuttering view of the cab. The driver rolled from behind the wheel and dove for the passenger side. Her slender form and dark hair left no doubt who she was.

Marion Ravenwood.

With no one behind the wheel, the truck swerved in an uncontrolled turn. Dovchenko stumbled to the side, catching himself on a pile of crates. He heard a feminine cry as the woman leaped after her son through the passenger window. Outside, the duck's engine roared as it fled away from the side of the driverless truck.

Dovchenko lurched toward the open door to the cab.

Through the cracked windshield, he saw to his horror that the unguided truck was headed straight for a massive tree. His heart hammering, Dovchenko dove through the door and shoved into the driver's seat. Grabbing the steering wheel, he yanked it hard and lifted the troop transport up on two wheels in a sharp turn. He missed the tree trunk by less than a foot, then slammed back down on four tires.

With a squeal of brakes, he slowed the large truck. He could go no farther. The wreckage of the convoy blocked the way forward. He was trapped behind it.

Up ahead, the Americans raced away in the stolen duck. The amphibious vehicle swerved this way and that around the stalled convoy, like a racing boat in a choppy sea. As Dovchenko watched, it headed off around the curve of the road.

Dovchenko's fingers tightened on the wheel.

This was not over.

THIRTY-SEVEN

WITHOUT SLOWING, Indy cleared the smoking wreckage of the jungle-cutter. Beyond the blasted vehicle, the trail narrowed into a tortuous overgrown path, thick with patches of wild undergrowth and treacherous with fallen logs. It would be madness to traverse this at breakneck speeds.

Still, Indy shoved the gas pedal to the floor. He had no choice. Oxley needed to be rescued, and Indy refused to leave that crystal skull with Spalko.

And besides—

Gunshots rattled across the back of his vehicle.

—he was being chased by a jeepful of Russians.

Indy gunned the engine and banked around a bend in the trail. His back end fishtailed, but he cleared the sharp turn, only to face another.

"Hold tight!" he yelled to Marion and Mutt as he hauled on the wheel.

Around they went again, this time up on two wheels.

"I think I'm getting seasick," Mutt shouted.

"Can't stop now, kid!"

After they rounded the bend, the trail went straight for a stretch. Indy spotted the fleeing jeeps as they disappeared around the far turn.

He flattened the accelerator again.

They buzzed through undergrowth as high as the flanks of the vehicle. It was like jetting through a verdant sea. Though the others had a head start, he had an advantage over the jeeps ahead. They had to forge a trail across the rough terrain. All he had to do was to follow in their wake.

Speeding down the straightaway, he hit the next corner too sharply. Momentum threw them off the forged path. He fought to keep from crashing sideways into the dense forest. Their port side grazed a tree.

Mutt yelled, but then they were clear.

Indy pounded back to the center of the path.

Speeding around the next corner, Indy discovered the two jeeps directly ahead. A fallen tree blocked the path, and they were slowly edging around it.

Flying too fast to get out of the way, Indy's duck blasted straight toward the two jeeps. They were going to collide.

Worse yet, a figure stood in the back, a rifle leveled at them.

Spalko.

"Get down!" Marion yelled.

Indy ducked as the windshield splintered and shattered under a hail of bullets. Blindly, he yanked the wheel to the left. The duck swerved out of the line of fire.

He heard screams behind him and looked up.

The jeepful of Russians that had been chasing after them, taking potshots at the escaping prisoners, had swerved around the last corner and come directly into the line of Spalko's fire. Inside the jeep, bodies jerked and bled. Uncontrolled, the vehicle slammed into the back of Spalko's jeep. She went flying across the hood and smashed into the windshield.

Indy regained his seat as he shot ahead. He glanced into the rearview mirror.

Behind him, Spalko pushed to her feet and glared at him.

Indy grinned and punched the gas. Just ahead, the lead jeep bounced and rattled. It had cleared the fallen tree and sought to escape.

Not today.

Indy swung the duck to the right and drew even with the other vehicle. Oxley sat in the backseat, but the jeep's bed was crowded with Russian soldiers.

"Take the wheel again!" he shouted to Marion.

"This is becoming a bad habit, Jones!"

But Indy was already moving, hauling his feet under him. He waited until the jeep crashed through a low-hanging section of the forest. The vehicle was slapped and whipped by leaves and vines.

Taking advantage of the confusion, Indy leaped.

He crashed in a sprawl across the front seat of the jeep. He caught a brief glimpse of Oxley, flanked by soldiers, in the backseat—mostly because the man waved good-naturedly at him.

Unable to return the greeting, Indy rolled to the driver and slammed an elbow into his face. As the driver let go, Indy grabbed the wheel with one hand and punched out in the other direction.

His fist struck the passenger, who was just straightening up, square in the face. The man crashed into the dashboard, crumpled into the foot well, and cradled his nose. He spoke through his fingers.

"Goddamn it, you broke my nose again."

It was Mac.

But Indy had his own problems. The driver reached for him, and the soldiers in the back lunged. Luckily that meant they weren't holding on to anything. The jeep struck a buried log.

Soldiers flew high.

Indy yanked the wheel, swerving—and the soldiers went tumbling out of the jeep and into the underbrush with wild screams.

With one hand clamped to the wheel, Indy gained the driver's seat. A peek at the rearview mirror revealed Oxley safe and sound, belted in his seat. His hands were held up high in the air. Then a heavy burlap sack, tossed aloft like the soldiers, landed safely in the professor's hands. Indy caught a glimpse of bright crystal inside it.

The skull!

Movement on the passenger side drew his eye. Mac struggled back into his seat from the foot well.

Indy cocked his arm back, ready to pop Mac again.

Mac cowered back into the passenger seat, both palms raised. He shouted at him. "INDY! Listen to me, you dumb son of a bitch! I'm CIA!"

Back in the duck, Mutt continued his search of their amphibious vehicle, looking for a weapon . . . any weapon.

"Check the back!" his mother called to him.

Swinging around, Mutt leaned over the front seat and searched the rear compartment. On the floor, he spotted a familiar rosewood box.

Stretching, he unlatched the case's lid and flipped it open. Silver gleamed back at him from inside the velvet-lined box. He smiled down at the assortment of swords, sparkling brightly in the dappled sunlight.

"What are you doing?" his mother called from the driver's seat.

He answered as he reached down toward a rapier's grip.

"Just finding myself something to do."

"*CIA?* Mac . . . you?" Indy could not keep the incredulity from his voice.

"Yes, you dense son of a bitch!" Mac glowered at him from the passenger seat, holding a hand protectively over his nose. "I practically shouted it at you in the tent. I said *Like in Berlin*! Remember? Back in the tent when you woke up here!"

Indy frowned. He did remember Mac leaning forward as Spalko entered the tent. Mac had whispered in his ear conspiratorially.

—like in Berlin. Get me?

He hadn't gotten Mac then, and he didn't now, either.

Mac sighed in exasperation. "What were we in Berlin, mate?" Mac's eyes widened on Indy. "We were *double agents,* yeah?"

Indy thought back, then his eyes grew larger, too.

That's right! They'd been pretending to be Nazis to gain the Enigma Code.

Mac continued to plead his case. "And you think General Ross just *happened* to be in Nevada to bail you out? I *sent* him, Indy! He's my control agent."

Indy's mind spun, trying to recalibrate to all these new revelations. Before he could settle his thoughts, Spalko's jeep shot forward out of nowhere, crashing through underbrush and pulling up alongside him. Spalko stood in the backseat of the jeep and shouted at Indy in Russian.

He frowned. Why was Spalko yelling at him in Russian?

Then he noted motion in his rearview mirror. He spotted the top of a lone soldier's head popping into view beyond the rear guard. The man clung to the back of the jeep. It seemed not *all* of the soldiers had been thrown clear.

The soldier hauled himself up and lunged forward, clambering toward the backseat. He struck Oxley and knocked the professor down. His hand grabbed for the burlap sack as it rolled across the seat.

No!

The soldier snatched the prize and underhanded the sack over to Spalko. She caught it with a triumphant cry. Her jeep slowed, dropping back. She had what she wanted.

Behind Indy, the soldier reared up with a long serrated dagger in hand—but Mac punched him square in the nose. The soldier fell backward and tumbled out the rear.

"Hurts, don't it?" Mac called after the Russian. He returned to his seat. He cocked an eyebrow. *See?*

"Why didn't you just tell me, Mac?" Indy yelled.

"What did you want me to do? Paint it on my ass cheeks?"

Indy smiled at his old friend. "There's plenty of room back there!"

THIRTY-EIGHT

SPALKO SECURED THE SKULL in the back of the jeep—then yanked out her sword from its scabbard and focused on the fleeing jeep.

And Dr. Jones.

She'd had enough of the American. She barked an order to her driver and her vehicle surged ahead, hurtling down the overgrown trail toward her adversary. She rose to her feet and brandished her rapier. The distance between the two vehicles narrowed.

It would be over soon.

As her jeep drew even with the American's vehicle, she raised her blade for a killing stroke—then the hairs on the back of her neck twitched. Sensing danger, she spun around and backed half a step.

A sword's razored tip sliced through her shirt and grazed a bloody line across her midsection. She stared up at her assailant.

"You!"

Mutt Williams balanced on the rear half of a rampaging duck. The amphibious vehicle had raced up on her blind side. She parried the boy's blade with a smack of her own.

He dropped his guard—and she lunged. She had no patience for any further interference, especially from a nuisance like this boy. But the young man's wrist turned with some skill and blocked her attack, making her stumble.

It had been a feint . . . *clever.*

She regained her balance and eyed her opponent across the gap between their bouncing vehicles with renewed respect. He beckoned to her with his sword. He wanted a challenge.

So be it.

Across the chasm, the two swordsmen exchanged a flurry of blows, parries, feints, and ripostes. The boy completed a dancing bit of footwork known as a *flèche,* French for "arrow." Impressive. Especially on a moving vehicle. She hesitated, and he used the advantage to push off his rear foot and lunge at her.

She knocked him back with a stinging beat-parry.

Impudent boy.

"You fight like all young men," she called to him. "Eager to begin, quick to finish. A true master knows the pleasure of the long game."

He glared over at her. "We're still talking about sword fighting, right?"

With a flash of steel, he attacked as the vehicles drew closer again. He sprang up and got one foot on each vehicle. They parried and attacked. Steel rang out. They fought as the boy balanced precariously. There was no room to maneuver. It was all a matter of pure sword skill.

Glissade to forte . . .

Counter-riposte . . .

Coupé followed by an *arrêt a bon temps* . . .

The boy attempted to entrap her sword, but she avoided it with a perfect *derobement.* She counterattacked and stabbed forward. He blocked and shoved her back, but the vehicles began to drift apart under his hips, splitting his legs apart like a wishbone.

She paused, amused. "I adore young men's minds. So open—so quick to expend their energies."

It seemed unfitting to finish this match with her opponent so disadvantaged, but she had more pressing matters. She lunged for a killing blow, intending to spear him through the heart.

But at the last second, the two vehicles nudged back together—and the boy jumped high and twisted. Her rapier missed its target and sliced through empty air. Off balance, Spalko fell forward—toward the gap. The only way to avoid a deadly fall under the churning wheels of the two vehicles was to leap across to the neighboring duck. She crashed headlong into the backseat.

Her opponent fared no better. The boy landed in a stumble and toppled face-first into the backseat of *her* jeep. They had changed places. She sat up in time to see him scramble up with his sword in one hand. As he straightened, he lifted the burlap sack with the skull in the other.

He had captured her prize.

No!

Marion watched her son tumble into the other vehicle.

"Mutt!" she called out. "Get back in here!"

The Russian soldier behind the jeep's wheel grabbed blindly into the backseat and managed to snatch a handful of her son's collar. Mutt was yanked down. Their jeep slowed, while Marion's duck still shot forward.

Fearing for her son's life, she twisted around—and saved her own life. A sword stabbed through her seat back and lanced out where she'd been sitting.

Spalko.

So focused was she on Mutt, Marion had forgotten about the Russian stowaway aboard her duck.

Marion stomped the brakes hard. The duck jerked to a skidding stop, and the Russian woman went flying out of the backseat. She smashed clean through the windshield and rolled empty-handed across the flat, prow-shaped hood of the duck.

The only thing that stopped Spalko from plunging off the front end was the machine-gun mount.

The Russian woman slid into it and spun the weapon around.

The machine gun's muzzle pointed straight at Marion.

Spalko fired a wild chattering volley, shattering what was left of the windshield—but Marion ducked low and hit the gas. The duck shot forward again.

Thrown off balance by the sudden acceleration, Spalko stopped firing and held tightly to the gun mount.

Marion risked a peek up—and saw that her duck was barreling straight for the rear of the other jeep. She spotted Mutt staring back at her, his eyes wide with surprise. After Marion had stomped the brakes, the other vehicle had shot directly ahead of them.

The driver was still struggling with her son. Rather than slowing to avoid a collision, Marion punched the gas. Noting this, Mutt swung his heavy burlap sack and struck the driver in the back of his head. The soldier slumped, and the jeep suddenly slowed. Marion didn't have time to react.

Her duck smashed into its back end.

Spalko went flying forward again, this time landing in the backseat of the jeep.

Right next to—

"Mutt!"

THIRTY-NINE

KNOCKED OFF HIS FEET after being rear-ended, Mutt heard his mother yell.

He turned in time to see Spalko lunge at him. Mutt scrambled to his feet and out of her way. Clutching the burlap sack behind him, he crouched and cocked back his other arm. He balled up a threatening fist. He had lost his sword, but he was not about to give up the fight.

Spalko barked to the dazed driver in Russian, and he pounded the gas and sped their jeep onward. Then she turned her full attention to Mutt, staring at him from across the span of the backseat.

"Hand over the skull," she said with icy warning. "Perhaps I can use a boy like you, with your skill."

"Fat chance, sister." He lifted his fist higher.

Without even a menacing quip, she attacked with a flurry of kicks and flat jabs with the knuckles of her hand. He did his best to block her, but he failed as often as he succeeded. She was obviously skilled in martial arts. As his ears rang from a blow to the side of his head, anger blazed through him. He was tired of being a punching bag. With a growl, he took the offensive. What he couldn't match her with skill, he'd have to make up for in brawn.

Mutt swung the burlap skull into her side, then followed it with a roundhouse punch to the jaw. She fell back, but not before snapping a kick into his stomach. He coughed, lunged, grabbed a fistful of her hair, and slammed her face into the front seat's headrest.

They now seemed evenly matched.

Until . . .

As she turned and straightened, the top two buttons of her tunic popped open.

Mutt's attention faltered . . . just for a split second. His gaze dropped for the fraction of a heartbeat. He was a guy, after all.

Spalko took advantage, smashing a fist at him. He yanked his head back, but he was too slow. Her knuckles pounded into his face, splitting a cut under his eye.

Blood flowed hotly down his cheek.

Spalko smiled at his stunned expression. "First time?" she asked slyly, seductively. "Your wound, I mean."

His face heating up, Mutt attacked. Fury fueled his blows. But Spalko anticipated his reaction and used her skill against his wildness. Outmatched now, Mutt dropped back to the edge of the jeep. She closed in.

"To win a fight like this, you need balance," she whispered at him. "Not force, not skill—*balance.*"

She attacked with a flurry of blows, using all her strength. A foot struck Mutt square in the chest with enough force to send him flying off his feet. He toppled backward and tumbled out of the racing jeep, arms cartwheeling. Spalko's hand lunged out—and she plucked the burlap bag out of his fingers.

No!

But Mutt could do nothing to stop her from stealing the skull. He plummeted, expecting a hard collision into the underbrush. Instead, he struck with a clang onto the steel hood of a jeep racing alongside Spalko's vehicle.

Twisting, he turned and spotted a familiar face behind the wheel.

"Dad?"

"Can't stay out of trouble, can you, kid?"

Mutt spotted Oxley in the backseat, staring calmly at the passing scenery. The guy named Mac stood up from the passenger seat and offered a hand to help him over the windshield.

The jeep slowed under him.

Instead, Mutt swung around and pointed an arm toward Spalko's fleeing jeep.

"What are we waiting for, old man?" he yelled to Jones. "She's getting away with our skull!"

"That's my boy," he heard Jones mumble, and they leaped forward.

Mutt crouched atop the jeep, a living hood ornament. The canopy dropped lower through here. Leaves slapped at him. He lifted an arm to protect his face against the stinging barrage. He turned his face away and glanced behind. He spotted his mother's duck trailing them, trying to catch up.

Mutt risked pushing a little higher to wave to her, to encourage her to hurry.

It was a mistake.

A low-hanging vine hooked his upraised arm and scooped him straight off the hood. A scream sailed from his lips as he was flung high and swept up into the treetops. The world spun in blurry shades of emerald.

Reaching the apex of his swing on the vine, he prepared to plummet to his death—but instead landed square on a thick tree branch, out of breath and off balance. He froze, riding on pure adrenaline, arms out for balance, fingers clenched in terror.

Below, the jeeps raced away without him.

Perched on the branch, he turned.

Fifty small faces stared back at him.

Startled, he screamed.

Fifty faces screamed back at him.

Monkeys.

They scattered, leaping onto vines and swinging away.

As they fled through the upper canopy, it gave Mutt an idea.

When in Rome . . .

Mutt grabbed a nearby vine and gave it a fierce tug, testing his weight against it. It held. Satisfied, he clutched hard and kicked off the branch.

He swung through the air after the monkeys, matching their stride and rhythm, moving from vine to vine, following their flight.

With this strange band of brothers, Mutt headed after the fleeing jeeps.

"Now, weren't we chasing *her* before?" Mac asked.

Indy scowled and twisted around. He had caught up with the Russian woman's vehicle a moment before. Then the overgrown trail had suddenly narrowed, one side falling away into a steep ravine, and Indy had been forced to shoot ahead of Spalko to avoid tumbling to his death over the cliff. The pair now raced along a tortuous course at the edge of the ravine. Sections crumbled with their passage. He caught glimpses of sharp rocks and white water far below.

At the moment, Indy was at a disadvantage—not only did he have to forge a fresh trail through the fallen trunks and rocks, but Spalko, who had taken the wheel, could ram him from behind and send his vehicle careering off the edge.

And apparently that idea had not escaped her.

Spalko gunned her engine and sped toward them.

"Maybe we should have let her go ahead of us," Mac said. "Ladies first, and all that."

"I don't need a backseat driver."

"I'm not in the backseat." Mac leaned out his door and looked straight down to the rocks below. "Though I wish I was."

Unable to go any faster, Indy was helpless to prevent their being rear-ended by Spalko's jeep. He fought the steering wheel to keep them on solid ground. The jeep fishtailed. One of the back wheels sailed out over open air and spun.

"C'mon, c'mon . . . ," Indy urged.

Spalko revved her jeep again behind him, clearly intending to knock them off the cliff. It was just the two of them. They'd left the rest of the convoy behind. Marion had slowed to search for Mutt amid the canopy. Hopefully she had found him, and the pair had made their escape. Indy intended to do the same.

He popped the gears, frantic to get moving, to get away from the edge, but his engine stalled.

Bloody hell.

He glanced over a shoulder and saw Spalko grinning behind her wheel. Her jeep lurched forward, gained speed, and barreled toward him.

Indy restarted his own engine, threw it into first gear, and punched the accelerator. Wheels spun, churning up the cliff's edge, and a large section of the cliff broke away behind him. It forced Spalko to momentarily veer off her deadly trajectory. She slowed, cleared the crumbling section, then sped at him again. There was no stopping her.

That is, until a large shape dropped out of the trees that over-hung the trail.

Indy noted the flap of a biker's jacket as the form fell.

It was the kid!

Mutt crashed on top of Irina Spalko and knocked her out of the driver's seat. Uncontrolled, her jeep swung straight for the edge of the cliff.

"Mutt!" Indy hollered.

What was it with people yelling at him today . . .

. . . especially parental figures.

Mutt knew what he was doing. *Well, mostly.*

He yanked the wheel with one hand and pulled the jeep away from the cliff's edge. With his other hand, he reached over and snatched the burlap sack, snagging it off the seat where it had rolled.

A soldier in the backseat lunged for him—but Mutt had not come alone. Monkeys rained down out of the treetops. Angry monkeys. No one messed with one of their own. With screams of fury, they bit and clawed into the Russian.

"Thanks, *amigos*!" Mutt called out.

He shoved up onto the driver's seat and hurdled over the windshield and onto the hood. He danced across the front of the jeep as it slowed underfoot. Once close enough, he bounded from Spalko's jeep and landed in the back of Jones's foundering vehicle.

Still rolling, Spalko's jeep tapped the rear bumper of the other vehicle. The impact was just enough to shove Jones's jeep onto more solid footing.

It shot forward.

"Are you nuts, kid?" Jones scolded.

"No more than you!"

Mutt dropped into the backseat right next to Oxley and patted the professor's knee. Oxley stared at the gift that Mutt had delivered. The professor ever so gently took the burlap bag, peeked inside, and with a contented smile slipped the skull free. It shone brilliantly in the dappled light.

They'd made it.

Mutt glanced behind him—just in time to see Spalko rise up in the passenger seat of the jeep. She hiked back her arm, a *sword* in hand—the one Mutt had lost when Marion had rear-ended the jeep. She hurled the blade like a javelin. It sailed straight for the back of his father's head.

Mutt leaped to block it with his own body.

If anyone was going to kill Jones, it wasn't going to be *her*!

But Oxley merely lifted the skull high into the air. The sword's trajectory shifted—drawn by the strange hypermagnetic properties of the skull—and slapped against the side of the crystal with the ring of a struck bell.

Indy glanced back, oblivious of the close call. "Ox, quit playing with that thing before someone gets hurt."

Behind them, Spalko's jeep roared back to life and chased after them down the trail.

It wasn't over.

A mile back, Dovchenko followed in the wake of the chase, trundling along in the troop transport with the sheared-off top half.

Seated behind the wheel, Dovchenko crouched forward. His lips were set into a hard line. His eyes were twin spears of ice.

As he drove, he gathered stray soldiers along the trail, slowly building a force, massing like a storm front. And also like a storm, Dovchenko sought his own path, regardless of the contours of the land.

Once he had retrieved enough men, he turned the troop transport off the winding, meandering trail and headed across the raw jungle. The truck aimed in a straight line toward Jones. Dovchenko had one goal in mind as he wiped the drip of blood from under his nose.

The American would suffer.

FORTY-ONE

INDY FLEW ALONG the edge of the cliff. Off to the right, the ravine grew less steep. He caught more and more glimpses of white water. A river, flowing heavily, churned in the channel below.

Ahead, the trail suddenly swung away from the ravine and climbed up a steep rise. Indy gunned the jeep and flew up the trail. He could not see what lay over the crest of the hill, but he knew what chased behind him. Occasional rifle blasts echoed. It was only the twists of the trail that had kept them alive.

Yet Indy also suspected that Spalko pursued them with a measure of caution. She no longer sought to ram them. Even the shots were more threatening than serious. She could not risk having the jeep go tumbling over the cliff. Not as long as they possessed something she did not want lost to the river.

Indy glanced to the rearview mirror. Oxley cradled the crystal skull in his lap, as if holding a child. The professor wore a beatific smile of contentment. At the moment, the skull was protecting them from the worst of Spalko's wrath. But she would never stop pursuing them until she recovered what had been stolen from her.

Their only hope lay in losing her in the jungle.

With this in mind, Indy pushed the accelerator to the floor. The jeep shot ahead faster. Cresting the top of the steep rise, his vehicle went airborne for a few feet—then struck hard, jarring them all.

As they careened down the far slope, Indy spotted a sight ahead that made no sense.

Filling the jungle before them, crossing the entire breadth of the trail, rose a mountain of loose dirt and sand. It was as if a hundred dump trucks had come out into the middle of the jungle and unloaded.

Indy couldn't brake in time.

The jeep hit the slope and climbed halfway up it—then they lost all traction as the tires churned the loose dirt. The jeep sank in up to its axles. The engine stalled.

In the sudden silence, the roar of a second engine sounded behind him.

Indy stared back at the ridgeline.

Time had run out. They'd never make it over this sandy hill. The footing was too loose, the slope too steep. They'd have to double back the way they'd come, find somewhere to hide.

"Time to go!" he yelled.

The group piled out different doors and slipped and skidded down the slope, retreating the way they'd come. Mac helped Oxley, who clutched the burlap bag with the skull. Indy grabbed Mutt by the elbow and dragged him faster down the hill.

But they were too late.

Spalko's jeep shot over the rise, going airborne. She must have taken the hill at twice the speed Indy had. Sailing high, the jeep crested the sandy mountain—then smashed flat atop its summit, sinking to its bumpers.

Indy didn't stop to gawk. He hurried them on.

Mutt pointed down to his feet. "I told you there were giant ants out here!"

Indy frowned but looked where the kid pointed. A couple of red fire ants, as long as his outstretched fingers, scurried about their business.

Indy glanced from the giant pincers of the ants to the sandy mountain behind him. He suddenly understood what they'd crashed into and pushed Mutt even faster. He waved a wild arm to Mac and Oxley.

"Run!"

Atop the hill, Irina Spalko straightened in the driver's seat, still dazed from the impact. She fought through the shock and employed an Inuit deep-breathing technique to focus her full attention back to the situation. Twisting around, she spotted the Americans' jeep farther down the mound.

She also noted the flight of Dr. Jones and the others.

They seemed especially panicked.

And well they should be.

She swung to the soldier next to her. He groaned and rubbed his forehead. It was already swelling up into a knot from where he'd struck the dashboard.

She would have to do this herself.

Reaching over, Spalko relieved the soldier of his sidearm and turned back toward the fleeing prisoners. She extended her arms and cradled the pistol with both hands. Holding her breath now, she steadied herself and aimed down the sights.

She centered on Dr. Jones.

She no longer had to worry about inadvertently sending him—and thus the skull—into the raging river. Having the high ground, she would pick off each one, then collect the skull.

As if sensing her attention, Dr. Jones suddenly stopped and stared back in her direction. Their gazes locked.

Good-bye, Dr. Jones.

Before she could fire, the walnut-sized head of an insect popped over the end of her gun's barrel, blocking her view and waving long antennae. Startled, she leaned back as the creature climbed fully into view.

It was a massive fire ant.

Aghast, her finger spasmed on the trigger, and a round blasted out into the jungle. The noise surprised her—and the ant.

The creature raced forward over the weapon and sank its pincers into the meat of her thumb.

The pain drew an agonized gasp from her.

She smashed the ant against the doorjamb and scrambled to her feet atop the driver's seat. More giant ants appeared, crawling from air vents, pushing out from around the pedals. More and more materialized and swarmed into the jeep, coming for her.

Seeking higher ground, Spalko jumped over the windshield and landed on the hood. All around, ants boiled up out of the sand. Off to the left, from a gaping maw at the top of the hill, poured thousands upon thousands of ants. They writhed out in a churning, pinching pile, spreading in a sea toward the jeep. As they surged forth, a waft of fetid odor came with them, billowing out of the dark tunnel.

It smelled like rotting meat. Spalko knew what it was.

Food.

The horde was carnivorous.

Seated in the front of the jeep, the dazed soldier suddenly bellowed, pawing at his face. Pain drew him back to full alertness. With a cry, he turned in Spalko's direction. Half his face was covered in flailing ants. Blood poured down his neck. Frantic to escape, he fell out of the jeep and into the sand.

A mistake that doomed him.

Immediately a wave of ants swept over his body.

He crawled on, blind and screaming.

FORTY-TWO

"IT'S A GIANT ANTHILL!" Indy gasped, and pushed them all down the slope.

"Bloody hell," Mac moaned.

As the group reached the bottom of the mound, Indy swung around. He spotted Spalko standing on the hood of her jeep. A surging red sea raged around her and flowed downhill, a boiling volcano of hunger and anger.

"Siafu," Indy mumbled.

Mutt glanced to him.

"Army ants," Indy explained and hurried them away. "Even the little ones can strip flesh from bone. We have to get to the river."

Indy had encountered army ants before, in the jungles of central Africa and Asia. They formed colonies as large as twenty million. And once on the move, they were an unstoppable force. During feeding swarms, an entire jungle would flee from their path. Even elephants with their tough hides stampeded out of their way.

And those had been only the small cousins of these giant ants.

Indy glanced back one more time. Up on the anthill, Spalko still had not moved. She stood in exactly the same position, staying quiet as a statue. She met his gaze across the deadly sea. He sensed her hatred, her desire to kill him. She even held a pistol in one hand, aimed at him—but she dared not shoot it.

Not if she wanted to live.

The blast would draw the aggressive ants straight to her. Her only hope for survival was to hide in plain sight, to offer no sign of hostility or threat.

And it served Indy just as well.

Safe from her for the moment, he led the others up the neighboring ridgeline. They had to hurry. Mac and Mutt hauled Oxley between them. Reaching the top of the rise, Indy glanced back at the churning red sea. The colony washed to the bottom of the anthill and flowed up the ridge after them, surging at an amazing speed.

Indy swung around. "Faster!" he screamed.

As they fled down the far side of the ridge, a strange rumbling roar grew in volume. At first Indy thought it was the surging white water of the river. But it came from the wrong direction. He searched the sky.

Was it a distant thunderstorm?

As Indy reached the bottom of the ridgeline, he had his answer. From the jungle to the right, a massive vehicle plowed out of the dark forest and onto the trail, its horn blaring.

It was the damaged Russian troop transport, its roof missing and shredded.

The vehicle crashed across their path with a squeal of brakes. It skidded and fishtailed to avoid plunging into the ravine. Then with one last rattle it settled to a stop, spewing exhaust and blocking the way to the river.

The driver's door slammed open, and a familiar brute bounded out.

Colonel Dovchenko.

The Russian barreled straight at Indy like a runaway locomotive, his face locked in a cold mask of rage and vengeance.

Backpedaling away from the others to draw the Russian colonel off, Indy yelled to Mac and Mutt. "The river! Get down to the river!"

Oxley nodded and promptly dropped flat to the dirt instead, sprawling out on his stomach amid the weeds, lying on top of the burlap sack.

Mutt tried to get him back to his feet.

Indy knew the boy wouldn't abandon the professor. He yelled to Mac and pointed toward the ravine. "Get the kid down to the river."

Mac nodded, grabbed Mutt by the elbow, and hauled him bodily toward the chasm.

Then the locomotive hit Indy.

"Let me go, man! I need to get to the Ox!"

Mutt struggled, but the older British man was stronger than he appeared, though maybe it was a strength born of terror. Still Mutt fought. He wasn't going anywhere without Oxley.

Finally Mac pointed toward the neighboring ridgeline. They would be swamped in a matter of moments: Ants were cresting the top and surging downward. "Got company coming, mate! You're not going to help anyone if you're ant food. Got it? Leave Oxley to Indiana."

Mutt hesitated.

"You may not know it yet, mate, but your father has gotten out of tougher scrapes than this."

Mutt turned in time to see Jones take a fist to the belly that lifted him off his feet.

Mac tugged Mutt onward. "Okay, maybe not tougher than this. But if anyone can come out of this smelling sweet, it's Indiana."

Mutt finally nodded.

Together the two barreled toward the ravine. But there was one problem.

The troop transport.

It blocked the way, and rifles bristled at them. The soldiers were not going to let them escape again. Mac and Mutt tried flanking to the left, but the rumbling truck edged along with them, keeping them hemmed in.

Mutt glanced back to the rise.

The ant army rolled toward them.

They were trapped.

Mac frowned at their predicament. "Looks like Indy will have to save us, too."

Marion took in the situation with a single glance.

Her duck idled under her. She had swerved the amphibious vehicle into the shadows when the troop transport blasted out of the jungle.

Bastard must've taken the direct route. Never trust a Commie to play by the rules.

Marion dared wait no longer.

She floored the gas, and the idling duck rocketed forward. She arrowed the prow straight between the Russian transport—and her son.

As she'd hoped, the noise and sudden appearance caught the soldiers aboard the truck off guard. Plus she was riding in one of their own vehicles. The Russians hesitated long enough for her to plow between her son and the guns.

"Inside!" she yelled to Mutt and Mac.

Realizing Marion was not one of them, the Russians finally reacted and opened fire. The noise was deafening.

Marion crouched low in the duck. Rounds ricocheted off its armored side. Shielded behind the bulk of the duck, Mutt and Mac clambered inside and fell flat to the floor.

"We have to get to the river, Mom!" Mutt hollered.

"That's the plan, but first—" Marion popped into reverse. "—we have to fetch Ox and your dad."

Mac spoke up. "Marion, Indy *ordered* us to go to the river without him."

She hit the gas. "Mac, since when do I ever listen to Jones?"

FORTY-THREE

INDY WAS SORE from head to toe with nothing left to bruise. By now he was definitely well tenderized for the ant army. Though he and Dovchenko had been exchanging blows, Indy's fists had seemed little more than pats on the back to the Russian.

A moment ago Indy had heard gunfire and feared to look around.

Then he heard Marion yell and knew everything was fine.

Off to the side, Oxley remained sprawled out across the ground on his belly. He had his arms wrapped around the crystal skull. Not far away and moving closer, a river of fire ants poured down the ridge and flowed straight for the prostrate professor.

Indy positioned himself so that each punch or roundhouse kick from Dovchenko drove him closer to Oxley. He had to get his friend moving.

Dovchenko bore down on him. The only things bloody on the man were his knuckles, and Indy suspected most of that was *not* the Russian's blood.

Indy swung at Dovchenko, but his arm was just batted aside. A heavy fist followed and struck Indy square in the sternum. Indy flew backward and landed flat on his back next to Oxley.

"Henry Jones Junior," Ox said, staring over at him with a winning smile.

Indy gasped—that's all he could do. He rubbed his chest.

Okay, so Dovchenko *had* found a new part of his body to bruise. He'd felt that blow all the way through to his heart.

Rolling back to his feet, he coughed and glanced over a shoulder.

How close were the—?

—ack—

Only yards away, the ants swarmed in a wide swath straight at them. There was no chance to get clear in time, but Indy had to try. He bent down and pulled Oxley up. Resisting the effort, the professor shook free and instead raised the crystal skull up into a patch of sunlight.

The skull fired with brilliance.

As if shy of the radiant glow, the river of ants parted around the pair and flowed to either side, leaving them in a clear island.

But they weren't alone there.

With a roar, Dovchenko charged like a bull.

Indy was ready this time. He'd had enough of the Russian colonel. He faced the bull, waited, then ducked under Dovchenko's long arms.

As the giant struck, Indy flipped the Russian over his shoulder, letting his opponent's mass and momentum carry him up and over. Now it was Dovchenko's turn to land on his back.

In the middle of the river of ants.

Dovchenko jerked up onto his elbows, but in a matter of seconds the ants completely swarmed him. He screamed one piercing note—and then his voice was cut off as ants flooded into his mouth, streamed up his nostrils, and dug into his ears. He crashed backward, writhing, consumed under their mass, thrashing in silent agony.

His body began to slide across the ground.

At first Indy thought the Russian was crawling, and was amazed at his fortitude. Then he noted that the body seemed to be floating a couple of inches off the ground.

His large mass headed for the anthill, carried aloft by the sea of ants.

Apparently the dinner bell had been rung.

On tonight's menu:

Russian.

Marion drove the duck in reverse.

In the rearview mirror, she spotted Indy as he picked up Oxley in his arms. The professor held aloft the crystal skull. Burdened by the man's weight, Indy waded slowly toward her. But with each step, the ants parted from his toes, as if he were Moses crossing the Red Sea.

She and the others were not so lucky.

The ants covered the entire plateau in a solid mass. They swarmed over anything in their path, including both the Russian troop transport and the smaller duck.

Mutt and Mac yelled and slapped.

Several ants ran up and down Marion's legs.

Off by the ravine, the Russians poured out of the swamped transport, fleeing with ropes and climbing gear, anything to escape the ants. They had the same idea as their enemies.

Get to water.

Finally Marion reached Indy's side. "Need a ride, stranger?" she asked, but she had a hard time hiding the relief behind her words.

He was beaten, bloody, and bruised. Still, she expected some snappy comeback from him . . . but he just smiled, tired, weary, scared around the edges. That frightened her more than anything.

"Thanks, Marion."

Indy passed Oxley to Mac, then scrambled into the front passenger seat.

As he sat down, Indy's hand secretly reached across the front seat, found her fingers, and squeezed them. It was a private gesture that warmed through the cold terror clutched around her heart.

"Where now, beautiful?" he asked.

Reassured and confident, Marion hit the wipers, scattering ants. She punched the gas and aimed straight for the ravine.

Noting the direction of their flight, Indy's fingers tightened harder. "Honey, you gotta stop this thing or we'll go off the cliff."

"That's the idea, Jones."

He turned to her. "That's a *bad* idea! Give me the wheel!"

Marion offered him one of his own devil-may-care grins, an expression she had seen all too often. She also returned the words that usually accompanied that grin: "Trust me!"

Gunning the engine, she raced faster. Russian soldiers fled to either side. She ignored them, shot straight for the cliff, and sailed off its edge.

FORTY-FOUR

SPALKO LISTENED TO THE SCREAMS that flowed over the neighboring rise, but she remained calm. She waited perfectly still atop the hood of her jeep, using techniques developed by Nepalese monks to control heart rate, breath, and body temperature. They had taught her how to achieve *nothingness.*

She sought that same state here.

She was nothing, nothing to notice.

So far, the ants had ignored her stillness.

She waited while they emptied from their nest. As she stood quietly, the river flowing out the top of the anthill slowed to a dwindling trickle. Knowing she had a narrow window of opportunity before the colony returned, she finally moved. With great care, she edged off the hood. Stretching down, she tested the loose sand and dirt—first with one foot, then the other.

Nothing attacked.

Satisfied, she headed gingerly across the mound, treading lightly. She slipped cautiously down the slope, still controlling her breathing. She kept an eye on the ant army. Once well enough away from the hill's opening, she fled faster, skidding to the bottom.

Reaching solid ground, she stopped and considered the best path. Screams still echoed over the rise. *Not that way.* She turned her back on the cries and crossed toward the jungle by a different path. She knew the general direction to the river and headed for it. She kept her goal in mind, pushing back fear and doubt.

She would rejoin her comrades.

Then find Dr. Jones.

As the duck flew off the edge of the cliff, Indy clutched Marion's arm in one hand and his door handle in the other.

The vehicle shot out into open air and seemed to hang there for a breath—then it dropped in a stomach-in-the-throat plummet. The cliff wall sped past, draped with soldiers on ropes.

Indy gave a strangled cry. *"Marrrrrion!"*

A second later the duck struck something halfway down the cliff and jolted to a stop. Indy was thrown forward, and his forehead struck the dashboard in a stinging blow.

What the heck . . . ?

Dazed, Indy pushed back upright in his seat and leaned over the edge of the door. Had they hit some ledge on the cliff face? But peering down, all he saw were branches and leaves, and somewhere beyond that a churn of water over sharp rocks. He gaped back at the cliff, then over to Marion. He realized where they had landed. It stuck straight out of the wall like a leafy catcher's mitt.

"A tree?" he gulped out. "You landed us in a bloody tree?"

With a shrug, Marion goosed the engine. Tires spun in the air and tore leaves off branches. "Saw the tree earlier! When I was driving up! Cliff's not that high at this spot!"

Indy craned up. *High enough to scare a year off my life.*

And they weren't out of trouble.

Russian soldiers continued to drop toward them, sliding down on ropes.

And behind them—ants swarmed and poured down the wall in a crimson waterfall.

"We can't stay here!" Indy yelled over the whine of the revving engine.

The duck lurched as the tree slowly bent under its weight. Behind the rear wheels, its massive roots ripped from the cliff face. Chunks of rock crashed below. The tree slowly sagged, the vehicle tilting precariously.

Down, down, down . . .

As they all held their breath, the first wave of Russian soldiers swept past them. The men ignored the foundering duck. Immediate survival overwhelmed old grudges. The ant colony swarmed after the fleeing soldiers. One body toppled from above, screaming, coated with ants.

All the while, the duck slowly tilted nose-first, shifting toward vertical.

Through the windshield, Indy spotted a sandy beach below, bordering the swollen river. It was not far. In fact, the front of their vehicle was only a yard from the shoreline. As the tree continued to bow, their center of gravity shifted. The duck began to slide down the bowed tree trunk. Branches snapped and fell. Leaves rained to the sand. The duck was about to follow.

"Hang tight!" Indy called out.

The warning proved needless. The tree continued to bend, the duck to slide, and a moment later the front tires touched sand. They drove smoothly onto the shore with hardly more than a bump.

The Russian soldiers who had gathered below gaped at the strangeness of their landing. Still, rifles slowly rose in their direction and pointed at them.

But as soon as the duck dropped free of the tree and released its weight from the massive limb, the tree snapped back and slapped the wall like a giant flyswatter. The impact knocked two soldiers off their ropes.

Worse yet, the tree also swept the ant army off the cliff face.

The biting horde rained down upon the gawking Russians below. Weapons were forgotten. Cries and screams chased Indy and the others as the duck raced across the sandy shore and crashed into the river.

Hitting the water, the duck proved its amphibious nature and jetted out into the wide river, floating and bobbing on the surface. The swift current grabbed the vehicle and hauled it safely away from the two battling armies: ants and Russians.

They had made it.

His heart still pounding with adrenaline, Indy's face broke into a broad grin.

Oxley pointed downriver, shaking with excitement, apparently just as hyped up from their narrow and precipitous escape as Indy. "The way down!" the professor yelled. "The way down!"

The boat spun in a circle, and Marion seemed to have no control over their draught or direction. She twirled the wheel this way, then that. But nothing changed. They continued to be slaves to the current.

"The way down! The way down!" Oxley insisted and pointed again, jabbing an arm in his enthusiasm. He clutched the skull under his other arm.

Indy checked where Oxley pointed. At least the current was carrying them in that direction. He patted his friend's shoulder. "That's the way we're going, pal. Calm down."

Mac helped Oxley sit back down, but then leaned forward from the backseat and pointed to a switch on the dashboard. He spoke to Marion. "Flick that, my dear, and you'll miraculously transform from driver to motorboat pilot."

With a glance over her shoulder, Marion eyed the man, but she obeyed and thumbed the switch up.

A new motor engaged. The seat under Indy rumbled. He leaned over the starboard side of the duck and watched the vehicle's wheels retract into its sides. A churn of water erupted behind the stern as a boat propeller engaged.

With one hand on the wheel, Marion straightened their spin. She grinned over at Indy. He shrugged, grumpily impressed.

Mutt leaned forward. "Way to go, Mom!"

As Mutt dropped back, Indy slid his arm over and twined his fingers around Marion's free hand. He squeezed tightly. He wasn't letting go.

Not this time.

FORTY-FIVE

As THE BOAT MOTORED slowly down a flat section of the river, Mutt leaned back in the seat. He sat with his legs propped on the rear door, his ankles crossed.

Even though his gaze was on the river, he sensed eyes on him. Turning, he found Jones staring back at him from the front seat.

"What?" he asked.

"I saw you with Spalko." Jones made a motion of wielding a sword. "You learn to fence like that in prep school?"

Mutt shrugged. "Just one more useless experience."

"I'm not sure I'd call that one *useless*."

His mother spoke as she guided the boat along the current, her voice ringing with pride. "He was fencing champ two years in a row, but he got kicked out for betting on the matches." She cast a glare back at him over her shoulder.

"What?" Indy exclaimed. "He got kicked out for that? That's outrageous!"

Mutt straightened in his seat and pointed a thumb to his chest. "I bet on *myself* to win. I made a fortune. What's wrong with that?"

Mac smacked Mutt on the back. "Attaboy!" Then the Brit leaned over and added in a more serious tone, "But you *did* do something wrong, young man."

"What?"

"Always have a little action on the downside. In case you gotta throw one."

Mutt considered the advice, then slowly nodded. *That makes sense. Cover all angles.* Why hadn't he thought of that?

In the front seat Jones rolled his eyes and looked like he was about to say something, but the boat suddenly began to shake and rattle. Everyone tensed, expecting the worst.

"Water's getting rougher," Marion warned.

Mutt scooted up, searched downriver, and pointed. "Rapids ahead. But they don't look too bad. You can do it, Mom."

His mother patted his arm and smiled back at him. She guided the boat to smoother water, but there the current also ran swifter, and the duck flew down the river.

As they raced, Mac leaned up next to Mutt and thrust an arm out at Marion, offering his hand to shake. "By the way, the name's George McHale. Sorry about the first impression. Double agent and all that. I'm actually rather a—"

Jones pushed the Brit's arm away. "Will you back off her already?"

"What?"

Jones glared back at the man. "Don't think I don't notice the way you keep smiling at her, buster. Like your lips are stuck to your teeth."

Just then the duck entered the rapids Mutt had seen a moment before. Hitting the first swell, the boat's nose shot up, then dropped and dipped underwater momentarily. The river rushed over them.

Hit in the face by a wall of water, Mutt got knocked to the floor. He took a mouthful of river. Fighting to rise, he coughed and spit. As the duck righted itself, Mutt found himself sitting in a small pool of water on the bottom of the boat. He started to shift to a higher spot, then felt a biting pain flare in his hand. He yanked his arm out of the water and found a rainbow-bellied fish hanging from one of his fingers. He shook his hand in disgust.

"Ack!" he gasped out. "Piranha!"

The others screamed, too.

Mutt whipped his arm out over the side of the boat. The fish went flying and plopped into the river. He pulled his bleeding hand to his chest.

But the screaming continued from the others.

"It's okay! I'm okay!" he assured them.

But no one aboard the small boat was looking at him. They were all staring forward. His mother spun the steering wheel, her concentration fierce.

Curious, Mutt scooted higher and looked downriver. His eyes widened as he realized the source of the others' terror. The river ended a few yards ahead—and went plummeting over a waterfall.

Off to the side, Oxley shouted, excited, "*Three times* it drops!"

Though his mother continued to fight the current, they could not pull free. The engine was at full throttle, the stern propeller tore into the chop, but the duck raced onward, trapped in the heavy flow.

With no escape, Mutt braced for the plunge.

Spalko stood with the remainder of the Russian contingent on the bank of the river. Three vehicles were slowly being brought down a steep road toward the gathered soldiers. She studied the men, now fully under her command. Somewhere along the chase, Colonel Dovchenko had vanished.

So few remained.

Three-quarters of her forces—the finest of the Russian *Spetsnaz*—had been wiped out by a woman, a boy, and an old archaeologist. She shook her head at the impossibility of it all. Still, she accepted the reality of it, too. Undaunted, she would forge ahead. Her enemy was on the river. With no other choice, she would follow the river's course and hunt for the others.

As the vehicles drew up beside Spalko, she did not wait. She swung to the lead vehicle and climbed inside.

"Load up!" she bellowed to her soldiers.

Over the waterfall they went.

Indy clenched his fingers to handholds and braced his legs as the duck dropped in another gut-wrenching moment of free fall. The screaming from the boat seemed to hold them suspended in the air, borne aloft by pure terror—then the duck fell and struck the river again, plunging deep, but bobbing back up quickly.

That wasn't too bad.

Spitting water, Indy sighed with relief—until he saw the river rush over a second waterfall just ahead. Their boat, slave to the savage current, shot toward it.

"The way down!" Oxley screamed from the backseat.

They were airborne again. Indy felt the boat drop out from underneath them. He hung above his seat for a breath. Then the boat struck the river. Indy crashed back into his seat as water swamped the vessel, almost washing him out.

He grabbed a door handle to steady himself.

He checked the others. Everyone was shaken but still in the boat.

Oxley sat straight in his seat. "The way down!"

"Take it easy, Ox," Indy said. "You wanted us in the river, right? *Three times it drops*?"

Oxley lunged forward and pointed frantically. "The way down, the way down . . ."

Mac shifted. "He's not pointing to the *river,* Indiana."

Indy saw Mac was right. Ox was pointing to the shore, at a path that switchbacked down beside the waterfalls.

The way down.

As he stared, Indy also spotted a handful of vehicles cautiously traversing the path, heading down. He knew those trucks and jeeps.

Russians.

"Aw, nuts."

Marion glanced to him. "What?"

Indy recognized his mistake. "The way down isn't *in* the river . . . it's *next to* the river. And we've got company coming."

He glanced back to Oxley. The professor trembled and shook, quaking all over. Indy had attributed Oxley's attitude to *excitement*. Now he understood the truth.

It wasn't excitement—it was terror.

Without turning, Indy heard it.

Distant thunder, growing louder, swelling.

The *third* drop.

He turned and faced the monster ahead. The entire river rolled over a churning edge. Beyond, there was no sign that the river even continued.

Just sky and more sky.

"We won't make it," Indy mumbled. "Not in the boat."

"Indy?" Marion's voice was strained with worry, fearful at what he might be about to propose.

Indy faced the others. "As soon as we go over the falls, everyone abandon ship! Leap clear of the boat! It's the only chance!"

Eyes just stared at him, but Indy knew they understood. He faced forward, readying himself as the boat raced for the abyss.

There was no screaming—what came next was beyond screaming.

With no other recourse, they all held their breath as the boat hit the edge and went shooting out into open space. The duck tipped its nose downward. The river came in sight again, impossibly far below.

Indy knew they had only one hope.

"*JUMP!*"

PART SIX

THE LOST TEMPLE

FORTY-SIX

INDY CLAWED for the river's surface, kicking and pulling. He had lost all sense of direction and instinctively fought out of darkness and toward the light. His lungs burned, and his muscles cramped. With one last fierce kick he broke through the surface of the water. He shoved high with a great gasp of air.

As he reentered the world, it greeted him with a thunderous applause.

Indy treaded water and searched in a slow circle. He discovered the source of the noise. The giant waterfall pounded a few yards off. Fearful of the crashing waters, he swam away. Luckily the river pooled into a deep lake below the falls before continuing onward.

Indy felt the current's tug, but he kicked against it.

Through the fall's mist, he spotted splashing in the water. Voices called. He heard his name. "Indeee!"

Marion!

He swam in the direction of her voice. Drawing closer, he made out both Marion and Mutt. Mother and son were swimming for shore.

He waved to them. "Marion!"

She stared back, and her face bloomed with relief.

"Get to shore!" he called to them.

Indy searched both banks and the open stretches of water.

Where were Mac and Oxley?

As if summoned by his fear, two figures stumbled from the very edge of the waterfall, already ashore. They looked like drowned rats, leaning on each other.

Indy kicked toward where Marion and Mutt were climbing out of the river. The pair collapsed onto the mossy bank.

Swimming toward them, Indy fought his water-laden clothes while taking in his surroundings. The air seemed cooler here, yet also moister, due to the falls. The shoreline was covered with jungle trees and flowering orchids. A scarlet macaw took wing in a brilliance of fiery plumage. Monkeys hooted deeper in the forest, calling questioningly at the intruders.

Indy finally reached the shoreline and hauled himself out of the river. He felt four times his normal weight and half as strong. He shook his satchel off his shoulder and let it drop to the shore. Before he knew it, he was on hands and knees, too exhausted to stand upright. He crawled over to Marion. She did not even lift her head to greet him. He slid next to her, scooping an arm beneath, pulling her to him. It was as familiar as coming home.

Indy turned to her, staring down into those eyes. He ran the back of his thumb along the edge of her eyebrows. Soaked, exhausted, and nearly drowned, Marion had never looked more beautiful.

She noted his attention and allowed a ghost of a warm smile to tease her lips. "Not tired, are you, Indy?"

"Baby, you have no idea."

"Sure I do. The way you live? Running off to every godforsaken spot in the world and back again twice?"

He sighed, returning her gentle smile. "It ain't the mileage, honey. It's the *years*."

They stared at each other. For once, Indy was too tired to fight, too worn to hold back. "Marion . . ."

Her name was a promise and a wish on his lips.

Before he could say more, a rustling erupted in the underbrush.

Mutt jerked up from his half-drowsing state. His hair stuck out every which way as he glanced frantically all around. "What the hell was that?"

Indy rolled to his back and up on an elbow. "Calm down, kid. Probably just a deer or tapir."

Oxley and Mac arrived at their riverside camp.

Joining them, Mac fell flat onto his rear end, then collapsed back. "Let's *not* do that again," he mumbled to the sky.

Oxley wandered past, carrying the drowned burlap sack. Despite the long fall, the professor had not let go of the crystal skull.

As Indy watched, Oxley crossed to the river's edge and sat down, his back to the river. With the sack in his lap, he fingered it open, pulled out the crystal skull, and placed it on the pebbly shore.

Curious, Indy stood with a groan and stumbled over to his friend.

Marion and Mutt followed.

Oxley had positioned the skull so that it stared in the same direction as he did. Indy heard or maybe just sensed a vibration in the air. It grew stronger.

"Look!" Mutt exclaimed.

Small pebbles and sand had begun to quiver and jump, slowly stirring in a slow circle around the skull.

Marion slipped her arm into Indy's. "It's both beautiful—and horrible."

Indy lifted a hand to shield his eyes. He followed the path of the skull's gaze and pointed his arm. Beyond the fringe of rain forest, black cliffs rose high. They were craggy and streaked with patches of moss and trails of blooming orchids. But where the skull stared, the entire cliff had been carved into the relief of a colossal stone head. Its eyes were huge, oversized for its face.

Like the crystal skull.

Oxley intoned next to them: "*Through eyes that last I saw in tears . . .*"

The golden vision reappears . . .

Mutt stirred at Oxley's side, filling in the last half of the verse in his head. He recognized that poem!

"He's quoting T. S. Eliot!" Mutt said aloud.

Everyone stared at him.

Ignoring them, Mutt pushed forward and bent next to Oxley. "Ox, you made me read it, remember? *Eyes that last I saw in tears, through division, here in death's dream kingdom, the golden vision reappears.*"

Oxley showed no sign that he'd heard anything Mutt said.

But someone else had.

Mac came over, drawn by the commotion. "*Golden* vision? I like the sound of that! You can count me in."

Disheartened but not giving up, Mutt straightened and positioned himself in front of the skull. He stared in the same direction as the skull's eyes and squinted with concentration. Jones joined him, matching his expression.

Studying the cliff face, Mutt slowly lifted his arm. "If you look closely, there's a thin waterfall flowing from the left eye. *Like tears.*"

Jones squinted harder at the cliffs, but eventually shook his head in defeat. "You got sharper eyes than mine, kid. I'll have to take your word for it."

"*Through eyes in tears,*" Mutt mumbled.

As Mutt chewed on the puzzle, he felt Jones studying him, as if waiting to see if he could figure it out. Mutt hated that he even cared what this man thought . . . yet at the same time, he knew that he *did* care.

He finally faced Jones. "So that must mean we have to go through that waterfall . . . through the *tears*?"

Jones clapped him on the shoulder. "You got it, kid. That's where we're going."

"Up there? Without any gear? Are you nuts?"

Jones strode toward his discarded satchel at the river's edge. "Nobody else has to come. But that skull has to be returned."

"*Returned,*" Oxley echoed.

Mutt trailed after him, bone-tired and a little scared. "Who cares? That thing's brought us nothing but trouble." He pointed to Oxley. "I mean, look at him!"

Jones shouldered his satchel. "I have to return it."

His mother put her arm around Mutt. "But why you, Indy?"

He shrugged. "Because it asked me to."

Mutt shook his head in disbelief. "It *asked* you to? A hunk of dead rock?"

Jones headed out. "What makes you think it's *dead*?"

FORTY-SEVEN

INDY CLUNG TO THE DAMP ROCK, bathed in mist. He ached down to his bones. It had taken half the day to cross the jungle and scale the cliff to this point. The way grew steadily steeper and more treacherous; each toe- and foothold had to be tested. Slippery moss, leafy ferns, and crumbling stone threatened to toss them all back to the jungle below.

Gasping, Indy stared out toward the lowering sun. The angled light had turned the valley below into a world of shadow and emerald, split by the shining silver snake of the river. Low mists hung like ghosts, while the jungle cawed and howled and cried. Here was a world primeval.

"GET YOUR FOOT OFF MY HAND!"

Okay, maybe not completely primeval.

Indy looked down. Marion climbed directly below him, hugged tight to the wall. Beyond her, Mutt and Mac struggled. The kid was shaking his fingers, balanced on his toeholds.

Mac, red-faced and streaming with sweat, wore a wounded expression. "Sorry, mate, I slipped."

"Quit bellyaching!" Indy called down with more verve than he felt. He pointed to Mutt's precarious perch. "And remember, kid, three points of contact with the rock at all times. Safety first!"

Mutt gawked up at him. "How's any of this *safe,* man?" The kid shook his head, but he did stabilize his grip and mumble under his breath, "You and your talking skull."

"Just keep moving!"

Indy headed up again. Earlier, as they trekked through the jungle, the others had questioned him about his statement that the skull was more than rock crystal. But he didn't elaborate—*couldn't* elaborate. While the skull hadn't actually *talked* to him, he had sensed something, a drive to come here, a compulsion instilled in him. Even now it felt like a pull at his sternum.

Return . . .

Indy also remembered staring into that skull, being lost in its light, a light that *stirred* as if it were living. If only he'd had more time . . .

Marion called down from below. "Indy! Look!"

She pointed higher.

Indy craned up. The final member of their party scaled the rock ahead of them all. Oxley moved up the cliff face as if he were on a morning stroll around the park. He'd even stopped to pull some extra feathers for his hat from the rocky nest of a harpy eagle.

Above the professor, a giant carved eye gazed out over the valley, solemn, stoic, but also melancholy, mostly because of the springwater gushing out of the tunnel that formed the eye. The stream tumbled in a sheer waterfall and trailed off into a series of silvery cataracts flowing down the stone face.

They'd been following those *tears* up the cliff. Indy had been matching Oxley's toeholds and finger grips. The professor had been here before, and Indy was happy to give him the lead.

With Marion's warning, Indy now watched Oxley leap from a small ledge and straight through the waterfall under the eye.

Mutt had been right!

Through the tears.

Invigorated by the revelation, Indy climbed faster. He reached the ledge and stared at the rush of water. He saw no opening, no sign of a passageway or cave. Still, Oxley had shown them the last step, one of faith.

Crouching, Indy dove through the water.

A shock of pounding cold jolted through him—then he half rolled into the mouth of a tunnel. He stood up, amazed and relieved.

"Indy!" Marion called through the roar of the falls. He could just make out her shadow through the screen of water.

"I'm fine!" Indy called back to her. "Just jump! I'll catch you! All you have to—"

Before he could finish, Marion came flying through the falls, soaked to the skin, and right into his arms. She stared up at him, grinning, with water streaming over every surface. "What were you saying?"

"Never mind," he said and shifted her deeper into the tunnel.

Mac yelled, "Here I come!"

With a few more shouts and leaps, they were soon all gathered at the mouth of the tunnel. Indy had prepared torches using sap from the copalli tree. The natives of the Amazon used it for wound healing and treating colds—but it was also rich in flammable hydrocarbons. With the touch of a match, flames burst from the ends of their torches. The smoke curled to the roof, smelling acrid and medicinal.

Indy raised his torch, lighting the tunnel.

"Where's Oxley?" Marion asked.

Frowning, Indy swung his torch and searched around. The professor had been at his side a moment earlier. Now he was gone. Far down the passageway, a pinpoint of sunlight marked the end of the tunnel.

Indy pointed. "There."

A figure danced in that light, waving an arm. "Hennnry Jonnnes Junnnior!"

"We'd better get going," Indy said. "Before we lose him."

Mutt had wandered off. He lifted his own torch high toward the wall. "Hey, you might want to see this."

Indy crossed to the kid's side.

Along the entire expanse of the wall, elaborate cave paintings covered the rocky surfaces, divided into panels, each with its own artwork.

"Over here!" Marion called from the opposite wall. She lifted her torch.

The wall on that side was also covered in ancient art. Indy had once visited caves in Lascaux, France, where prehistoric cave paintings dated back to 15,000 BC, depicting horses, bulls, rhinoceroses, and giant cats. Throughout human history, cultures had sought to capture and memorialize what was important in their lives through their art.

The same seemed to be true here.

Indy moved down the passageway, waving his torch from one wall to the other. The paintings continued all the way down the tunnel. They were perfectly symmetrical, intricate, detailed. The torchlight also revealed that the tunnel was in reality a series of adjoining chambers, lined up one after the other like a primitive art gallery.

Each chamber was elaborately decorated.

But by whom?

Spalko stood at the riverbank, her hands on her hips. She stared at the wreckage on the water's edge. Though it was dented, crumpled, and waterlogged, she recognized one of the convoy's ducks. According to her men, the vehicle had been used by the prisoners to escape into the river. She studied the drowned duck.

Had Dr. Jones and his party been killed?

She took a deep breath.

No matter. Her team would move on.

But to where?

Turning her back on the river, she inspected the men gathered there. Only a dozen of her original sixty were fit to carry on, and even these bore bandaged wounds or had faces and limbs swollen from ant bites. Not all would be able to make the climb. Still, those who could were the best of the best. They'd come through fire and terror to this place. Like her, they'd proven their worth. The soldiers were already dividing up the climbing harnesses and ropes. They'd had to leave the vehicles at the top of the last waterfall, but they'd brought all their gear with them.

Including their guns.

She prayed Dr. Jones was still alive because if he was . . .

A lancing flash of burning light exploded behind her eyes. Momentarily blinded, she fell to one knee on the riverbank. She felt agonizing pressure in her head, like diving deep underwater. She had never felt such force. It both frightened and exhilarated her.

Then it was gone.

No . . .

"Colonel Doctor?" her lieutenant asked, concerned.

Spalko shook her head and gained her feet. She recognized what she'd felt, a surge of power like a mental lightning strike. She stumbled away from the river. "They . . . they've found it! They've found Akator."

She could not say how she knew it, but she did. Her lieutenant passed her a handheld transceiver. She studied it and slowly scanned in all directions, but the needle remained fixed and steady, pointing only one way.

She stared where the needle indicated, toward a stretch of misty cliffs.

Of course . . .

Across the jungle, a towering face had been subtly carved into the cliffs. She studied the stony countenance. The eyes seemed to be gazing at her alone, daring her, challenging her. With her head still pounding, she recognized what lay ahead, knew it in her heart.

At long last, she'd found it.

The gateway to Akator!

FORTY-EIGHT

TORCHLIGHT FLICKERED over the panel of artwork.

Mutt watched Jones lean toward the cave painting, so close his nose was almost touching. On the wall, six human figures knelt in a row, arms upraised to the sun. Jones lightly ran his fingertips over the surface. Then he sniffed his fingers.

"Ochre . . . charcoal . . . iron oxide."

Mutt had been doing his own investigation. He'd found torch holders drilled into the wall. He jammed his flaming brand into one of the holes so he could examine the stone beneath it. It was black with soot. Following Jones's lead, he ran his fingers across the oily stain. It came off easily. He sniffed and smelled the turpentine-like odor of the sap used to fuel their own torches.

"This is fresh," Mutt muttered. "Someone's used these holders. And not too long ago."

No one paid him any attention.

Jones straightened from his observation of the art and stretched a kink from his back. "These must have been painted by the Ugha tribesmen, the original inhabitants of Akator."

Mac leaned on another panel of artwork, looking unimpressed. "How old do you think they are?"

"Some may be Neolithic. Possibly going back six . . . maybe *eight* thousand years."

As a group they moved down the tunnel, flashing their torches over the artwork. Jones stopped at another panel. This one depicted a larger group of humans, kneeling again, gazing upward. But here the sun had been replaced by a tall, thin figure floating in the sky, arms outstretched, radiating shafts of light.

"Somebody came," Indy interpreted aloud.

They moved deeper. Flames cast flickering shadows over the walls. Mutt felt a prickling sense of dread.

The panels continued to reveal more of the strange, tall figures, but now the visitors mingled with the human figures, pointing their long arms. The tableaux varied, demonstrating advancements in their daily lives: the construction of homes, the pounding of metal, the tilling of fields. In the last panel one of the figures sat cross-legged in the center of a group of loincloth-draped humans and pointed to a detailed starscape overhead.

Indy touched one after the other. "The visitors taught the Ugha . . . architecture, metallurgy, irrigation and farming, astronomy . . ."

Mutt's mother called out from farther ahead. She lifted her torch toward a large drawing. This one was life-sized. They all gathered around her. In subtle colors and shades, painted in loving detail, was a bust of one of the visitors, done in profile. The skin was smooth, painted in shades of white. The artistry captured the wisdom and sense of peace in the strange countenance. But it clearly wasn't human.

Jones reached, traced a finger along the elongated cranium, then outlined the large eyes, narrowing at the corners. "Just like the skull," he murmured.

In the next chamber every panel showed the strange tall figures. They were grouped together, robed and shining, among the populace. Each painting was a variation on the same theme.

Jones stepped along the wall, his eyes fixed on the artwork, one hand raised but not touching. "They're always together now. Thirteen. Always depicted in a circle. Always in a group."

"What could that mean?" Mutt asked.

Jones shrugged and pointed farther down the tunnel.

They continued into a larger adjoining chamber. Jones crossed to the center of the room. He turned in a circle, then waved the group over to join him. Mutt and the others gathered next to him. Shoulder-to-shoulder in a circle, they held their torches toward the walls.

In this chamber there was only one painting, encompassing the entire circumference of the cavern. No one spoke; they were awed and horrified at what was depicted here. Mutt had once seen a painting by Pablo Picasso titled *Guernica.* Picasso's monumental artwork showed a Spanish village under attack. It was a visceral representation of the horrors of war: screaming, suffering, bloodshed, atrocities, all encompassing the raw brutality of man.

Here in this chamber was the same theme on a massive scale.

Across a painted village, figures ran, fleeing on foot. Splashes of crimson dripped, looking almost wet. One woman held up a baby to the heavens. Blood poured down the anguished woman's arms. Everywhere across the village, bodies sprawled, piled one atop the other. More figures hung from ropes or were impaled on spikes. In the center of the bloody chaos stood the source of the bloodshed and horror, a shining figure in golden armor, surrounded by a cordon of warriors in breastplates and helmets.

"The conquistadores," Mutt said.

Around the painted Spanish figures, Ugha tribesmen attacked with spears and bore aloft strange whirligigs spinning from upraised arms. But the invaders had muskets and powderhorns.

"The conquistadores came looking for El Dorado," Jones said quietly. "They looted the city. Took whatever they could, including the skull."

It was a humbling and horrific account. No one protested as

Jones led them to the last chamber, glad to escape the bloodshed. Mutt could still hear the screaming in his head.

The final room was the largest of them all, a giant rotunda—with a dome so high their flames failed to do more than dance shadows around it. They crossed the chamber slowly. There were no paintings here.

Only bones.

Embedded in the walls, as if trying to push out, were the fossilized remains of ancient creatures. Along one wall, a pronged deer was caught in midflight, head thrown back in panic, while a skeleton of a saber-toothed panther chased behind it. It was a battle of predator and prey forever locked in stone.

Higher across the dome, skeletal birds soared and flapped; low to the ground, serpents coiled into and out of the rock. Beyond, buried deeper into the stone, lay hints of shadowy creatures, massive, suggested by only a bit of claw or the bony cavity of an eye.

But the most impressive feature of the chamber were the thirteen skeletal faces embedded eight feet above the floor. They circled the chamber on all sides, staring down at the intruders with a vague sense of menace.

Again a prickling of warning iced through Mutt.

As he stepped under one of the faces, he felt something trickle against his shoulder. He turned and held out his hand. It wasn't water, but a stream of sand and bits of rock. He gaped up at the skeletal face—

—then the eyes moved.

Stumbling back toward the center of the room, Mutt screamed, half in warning, half in terror.

The face smashed apart, and something squirmed through from behind—damp, wriggling, slick with mud. Mutt heard crashes from all around the room. Other skulls shattered. More muddy figures wormed out, dropping to land on bare feet. Behind them, others followed, sliding and birthing out of the worm-tunnels.

With a sting of terror, Mutt ran for the sunlit exit to the chamber.

From the corner of his eye, he saw one of the creatures rise up, whirling a length of cord threaded through fist-sized rocks. Mutt flashed to the cave painting, picturing the Ugha tribesmen attacking the conquistadores with whirligigs.

He immediately understood what the weapons were: bolas, primitive hunting tools. And when used skillfully—

The tribesman let fly. The deadly bola spun toward Mutt. He tried to duck away, but he was too slow. The bola struck and wrapped around his neck. The weight and impact threw him sprawling on the floor.

Panicked and choking, Mutt rolled to his back. One of the muddy attackers leaped high, a sharp rock raised over his head.

Mutt winced, knowing what was coming—then above him, a fist punched out like a piston and flattened the tribesman's nose, knocking him back.

Jones dropped down and yanked Mutt to his feet. "Time to go, kid!"

FORTY-NINE

All around, the chamber erupted into chaos.

Clutching the kid by the elbow, Indy turned. He caught a whirling flash, then ducked as a bola spun over his head. Ahead Marion and Mac sprinted for the exit. Oxley waved merrily to them, framed in sunlight, feathered hat in hand.

Oh brother . . .

"C'mon, kid. Stay low and follow my lead."

Indy hunkered down and barreled toward the exit. Bolas flew past overhead and struck at his feet, casting up sparks as rock struck rock.

Indy danced and jigged across the chamber.

Mutt kept up with him step for step.

Ululating war cries chased after them.

A moment later they burst out into sunlight.

Indy blinked away the glare and saw that they were standing at the top of a long staircase.

Marion and Mac were already pounding down the stone steps that led to a green valley below, chased by more warriors. Oxley was being herded in front of them, hopping along with hardly a care. Indy shoved Mutt after them and turned to face the tunnel.

Reaching to his shoulder, he grabbed a leather handle and unfurled his bullwhip. With a flick, he draped its full length down the stairs, ready to make a dramatic stand, to protect the others so they could escape.

Then from the mouth of the tunnel, a solid mass of Ugha warriors surged straight at him, shrieking with one voice.

Reconsidering, Indy turned on a heel and ran down the steps, taking them two at a time. More warriors boiled out of tunnels to either side of the stairs. Bolas struck all around like the mother of all hailstorms, clacking and clattering across the steps.

As he fled, Indy caught a glimpse of the valley below.

A vast plateau stretched across the hollow depression, covered with the ruins of a sprawling ancient city, half consumed by the jungle. Beyond the ruins, a massive lake seemed to float above the city—shining a brilliant blue in the sunlight, its surface frosted by mists.

Indy recognized it as a reservoir—engineered, not natural.

Despite the danger and terror, he was still an archaeologist. He spotted silvery blue lines spiraling through the city and understood what they were.

Aqueducts—flowing from the reservoir.

He followed the spiral of aqueducts to the center of the ruins, where a towering stone temple waited. It was a giant stepped pyramid, climbing in terraces. It had to be the fabled Great Stone Temple of Akator.

Indy squinted.

At the top, he could just make out—

Indy suddenly slammed forward, struck from behind, tackled by two of the small warriors. One leaped onto his back, wrapped a bola around his neck, and yanked his head back.

Serves me right for sightseeing.

A shout drew his attention to the right. Mutt came flying over, his arms straight out to either side. The kid clotheslined the pair of tribesmen across their throats and sent them tumbling off the stairs.

Mutt hauled Indy up. "Time to go, old man!"

They set off together, father and son, leaping two steps at a time, bolas sparking at their heels.

"Indeeee!"

Near the bottom of the stairs, Marion was down on her back. A warrior straddled her chest, pulling at her hair and holding a rock in an upraised arm.

"Mom!" Mutt yelled.

They were too far off, except—

kuh-RACK

Indy lashed out with his bullwhip. The leather sailed out to the very limit of its reach and wrapped once around the tribesman's scrawny neck.

Good enough.

Indy yanked and sent the warrior flying.

Together, step for step, Indy and Mutt hurried down to Marion. They scooped her up as they passed, carrying her between them.

A regular happy little family united again.

But they still had to contend with two crazy uncles.

Ahead Mac stood his ground, punching and gouging. He used elbows and kicks to the groin. The man was not above fighting dirty.

Indy, Mutt, and Marion bulled through to him, collected him, and kept going, expanding their family grouping. The last member was skipping ahead, waving his hat as if he were in a Disney film.

They caught up with Oxley, momentarily ahead of all the warriors.

To either side, lining the stone roadway, rose massive sculptures and statues, draped in vines and coated with lichens and moss. One appeared to be a dragon or serpent. It seemed to be struggling to rise out of the ground, but vines and roots imprisoned it, slowly dragging it back under the earth.

Farther out, ancient structures and homes were also succumbing to the relentless claw and creep of jungle—not to mention the inescapable march of *time*.

Only one structure appeared impervious to all.

It rose ahead of them, climbing in stone tiers, pristine, a testament to early mankind's ability to carve order out of chaos.

The Great Stone Temple of Akator.

But the shrieks and screams behind Indy reminded him once again that sightseeing was not on the schedule at the moment. Survival was the primary concern.

And only one man held the key to that.

Indy shouldered over to Harold Oxley. "Ox! You were here before! You got past them!" He waved back to the crush of Ugha warriors. "What do we do?"

The professor continued skipping, oblivious.

Indy grabbed his shoulder, stopping him. There was no reason to keep running. Where could they go?

"HAROLD!" he barked, trying hard to break through. "WE ARE GOING TO DIE!"

Oxley frowned at the tone of his voice, then turned to the warriors with a pained look of exasperation. He stepped away—toward the warriors.

The professor reached into the burlap sack tied to his belt and pulled the skull free. Standing before the rampaging tribesmen, he lifted the crystal skull high in both hands.

As a shaft of sunlight struck it, the skull ignited into a fiery rainbow of diffracted light. Shadows fell back. The sun itself seemed to shine a little brighter. Indy heard a slight humming that seemed to vibrate the very motes of light.

The leading edge of warriors skidded to a stop. Others piled up behind them. The whirl of bolas slowed and stopped. A low murmur of awe spread through them. There was no fear, or even abject worship, merely some understanding that both mystified and intrigued Indy.

Muddy arms pointed at Oxley. Heads nodded, and slowly the warriors retreated toward the cliff, leaving the intruders in peace.

Or maybe leaving them to do what must be done.

Mac stepped next to Indy and nodded to the skull. "I have to get me one of those."

Indy slowly turned and faced the Great Stone Temple of Akator. It towered ahead, an ageless sentinel with a forbidding mystery at its heart. He shaded his eyes as he studied the colossal edifice.

"Mac, you may change your mind about that."

FIFTY

"WELL, THERE's *got* to be a way inside!"

Mac stalked around the flat summit of the temple pyramid, plainly hot and irritated. He took off his hat and swiped the balding crown of his head with a handkerchief, then tugged his hat back on.

Mutt ignored the complaining man. He followed Jones, studying what the old man was doing. It had been a solid hour since they'd clambered up here, climbing from terrace to terrace, examining each tier, looking for a way inside the temple.

All along, Jones had hardly said a word. With each level gained, he grew more taciturn and lost in concentration, especially when they reached the top and found no doorway into the pyramid. The few square openings along the sides of the temple appeared merely decorative and dead-ended within a step.

The entrance to the heart of the pyramid had to be here, on its flat summit. But how to get inside? The answer had to be tied to the strange structure that surmounted the temple.

Jones circled it, so Mutt did, too.

In the center of the pyramid's plateau rested a massive stone box.

It took up much of the open space atop the temple. It looked like a giant planter box, each side composed of a single slab of raw black granite, roughly hewn. It stood shoulder height. Along the base, a series of holes had been drilled through the slabs, but these in turn were plugged by pieces of stone.

Jones frowned and, fists on hips, stared at the unusual structure. Then, as if deciding something in his head, he stepped forward and reached up to the edge of the box. Pulling himself up, he clambered to his feet atop the box.

Mutt followed, though it took him a couple of tries.

The planter box was open at the top, but rather than being full of dirt, it was full of sand. *A giant catbox*, the British man had described it when they first reached the summit and gave the strange structure a cursory examination.

Still unimpressed and growing more and more irritated, Mac stood at the edge of the pyramid's summit and waved an arm out over the city. "Where's all the bloody gold? Look at this place! It's a dump!"

Standing on the box, Mutt stared out over the valley from his higher vantage point. While the city lay in ruins, half consumed by the jungle, there remained to his eyes a tarnished glory to the place. The city must once have been a beautiful, vibrant metropolis. The statues, the spread of buildings, the open amphitheaters. It was a wonder of civic engineering. Centuries later, water still trickled through its aqueducts. Staring down from above, Mutt imagined the city full of gardens and fountains and laughing children.

His viewpoint was not shared by another.

"Just a pile of rubble," Mac groused.

Off to the side, his mother sat with Oxley. She occasionally stared over at Mutt and Jones atop the sandbox with a soft smile. Mutt could guess what she was thinking.

Father and son, working together.

Jones knelt and dug out a fistful of sand. Wearing a look of concentration, he let the grains sift through his fingers. Then he stood back up and studied what sprouted from the heart of the sandbox. Four granite obelisks—each triangular in shape and fifteen feet long—rose crookedly out of the sand. They leaned outward, like stone fingers pointing toward the cardinal directions: north, south, east, and west. While the obelisks' bases were buried in the sandbox, their far ends rested on square stone pillars that stood at each corner of the pyramid's summit.

From below, the structure appeared to form a strange granite crown atop the pyramid. Mutt knew it had to be significant. But what did it mean?

Standing in the center of the sandbox, Jones turned in a slow circle and stared out at the length of each obelisk. Remaining silent, he finally nodded. He lifted his arms, laying one forearm atop the other in front of him. He angled one arm up, as if pantomiming the needle of a meter, and turned again in a circle. His eyes grew wider.

"Four become one," he muttered.

Mutt frowned at the strange behavior. "What do—?"

Ignoring him, Jones patted one of the obelisks and turned. His eyes flashed in the sunlight. He had figured something out. He crossed to the box's edge and hopped down.

Mutt followed him, leaping off the box and onto the stone summit of the pyramid. "You know something!" he accused. "Don't you, Jones!"

The man ignored him and crossed over to Oxley. Drawn by the excitement, Mac joined them. The boredom in the British man's expression had been replaced by curiosity.

Mutt's mother stood up at Oxley's side. "What is it, Indy?"

Jones pointed to the professor. "Harold made it this far, reaching the valley, but he couldn't get inside the temple."

"No kidding," Mac mumbled.

"So Ox did the only thing he could," Jones explained. "He took the skull back to the cemetery and hid it where he'd found it."

Mutt remembered the underground burial chamber of the conquistadores and the two sets of footprints. Jones *was* on to something. The man's eyes danced with a fervent excitement. Mutt's own heart beat harder.

Oxley stirred and mumbled. *"To lay their just hands on that Golden Key . . . that ope's the Palace of Eternity."*

Jones nodded as if that made sense. He crossed to an overhanging length of one of the obelisks and pointed to its smooth surface. "These obelisks must have once been polished to a shine." He pointed to the sun. "To reflect the light of the rising and setting sun. Shining bright."

"A *golden* key," Mutt said.

Jones nodded. "We're looking at that key. But it's been broken."

"Broken?" Mac asked with a thread of worry in his voice.

Jones pointed to the lengths of stone, but before he could explain, Mutt had figured it out, too. It was so obvious. "The four pillars!" Mutt gasped and studied the triangular shapes of the granite columns. "If you stood them up together, they'd form *one* really big obelisk!"

"The golden key," Jones said, clapping Mutt on the shoulder. "We have to join the four pieces together and re-create that key."

Mutt's exhilaration died to confusion. "But how do we lift them? Each one's got to weigh four tons."

"More like five, kid."

Mutt sighed. "No wonder Ox couldn't get inside."

Mac snorted, unconvinced. "If that really is the key, I'd love to see the *lock* it fits."

"You're standing on it, bub!" Jones swung away and crossed to a stack of loose stones piled in one corner of the summit plateau. He searched around.

Mac crossed toward the box. He stared up and shook his head. "Madness if you think we can lift these stones," he mumbled. "First Oxley, now Indiana."

Off to the side, Jones straightened and heaved to his feet with a heavy rock in his arms. He lifted the boulder above his head—then with a roar of effort, he ran straight at Mac.

The Brit lunged out of the way. "What the hell? Are you trying to kill me?"

But Jones ignored him and continued straight to the box. He slammed the rock down onto one of the stone plugs lined along the bottom of the slab. The impact knocked the sliver loose. Sand began pouring out the unblocked hole.

"What are you doing?" Mac yelled at him, obviously still shaken.

"Emptying the catbox, Mac . . . just emptying the catbox." Jones turned to Mutt, grinning wildly. "Give me a hand, kid."

Mutt matched his grin as he suddenly got it, too. He pictured Jones pantomiming the needle on a meter.

Of course!

Grabbing up a heavy chunk of rock, Mutt joined Jones in knocking out more plugs along the base. Sand poured out of each, piling up.

"Mom! Ox!" Mutt called and waved. "Help us clear the sand away from the holes! Keep 'em flowing!"

Jones patted Mutt on the shoulder. "Smart, kid!"

They all set to work, even Mac.

While they scrambled, Mutt took a moment to step back. As the sand emptied from the box, the bases of the four columns dropped lower. Their ends swung up, balanced on the edges of the box. Their tips lifted off the square stone pillars at the corners of the pyramid and began to point higher and higher into the sky.

Soon all the plugs were out, and sand poured out of the holes on all the sides.

As a group, they backed away and watched in amazement as twenty tons of rock, aided only by gravity, swung upright in front of their eyes.

"Well, I'll be damned," Mac said.

With a final trickle of sand from the box, the four sections teetered and came together—forming a single obelisk, perfectly erect and pointing straight into the sky.

His mother hugged Indy. "You did it!"

Immediately a low rumbling shook the plateau. The grind of massive gears sounded. Under their feet, the entire top of the pyramid began to split apart. Sections opened like an iris before them, folding away from the obelisk, driving them all back.

"But *what* did you do?" Mac asked, retreating.

Jones urged them to keep moving. "The twenty tons of stone acted as a *pressure key*. The weight settling on the one spot triggered the mechanism."

As the floor opened farther, a cavernous space appeared below.

"The whole pyramid is hollow," his mother said, peering carefully over the edge.

"Not quite," Mutt corrected and pointed. "Look!"

In the center, the newly formed obelisk now rested atop its big brother. Its fifteen-foot length was now just the very tip-top of a *hundred-foot* obelisk. But that wasn't all.

"Stairs!" Jones called out.

Mutt had spotted them, too. A stone staircase spiraled down the massive obelisk's length. It consisted of small slabs sticking straight out of its surface.

But the opening iris was pushing the group farther and farther away.

"We'll have to jump now!" Jones said. "Or it'll be too far!"

Mutt's mother shook her head. Mutt knew she wasn't too keen on heights. So before she could forbid him, he ran and leaped. He sailed over the yawning gap and landed on the top step of the obelisk.

His mother pointed to her toes. "Mutt! You get back here, young man!"

Instead Mutt headed down and waved. "C'mon! This is why we came here!"

Jones and his mother shared a look. At the same time, both said, "He's definitely *your* kid!"

With no choice, everyone ran and leaped—even Oxley followed with a small whoop of excitement. They gathered together on the stairs and headed down, mindful of the eighty-five-foot drop.

"Slow and steady," Jones warned as they proceeded down the steps.

"You know," Mac said, "that wasn't so bad."

Jones swung toward him with a sour, worried expression. "Mac, you never say—"

The steps began to retract into the column.

Mac wore a chagrined expression.

Jones merely pointed and bellowed. "Run!"

Across the valley, Spalko stepped out of the dark tunnel and into sunlight. Stairs descended ahead of her, dropping into a wide bowl of a valley. She spotted the ruins of a city, and a distant lake. Behind her, the muffled pops of a pistol echoed from the tunnel.

Her lieutenant stepped to her shoulder. He carried a rifle that still smoked. She glanced back. The tunnel was littered with the bodies of tiny brown warriors. And some of her men.

"The rest have fled back to their tunnels, Colonel Doctor."

"Very good."

"Orders?" he asked.

She lifted the transceiver, seeking the trace. It blinked, confirming what she already knew. She pointed to the stone pyramid in the center of the valley.

There was only one order to give.

Spalko headed down the steps, trailed by her three best soldiers, Russia's elite. She rested her hand on the pommel of her sword.

At long last . . .

"We end this."

FIFTY-ONE

INDY FLED down the retracting steps, flying around and around the giant obelisk. He cursed the ancient engineers. Why were these places *always* booby-trapped? Couldn't solving the riddle of the obelisk be enough to gain entry?

Under his boots, the steps continued to pull into the obelisk. Each stair was now less than a foot wide and shrinking steadily.

"Faster," he yelled.

Panting, Indy rushed down the stairs. His knees stabbed with pain, but he dared not slow. They were still four stories above the stone floor. Mutt and Oxley were a full turn ahead of him. They should be fine.

Behind him, Indy heard Marion and Mac gasping. He heard occasional high-pitched cries of terror from Marion—or maybe some came from Mac, too. Indy knew Marion had a thing about heights. Like he had about snakes.

Around and around.

As the steps continued to shrink, Indy found he had to turn sideways, his arms out, hugging the sides of the pyramid. He sidled and scooted. And in another turn around the obelisk, he was running on his toes.

He risked a glance back to Marion and Mac. The pair were nowhere in sight. He prayed they were simply on the far side of the obelisk, that they hadn't lost their balance and fallen.

Then what the mind thought, the body made happen.

Indy lost his footing. He scrabbled for the wall, seeking some handhold, but there was none. He fell—but managed to get his legs under him just before he hit. It was only a ten-foot drop, but still he struck the floor hard. He was no longer as spry as he'd once been. He felt the impact all the way into his teeth.

Mutt and Oxley came running up to him. Oxley cradled the skull in its burlap sack against his chest. The pair had made it safely down—but where were the others?

Worried, Indy circled the obelisk, looking for Mac and Marion, Mutt and Oxley close behind. A yell and the shadowy drop of a body drew them around faster. They found Mac sitting on his backside, wearing a pained expression.

"Marion?" Indy asked.

Mac pointed up.

She was hanging from her fingertips from one of the steps, fifteen feet up.

Indy hurried to a spot under her. "Let go, Marion!"

"No!"

"I'll catch you!"

"I'm fine right where I am!"

Indy saw that the stairs were continuing to retract. She would not have a fingerhold for long.

"Babe, you've got to trust me sometime!" Indy called up.

She glared down at him. "Now? Now we're having this talk about trust?"

He held out his arms. "Just have a little faith!"

She turned away and laid her cheek against the stone. "Indy . . ."

"Marion, I won't let you down . . . not this time."

And in his heart, Indy knew this was one promise he meant to keep.

She closed her eyes—then in an act of blind trust, she let go.

Indy got under her and caught her cleanly in his arms. He might be exhausted, bruised, bitten, and bone-sore, but he would never drop her.

Never again.

Marion twisted in his arms and smiled at him. "This is familiar."

"Catching you?" He nodded and gently placed her on her feet, thinking back to a tomb in Egypt. "But last time, there were snakes. Lots and lots of snakes."

She grinned back at him.

She hadn't been talking about the Egyptian tomb.

He returned her smile. He knew it, too.

Mutt called from around the side of the obelisk. "There's a hallway or something over here!"

Indy turned and helped Mac to his feet. His friend had a limp, but he waved Indy forward. "I'll be fine." Mac stared up at the obelisk. The steps had fully retracted into the wall. "No going back that way."

Indy nodded. They would have to find another way out of the pyramid.

Together they circled the obelisk and found Mutt standing at the mouth of a cavernous hallway. As they neared, Indy noted that the tunnel extended far into the distance, possibly miles.

"Must head under the city," Mutt said as they set off down it.

The tunnel was gloomy but not pitch-black. Natural sunlight filtered into the passageway from above, shining through strategically placed fissures and shafts, reflecting off polished surfaces of crystalline rock.

The sound of running water drowned out their footsteps. Along one side of the tunnel, an open aqueduct flowed heavily, streaming with water under some pressure. No doubt it was fed, Indy thought, from the large reservoir he had spotted as they'd entered the valley.

As they continued, shadowy shapes appeared and revealed themselves to be giant bronze waterwheels set along the aqueduct. Dozens of them. The flowing water's current spun them.

"Turbines," Indy said with amazement.

He crossed to a humming copper conduit connected to one wheel. He lifted a palm close to it. The hairs on the back of his hand stood on end. He also caught a whiff of ozone.

"Electrical current," he commented. "This whole place is like a massive power-generating plant."

"Generating power for what?" Mutt asked.

Indy shrugged, but it was a good question.

As they continued, other passageways crisscrossed and branched outward into a veritable maze. It would take years to examine it all.

As he walked along, Indy's eyes widened, trying to take everything in. His mind spun as fast as the turbines, pondering who had built this place, why it had been engineered, to what purpose. A thousand and one questions burned through his mind as electric as the current running through the copper conduits.

Off to the side, Indy saw Mutt pick something off a shelf. It was a ruby-encrusted piece of silver shaped into a sunburst, and the kid held it up to one of the cracks of light, turning it this way and that. Indy understood the kid's curiosity. It was a magnificent piece of artistry. Its value to history—

But Marion also noted Mutt's attention. She slapped his wrist. "Put that down, young man! You should know better than that."

Mutt looked up innocently. "I was going to put it back," he said, and he did just that. Afterward, he stared over to Indy. "I'm not a grave robber."

Indy frowned at the kid, remembering the gold conquistador's dagger. He motioned to Marion: *Not in front of your mother, kid.*

Mutt hid a grin, and they continued walking.

Marion moved up next to Indy. "Do you know where you're going?"

Indy pointed to the copper conduit running along the ceiling from the bronze waterwheels. "Power's going somewhere . . ."

Trailing behind the others, Mac limped along. He passed the jewel-encrusted sunburst left on the shelf. While no one was looking, he stealthily scooped it up and dropped it into his pocket.

"Now, *this* is more like it."

FIFTY-TWO

"HEY, THERE'S A ROOM up ahead!" Mutt yelled.

He rushed forward, but Jones and his mother shouted at the same time:

"Hold your horses, kid!"

"You stay with us, young man!"

Mutt obeyed, but it took all his will. The hallway they'd been following ended at the chamber ahead. He vibrated with curiosity. What was hidden inside the pyramid? With the complicated unlocking mechanism and booby traps, it had to be something valuable.

As they approached, a burnt odor became apparent and grew more potent with each step. It wasn't the pleasant scent of a wood fire, but more like the time Mutt had singed his leather jacket with a cigarette butt.

Mutt glanced to the others. His mother crinkled her nose. They smelled it, too. Reaching the end of the hallway, Jones waved for them to hang back as he stepped forward and took the lead. He continued cautiously, motioning them to follow slowly.

Mutt followed in his steps, but he kept behind Jones. Just in case. No reason to be careless.

The chamber was shaped in a half circle. On the far side rose a giant set of red-metal doors that looked like they'd been carved out of a single block of iron ore. As Mutt took another step, it became clear where the burnt smell was coming from.

Across the open expanse of floor, row after row of desiccated corpses filled the room, radiating out from the doors in concentric half circles. They stood upright in various poses of horror and agony. Worst of all, all the heads had been burned down to the bone, revealing blackened, grinning skulls.

Like so many spent candles.

Mutt swallowed, sickened, trying not to throw up.

On the other hand, Jones seemed undaunted. He moved closer, plainly curious. Mutt had no choice but to follow, wanting to stick close to the old man.

Jones crossed to one of the figures. The corpse wore bronze armor that looked Roman, but the body inside was no more than a dry husk. And like all the others, his head had been charred down to the bone.

Mutt kept close to Jones, while the rest of their party cautiously edged into the room. Jones leaned closer to the Roman warrior's skull. The worst charring seemed to concentrate around the eyes. Even the bone around the hollow sockets had been burned away, giving the corpse a wide-eyed, surprised look.

Shuddering, Mutt finally had to look away.

He spotted Mac moving among the standing bodies, pausing to study gold rings and jeweled bracelets. Mutt suspected a few would go missing. Farther back, his mother was staying well away from the corpses. She drifted along the outer walls, where hundreds of niches were crammed with myriad bits of antiquity: goblets and swords, helmets and headdresses, carved tablets and stone tools.

Mutt turned in a slow circle.

The rows of bodies wore all manner of clothes—from different eras and different countries—like revelers at some macabre costume party. Mutt spotted the horned helms of Vikings, the beaten armor of ancient soldiers, the polished sheen of knights. Among them were men in robes, loincloths, and fancier dress, even a pair of Japanese samurai in full regalia.

But all of them had one thing in common.

"They're burned," Mutt mumbled to himself, needing to break the oppressive silence, wanting some answer to the horror here. "All of 'em. What happened?"

"Good question." Jones straightened and continued to move among the bodies. He waved an arm to the niches, then to the corpses. "There are artifacts here from every era of human history. Macedonian . . . Sumerian . . ."

As Jones went on, Mutt remembered the grave of the conquistadores. He pictured the chest of gold coins buried with them. Coins from different ages, different cultures. Mutt searched around the room. The conquistadores had been down here, too.

"And hit the mother lode," he mumbled.

Jones didn't hear him. He kept pointing out the various cultures. "Etruscan . . . Babylonian . . ."

Mac gazed with shining eyes at the archaeological treasures of the room. "There's not a museum on earth that wouldn't sell its soul for a day in here."

Jones continued, his voice full of awe and respect. "Stone Age . . . prehistoric . . ."

Mac's expression grew hungrier. "A *dozen* museums, a hundred."

Jones finally stopped. A dawning realization lit his face. He turned and faced Mutt and the others.

"They must have been collectors . . . perhaps archaeologists themselves!" Jones turned to the massive doors. "But who are they? Where did they come from?"

During all of this exchange, only one person seemed disinterested in the collection. Oxley stood at the entrance to the room, trembling from head to foot, a desperate look on his face.

Mutt finally noticed his distress. "Ox, man. What's wrong?"

As if released from a spell, Oxley started into the room. He carried the burlap-wrapped skull in front of him in his outstretched arms. The sack fell away and dropped to the ground. Oxley strode right over it.

The crystal skull exposed, the professor marched straight toward the doors. With each step, the skull grew brighter, the air around it seemed to shiver, and a strange thing began to happen.

Small bits of reddish sand began to fly into the air and cling to the skull. It shed from the floor, from the walls.

"Iron ore," Jones said.

Oxley kept going. As he got closer to the giant doors, more and more shavings and particles of ore covered the crystal. Step by step, the covering thickened and built upon the skull's surface, layer by layer, like a dissection run in reverse—muscles, fat, skin. It was as if the vanished flesh were re-forming on the skull. By the time Oxley reached the doors, the rough semblance of a bust had formed.

Mutt recognized the countenance from the painting in the tunnel.

It was one of the visitors.

Oxley stepped to the doors and lifted the skull.

They waited, holding their breath.

Nothing happened.

Mutt finally exhaled and voiced the question in all of their minds. "How do we open them?"

FIFTY-THREE

INDY PACED in front of the iron doors as the others waited. Upon the doors' surface, there were no distinguishing marks, no inscriptions, no decoration. They were as unreadable as the stone face on the cliff.

But there had to be a way to open them.

As a group, they had tried pushing and shoving. Mac had even found an old sword and tried to pry a way open. Nothing worked. The iron doors were too massive. As with the obelisk, they had to find another method to unlock the way forward.

Indy turned his back on the doors and studied the layout of the room. First, the bodies. The Ugha tribesmen must have positioned the corpses there, though Indy was fairly certain they'd died somewhere else. The corpses were posted as a warning to intruders against *opening* the doors.

Casting his gaze farther, Indy noted the niches in the far wall. None of them was higher than four feet, a comfortable height for the tiny Ugha tribesmen.

But wait . . .

Indy remembered something he had spotted earlier. He swung back around. He'd been so busy studying the doors that he'd almost missed it. Off to the right side of the massive doors was a single niche. He crossed to it and measured its height against the reach of his own arms. It was empty, but the niche had to be nine feet off the ground.

Much too high for the short tribesmen.

But not for someone else.

"They were tall," Indy mumbled. He remembered the tunnel paintings. The visitors had towered over the Ugha.

Rubbing his chin, Indy pictured the Chauchilla Cemetery. The secret entry to the burial chamber of the conquistadores had been guarded over by a skull in a wall niche. Even the *crystal* skull had been hidden in a hollow space behind Orellana's body.

Could that be the answer?

Indy crossed to Oxley. He leaned down to stare into the professor's eyes. His friend's face shone with worry and fear. Indy reached out and gently placed his hands on either side of the skull. Iron ore shavings crawled around his fingers like living tissue. He spoke softly to Oxley.

"I'll give it back," Indy promised. "But there's something I'd like to try, Ox."

The professor trembled from head to toe, but he slowly let go. "Henry Jones Junior."

"That's right, Ox." Indy stepped back to the wall and nodded to Mutt. "Kid, give me a boost."

Mutt trotted over and folded his fingers into a stirrup. He eyed the skull, then the niche. "Chauchilla?" he asked.

Indy's eyebrows rose in surprise, and he could not dismiss the spark of pride that flared in his chest. "Right on the button, kid."

Indy stepped into Mutt's grip and hoisted himself up. Once high enough, he shoved the skull into the niche, face-first, the same direction Oxley had been holding it. It fit perfectly, like a mold.

Then just a moment before dropping down, Indy noted a flash of ruby light. It seemed to trace down the skull. The words *retinal scan* popped into his head. Immediately the skull began to glow—at first dimly, then brighter and brighter, shining through the coating of iron ore particles.

Mutt and Indy backed away.

"What's it doing—" Mutt started.

The answer came as the iron shavings exploded off the skull, while at the same time a heaving groan moaned from the doors.

"Reverse magnetism!" Indy exclaimed, wiping iron shavings from his shoulders. He waved everyone out of the way as the doors began to part.

Through the crack, a blinding light pierced the room.

"Get back!" Indy shouted.

With a great rumbling, the doors continued to open. More and more light washed in as the thin line of brilliance widened. Indy shielded his eyes against the glare, but he could make out no details of what lay beyond the threshold.

He headed closer, into the light, like a moth to a flame.

"Indy!" Marion called to him.

"I know! Be careful!"

"No! Wait for me!" Bathed in the blinding radiance, he felt a hand slip into his own. *Marion.*

The others joined them.

The doors ground fully open and pounded to a stop.

Indy saw what waited for them. "Mutt, we'd better go fetch that skull first."

A moment later Indy returned the skull to Oxley. He sensed that the professor, the skull's chosen caretaker, needed to take it these last steps.

Now ready, they all crossed the threshold together.

The chamber beyond the iron doors was perfectly circular, built of stone blocks. The walls were filled with niches and recesses that housed objects of reverence: carved totems, fertility icons, stone urns and vases, strings of polished beads, bronze figurines, bone drums. All items of worship.

And there was no doubt for whom these tokens of reverence were meant.

On an upper level that circled the entire worship space stood thirteen immense thrones, each intricately carved and twined with serpent icons. Bodies sat on the thrones, upright and straight-backed, each easily seven feet tall. Their desiccated flesh had dried to leather over bone. Any clothes had long since rotted to dust. There were no crowns, but the skulls, elongated and prominent, were imposing enough.

Oxley stepped forward, speaking gently to the skull in his palms. "No more forever waiting soon now."

Indy noted that one of the thirteen was not like the others.

It was missing its head.

Mutt noted the direction of Indy's gaze. "Let me guess. It's his."

Oxley slowly walked toward the headless corpse.

They had reached their goal—then a sharp voice cracked out like a gunshot.

"STOP RIGHT THERE!"

FIFTY-FOUR

SPALKO TOOK GREAT SATISFACTION from the crushed look on Dr. Jones's face.

She stepped across the threshold, accompanied by her lieutenant and two other soldiers. They kept their Kalashnikov rifles leveled at those in the room. She rested her hand on her rapier's hilt.

She smiled grimly at her adversary. "I must thank you, Dr. Jones, for discovering the path here and unlocking Akator's secrets, but I believe we'll let more experienced *minds* proceed from here."

"How did you find us?" Indy asked, baffled.

As answer, Spalko thrust out her arm and held her palm open. No one moved at first; then slowly George McHale slipped from Dr. Jones's circle. He shuffled with a hangdog look and placed a tiny black box into her hand.

"A tracker beacon," she explained. "We've been following its signal. Sometimes technology has its uses."

"I'm sorry, Indiana," McHale said.

Jones sighed and placed a palm on his forehead. "Sheesh. Will you make up your mind, Mac?"

Marion Ravenwood looked just as exasperated and shook her head. "I'm *really* getting tired of this guy."

Jones eyed McHale with a pinched expression. "So let me get this straight, Mac. You're a *triple* agent?"

"Nah, Indiana. I just lied about being a double agent."

Jones rolled his eyes.

Tired of the exchange, Spalko headed over to Professor Oxley. She bore the man no ill will—the poor addled sot. So she gently removed the skull from his hands. It was easy to be generous in victory.

Behind her, she heard McHale speak. "Marion, you don't need to worry. You can come with us. The riches here—"

He was cut off by a vehement laugh from Miss Ravenwood. "Fat chance, buster!"

Spalko ignored such petty foolishness and lifted the skull. This was all that mattered. She turned its eyes toward her. Surely in this chamber, it would finally commune with her.

"Speak," she commanded it. "Speak *now*!"

The skull vibrated between her palms, growing warm as if it were real flesh. Something was happening. *Finally!* Her heart pounded faster, but she forced herself to remain calm. A deep glow suffused the crystal, rising from a seed of opalescence deep in its cranium.

At last . . .

She lifted the skull higher. As light filled her vision, pressure built inside her head, as if she were diving deep underwater. She did not fight it. Resistance against such force risked permanent mental damage. She'd seen ample evidence of that. To survive a riptide, you didn't swim against it.

As she relaxed into the glow, she began to understand. Following a silent instruction, she lifted her gaze and stared around at the thrones.

She spoke, explaining what she now understood. "Look at them. They could've gone home. But they still wait. Others came looking for them. The smaller scouts."

She pictured the tiny mummified remains stolen from Hangar 51.

"Hidden here, these twelve continued to wait—for the return of the one who was lost."

Between her palms, the skull grew brighter. "They're a hive mind. One mind shared across thirteen bodies. A collective consciousness. More powerful together than they could ever be apart."

Her feet, unbidden, moved toward the steps that led up to the headless body.

Her voice grew sharper. *"Imagine what they'll tell us!"*

"I can't." These negative words came from Dr. Jones, breaking through her spell. He waved an arm around the room. "Neither could the humans who built this temple . . . and neither can *you.*"

She frowned at the smallness of his mind. "Belief, Dr. Jones, is a gift you have yet to receive. My sympathies."

She returned her attention to the task at hand and climbed the steps that led up to the higher dais, where she belonged.

"Oh, I believe, sister," Jones said. "That's why I'm staying down here."

She reached the top step under the throne and held the skull out to the seated body. Between her palms, she felt a fire build inside the crystal. It flared up, too hot to hold. As she let go, it ripped out of her fingers, sailed through the air, and snapped into place atop the shoulders of the lost one.

They all held their breath. No one spoke.

Slowly a rumbling grew underfoot. It swelled louder and louder. The floor and walls began to shake. To one side, a vase crashed to the floor and shattered. Other objects danced and bobbled in their niches.

Unsure what was happening, Spalko retreated down the steps and back to the middle of the room.

On the thrones, the bodies also began to vibrate and quake. Faster and faster. Their images blurred at the edges. As she watched, mummified flesh turned to dust and shook away, shedding from the bones beneath.

No, not bones.

Crystal.

The vibration slowed and stopped, and it became clear what was hidden under the dusty flesh. Upon the thrones sat thirteen flawless crystal skeletons—living skeletons. Through their bones glowed viscous fluids, half light, half substance.

Spalko continued to sense the strange pressure in her skull. She was still connected to the collective mind. As the pressure grew, so did her understanding. She moaned, half in terror, half in wonder. She knew what was happening and voiced it.

"They wake . . . !"

FIFTY-FIVE

DURING ALL THE COMMOTION, Indy moved closer.

On the upper dais, the body to which the skull had been returned *stirred.* Its bones quivered like the wings of a hummingbird. Out of this vibration, flesh bloomed into being—soft, *living* flesh, with eyes that could see, and hands that could move. In moments its entire body had fully re-formed, sculpted out of nothingness.

Awed, Indy gazed up at the face, knowing they were the first to view this countenance in centuries. And the figure above seemed to gaze back down upon them all, studying them just as intently. A wise gentleness glowed from its large eyes, but also something else, something that turned Indy's blood cold.

An unnaturalness to this world.

At his side, Oxley had also been watching it all, unblinking. The professor suddenly began to speak, low and rapid. But it wasn't English. Indy faced Oxley, listening in disbelief.

"It's Mayan," Indy realized aloud. "He's speaking Mayan."

Spalko glanced back to them. "What is he saying?"

Indy leaned closer, but he was afraid to touch Oxley in this altered state. What was happening? He listened to his old friend as he spoke an ancient language with complete fluency. Words flowed from his mouth like water out of a burst dam.

Indy could guess the source of this torrent. He stared back over his shoulder at the seated figure. In turn, the being gazed back at Indy with those strange eyes.

One recognized the other. They had spoken before.

The being slowly raised its hands, placed its two white palms together in an X formation—then twisted them once, inverting the X.

Not understanding, Indy turned back to Oxley for some explanation, an interpretation. He listened, deciphering as Oxley spoke in Mayan.

"He says he's grateful—" Indy pointed back to the throne. "I mean *it*. It's grateful. It wants to give us a gift. A big gift."

Steps away, Spalko faced the throne and pleaded with the firm conviction of the resolute. "Tell me—everything you know. I want it all. I must know!"

The being turned to her, drawn to her.

Oxley continued speaking while Indy translated. "It heard," he called to Spalko. Indy could not keep the disappointment out of his voice.

Mutt had followed it all, too. He stepped forward. "They're going to tell us everything they know?"

The kid tried to step past Oxley, but Indy grabbed him by the elbow and shoved him back. "Hang on, genius."

Indy felt the hairs on the back of his neck quiver. He straightened and stared around. The other twelve skeletons had started to vibrate, just like the first. In moments, flesh grew over all their bones, too.

Something had begun.

"I've got a bad feeling about this," Indy mumbled.

At the foot of the throne, Spalko remained transfixed and locked her eyes on one of the thirteen. But all their eyes began to glow. Indy's hairs prickled. He sensed the flow of power among the seated figures. Pure mental energy, amplified across the thirteen skulls.

Marion joined him, staring around. "Indy! Their eyes . . . so beautiful!" When he didn't respond, she turned to him and found him studying her. She grinned. "Aren't you going to look?"

He matched her gaze. "I found what I was looking for."

The floor began to shake again—only more violently. A three-foot-tall carved totem of a fertility god fell out of its niche and struck the floor, breaking off what made it a *fertility* god.

Wincing, Indy searched around him. The walls cracked and crumpled away, exposing the thinness of their façade. Beneath the false layer of stone lay a strange luminous surface: smooth, silvery, metallic. Indy remembered the silvery shrouds that encased the conquistadores' mummies. Here was the same in thick, solid form.

Mutt gasped as sections of the ceiling crumbled, revealing a smooth domed roof. "What is going on? Are they spacemen?"

Harold Oxley turned to the kid. "In point of fact, Mutt, I believe they are *interdimensional* beings." He nodded as if this made perfect sense.

Indy gawked in surprise at his friend. All three of them stared at Oxley. The professor's eyes were sharp and bright. Frowning, the man picked the feathered hat off his head, stared at it with profound distaste, and threw it away from him with a shudder of disgust.

Indy smiled broadly at him. "Welcome back, Ox!"

Further conversation was cut off as the quaking and vibrations grew to a feverish pitch. More of the ceiling came crashing down in spattering sections.

"Um, Indy . . . ," Marion called out. "Something's happening!"

She pointed toward the upper dais—which was now *moving*!

Turning.

Like a Las Vegas roulette wheel, the upper arcade had begun to spin above them. Slowly at first, then faster and faster. The thrones and their occupants blurred away. All that remained visible was the glow of their eyes, now a continuous streak around the room's circumference.

A keening wail rose, almost ultrasonic.

And still the upper dais spun faster.

Overhead, the silvery dome of the roof shone brighter, forming a glowing, whirling cloud under it. Indy smelled ozone, as he might during a lightning storm, as if the cloud were building into a thunderhead.

And as if reading his mind, the cloud began to darken into something threatening, drawing down upon itself. And still it continued to collapse and spin, turning to ink. From the debris scattered on the upper dais, small broken pieces of stone façade floated up toward the darkness, swirling around inside the dome, slowly being sucked up and up into the black center.

Suddenly a piece of the wall at their level broke away and flew high.

Indy cringed. *That can't be good.*

"Keep low!" he yelled.

He dragged Marion down, while Mutt yanked Oxley down. They clutched together on the floor.

Indy craned his neck. It was like staring up into a tub's drain hole.

Only this drain hole was growing larger.

Marion shouted, "What the hell is that thing?"

"A pathway!" Oxley answered, gaping upward with awe. "A portal!"

"A problem," Indy finished for him.

He had seen enough. With the Russian guards' attention focused upward, Indy pointed to the unguarded exit. He gathered the others, and together they scuttled low across the room, then bolted for the exit.

Spalko and her cohorts ignored them, still awestruck, staring at the growing thundercloud.

As they fled, Oxley kept glancing back over his shoulders—at the glow of the spinning eyes. His feet began to slow. His head turned more fully toward the shining brilliance of that unearthly intelligence.

Indy frowned. *No you don't, buster . . . not again.*

He grabbed Oxley's elbow and kept him moving past the iron doors.

As a group, they dashed into the antechamber and bulled through the gathered bodies, knocking them down, shattering through them.

Oxley prattled as they fled. "Multiple dimensions! Fascinating to ponder, isn't it? Mignon Thorne wrote an interesting perspective. He teased out the notion of changeable physics—"

"*Not* a good time for this, Ox!"

"—a bit like eddies in water, with cold and hot spots. See what I'm on about?"

Mutt called from in front of them. "We got trouble!"

Indy sighed.

Of course we do.

FIFTY-SIX

MAC CRAWLED on his hands and knees across the floor of the throne room. He gathered anything that glinted amid the rubble: silver amulets, gold coins, ruby-encrusted jewelry. He stuffed them all into his pockets. He would sort it all out later. Now was *not* the time to be picky.

He reached for a tiny gold statuette of an Incan king, about the size of his thumb and worth the price of a beach house in Brighton. As his fingers reached for it, the statue floated off the floor—then suddenly zipped away, shooting skyward.

Mac reached after the fleeing king and watched his dreams of a beach house in Brighton vanish into the churning black maw overhead. To add insult, his watch was stripped off his wrist and sailed upward. Mac yanked his arm lower and flattened to the floor. All around the room, other bits of metal jittered and quaked, then shot up to the domed ceiling.

Rubbing his stripped wrist, Mac got the message and crawled toward the massive doors. It was time to get out of here.

As he reached the doors, he stared back over one shoulder.

Spalko's lieutenant, heavy with a belt of ammunition and iron-toed boots, floated off the floor. Mac stopped to watch, stunned. The soldier flailed his limbs, but he had nothing to grab onto but air.

One of his fellow comrades attempted to lunge for him. But he rose out of reach—though not out of range. From Spalko's scabbard, her rapier suddenly took flight, blasting out of its sheath like a missile from a silo. It shot upward and stabbed the flying soldier clean through the gut. Blood spilled out but pooled in midair, suspended by the iron in the hemoglobin. Both sword and soldier spun upward, trailing a swirling tail of crimson.

Then a moment later body, blade, and blood were all sucked up into the vortex.

Not good.

Having seen more than enough, Mac crawled faster toward the exit. He heard a scream from another soldier, but this time he didn't stop to watch. He could imagine the soldier was following his dear comrade.

Yet as he passed the throne room's threshold, a voice called out—loud and piercing enough to draw one last glance behind him.

Spalko stood in the center of the room, bathed in the glow of the swirling eyes. She pressed her hands against her ears as if trying not to hear something. Her face shone with an inner light, almost revealing her own skull beneath.

A cry escaped her, a mix of delight and horror.

"I can see! I can see it all!"

Indy ran with Oxley in tow. He joined Mutt and Marion in the long hall lined by the giant bronze waterwheels. The kid was right. What lay ahead certainly could be classified as trouble.

Big trouble.

The ground quaked underfoot. Distant explosions echoed to

them, coming from underground. Closer at hand, they faced a more serious problem.

As they sped down the long hallway, the turbines spun at maddening speeds. Overhead, the copper conduits they'd followed to the throne room crackled with dazzling arcs of electricity, like Saint Elmo's fire along the masts of ships at sea. The scintillating fire raced down the conduits in bursts, flowing outward from whatever was happening in the throne room.

Oxley continued a running dialogue on his own theories about what was happening. "Thorne called them 'post-inflation bubbles.' Of course, that presupposes universal expansion and therefore random pockets of extrinsic physics—"

At the end of the hallway the electrical display shattered out into a brilliant lightning storm. Power arcs snapped like bullwhips.

Unimpressed by the electrical show, Oxley only shouted louder. "—different realities reside in the same space at the same time, completely unaware of one another. It's all rather simple really."

The lightning storm pulsed larger yet. The air burned with ozone. Electrical arcs crisscrossed the tunnel and filled it like a fiery spider's web. It would be death to try to pass through there.

"We need another way out!" Marion called.

A loud boom of thunder knocked them all back. A section of the far tunnel fractured and collapsed. The lightning storm headed their way, blasting away more and more of the tunnel as it swept toward them.

"Back!" Indy yelled.

Turning, they fled down the hall. The water turbines spun like the wheels on Formula One racers, spitting electricity. Ahead, one of the bronze waterwheels exploded from its stanchions and came rolling right for them. There was no retreating. Lightning crackled at their heels.

"Keep going!" Indy yelled. He pointed ahead to one of the cross-passages. It led into the maze of corridors.

They sprinted for the turn as the bronze wheel rolled straight at them.

Mutt reached the corner, dragging Marion, and vanished.

Indy and Oxley would not make it. He tugged the professor to one side, and they flattened against the wall, arms out, heads turned to each other.

Oxley stared at Indy as the giant wheel rolled past them, missing them by less than an inch. "So what's your theory, Henry? About those beings?"

Indy rolled his eyes. "Not now, Ox."

Pushing off the wall, he grabbed the professor and headed after Marion and Mutt. All around, explosions rocked and tore the place apart. The entire complex was coming down.

They had to get out of here—but where?

FIFTY-SEVEN

SPALKO HEARD one of her soldiers scream—but it was no more than the buzzing of a mosquito in her ears. Inconsequential now. She was so much more now. She was beyond such petty concerns.

Before her eyes, she watched galaxies being born out of dust, only to die again in fiery collapses of blackness.

She stretched her eyes wider, wanting to see more. The upper arcade of the room sped to a blur that defied dimension. All that remained were the glowing eyes of the beings. Their light filled her skull and built into an exquisitely painful pressure. She breathed in through her nose and out her mouth. She employed ancient meditative techniques of yogis in India. She gave herself over to nothingness like the monks in Nepal. She relaxed her body to a limp receptiveness.

She did not fight.

She flowed with the light, accepted its burning glory with no resistance. Birth was painful, but ultimately it brought one out of darkness into life. Here was yet another form of birth. She would be the first of humankind to pierce that new barrier into a grander existence.

All would be known then.

As the pressure increased, it felt like the sutures in her skull were cracking open. She breathed harder, panting against the pain. Her vision widened in scope as if she were hovering just inches from her own body. Though she never looked away from the eyes, her vision expanded, widened.

Through her new eyes, she saw one of her men stumble across the room, wobbling, holding his head. Perhaps sensing her observation, he swung toward her. One arm reached out, searching blindly. His mouth stretched open in a silent scream, beyond pain into something worse. Blood poured down his cheeks. Smoke steamed from his eye sockets.

Despite the horror, she felt no pity. The man was untrained, unfit for the glory here. He had fought when he should have bent to the solar winds that blew out of the brightness from the swirling eyes.

The soldier hobbled toward her, pleading, warning.

Then he fell face-forward.

Dead.

But he never struck the floor. Instead he floated at half-mast, suspended over the ground. His body began to rise, drawn upward. She was surprised to find one of her own arms lifting toward him.

Then his limp body twirled and spun higher.

Though her physical eyes never shifted from the glowing eyes, still she followed the body's path upward with her expanded vision. That inner part of her craned high—and discovered a writhing blackness found only in the center of dead stars. The darkness screamed down at her with the cold fury of the unknown, the unknowable.

The horror of it blinded her new vision. Terrified, she collapsed back into her own mind, back into an agony that splintered the bones of her skull. As she snapped into herself, she found herself face-to-face with one of the beings.

It towered directly in front of her, its eyes blazing with galactic fires.

How had it gotten there?

She had never seen it leave the throne.

At the periphery of her vision, she also noted that the upper arcade of the throne room had stopped spinning. Something was about to happen.

More light blazed out of the eyes of the tall being before her and into hers. Understanding dawned as bright as the light and as painful as the pressure in her skull. Spalko suddenly knew the truth. This enlightenment was no gift. This creature was attempting to destroy her, using its knowledge like a dagger.

No . . . !

With a wrench that was as much mental as physical, she tore her head from the blaze of its fiery eyes. She turned her back on the creature—only to find another being standing there, appearing out of nowhere. Its eyes locked upon hers and raged with the fire of a thousand suns.

NO . . . !

She could not even blink. The flow of light held her lids open. All she could do was turn—

—to find that another being stood on her left.

—and on her right.

—and all around her.

NO MORE . . . !

They circled her completely, shoulder-to-shoulder, with her in the center. All thirteen pairs of eyes blazed down upon her.

"Cover them . . . Cover them . . . ," she gasped out, knowing in her heart that no one remained in the room.

More light and knowledge filled her. Her senses expanded again, unbidden now. Her temples throbbed. She felt a cascade of energy storm across the folds of her brain, crystallizing membranes in its wake.

All the better to conduct more power into her.

There was no stopping it.

From her lips, alien language babbled.

Faster and faster.

It poured out of her, spilling forth as if she overflowed.

With senses expanded beyond human endurance, Spalko felt more of her brain tissue harden into crystal. Hot tears flowed down her cheeks, leaving burning trails.

Not tears.

Blood.

Her senses expanded again. As before, she found herself floating, seeing the world from a foot above her own head. She remembered accounts of near-death experiences: how victims sensed themselves floating out of their own bodies, looking down from above. She did that now. She drifted higher, spinning—suspended in fiery agony. She was high enough now to be able to stare down at her own face.

Blood poured out of her eyes, which quaked and smoked.

She watched them turn black.

Watched them.

Her lips moved below—erupting in a scream of horror.

"I CAN STILL SEE!"

Even with no eyes, more light flowed into her.

She felt it as she floated higher.

With a final blast her brain turned to pure crystal and reflected back all that power in one blazing burst. Flames shot like geysers out of her sockets, a fire so hot it burned bone, hollowed out her sockets to a smoking husk.

Below, her body collapsed, all connections to it severed, like a blown-out candle. But like the soldier, her body never struck the floor. It drifted up after her, following her, her own corpse.

Dead arms flailed as if reaching for her.

She screamed in horror and twisted away—

—only to face the churning cauldron of dark energy, of impossible dimensions, of nothingness that waited for her.

Chased by her own corpse, she sailed up into it.

And away.

FIFTY-EIGHT

FED BY nether forces at the edges of the universe and nourished by the energy of vibrating atoms, the vortex grows. It swells outward along elliptical planes that shatter dimensions. It consumes all matter in its path. Deep in its heart, dark energies and dark matter churn, preparing for what must come.

But before that can happen, it needs to grow much stronger.

And to do that . . .

It needs to feed.

FIFTY-NINE

MAC FELT SOMETHING following him, a prickling at the back of his neck.

With his heart pounding, he ran faster, jangling down yet another corridor. Explosions rocked the floor under him. Distant booms echoed from much deeper underground. The air itself felt charged. It was as if he were running through the eye of a hurricane. Though there was nothing threatening that he could see with his eyes, he knew something pursued him, hunted him.

He also had to admit one other thing.

He was bloody lost.

So he ran faster.

It was the only thing he could think to do.

As he fled down an especially long corridor, cracks began skittering alongside him, racing with him, splitting walls, floors, ceiling. It was as if he were running on thin ice that was giving way around him. An especially loud grind of stone drew his attention behind him. Glancing over a shoulder, he watched a dark shadow flow into the far end of the passageway.

He blinked and squinted. Whatever was back there was slippery to the eye, hard to focus on. He dismissed it.

Just a trick of the light.

Still, his slowing feet sped up again. Ahead, the passage dead-ended into another corridor. A familiar figure shot past along that distant corridor, holding his fedora to his head.

Brilliant.

If anyone could find a way out of here . . .

Indy fled down the hallway. He was losing ground, his hip aching. Oxley was keeping up better than he was. Ahead, Marion and Mutt vanished around another corner. There were a lot of damn corners down here.

A large quake lifted the floor and dropped it.

Unprepared, Indy fell to a knee. Cries echoed to him from up ahead. That was a big quake. The vortex and its energies must be tearing apart the foundations of the city. If it continued, it threatened to drop the whole place down on top of them. Their only hope was to find a way out of this subterranean maze before that happened.

Indy shoved himself up and kept going, determined to survive. He had just reunited with Marion and discovered a son. He would not lose them again. He started forward, but before he could take two steps someone clapped him on the shoulder, scaring the wits out of him.

"We did it, Indiana!" a familiar voice shouted.

He groaned inwardly. *You've got to be kidding.* Still, he shouldn't have been surprised.

"Rats and sinking ships," Indy mumbled as he glanced over sourly at Mac.

As Indy fled, he had been praying for a miracle. This wasn't it. But he was too exhausted to do more than glare. Still, he had broken Mac's nose *twice.* And as they say, third time's the charm.

Indy cocked his arm.

Mac held up a hand. "Wait! You knew I was with you all along, right?"

Though Indy didn't believe a word of it, he still lowered his arm. What was the use? He scowled. "It's whoever's in the room, isn't it, Mac?"

His friend smiled, unapologetic, no remorse. Mac had always been a man who fought dirty and Indy had known that about him—so why not this, too? Besides, Indy had a soft place in his heart for scoundrels. And despite Mac's recent betrayals, the man *had* saved his life a few times over the years.

Indy finally relented and waved ahead. "C'mon, Mac. Let's get the hell out of here."

They ran for another minute in silence, just like old times. Indy even began to outpace his companion, which helped soothe his own wounded ego.

Mac called out behind him. "Indy?"

Indy turned at the strange note in his voice. Mac had stopped following. He had one foot out, leaning forward, but he was unable to move. Strain showed in his reddening face, panic in his wide, shining eyes.

Behind him, darkness churned at the end of the hallway, shifting and swirling with gravitational energies.

The vortex had found them.

Indy felt the force of it now, too—like a wind in the face that had been growing steadily stronger, blowing against him, trying to force him back.

Mac, farther down the hall, struggled against that power. He leaned with his arms toward Indy, grasping for some hold in the empty air. Indy noted that Mac's jacket extended behind him, stretched by pockets heavy and full.

Gold glinted there.

Indy now understood what held his friend trapped.

"Mac! Get rid of your metal!"

The darkness crept closer with swirls of ink and gravity. Loose rocks rattled and rolled toward its black maw. Cracks splintered across the floor and chased straight for them. At the back of the hall, the walls began to buckle and collapse, dragged down the black gullet.

Closer at hand, one of Mac's jacket pockets ripped at the seams. A cascade of gold and jewels flew out, jetting through the air to the vortex.

One of Mac's hands reached for the emptying pocket.

"Mac!"

His friend realized his foolishness, his eyes back on Indy. "Can't blame a guy for trying."

Mac's foot slipped, tugged by a laden pants pocket. He fell hard on his belly and began to slide backward. His hands scrabbled on the smooth stone floor, but he found no purchase.

"Indy!"

Despite his cry for help, Mac knew his doom.

It writhed with darkness and dread energies. Fighting against it, he flipped onto his back and braked with his feet, but still he kept sliding, if anything even faster. Rocks shot past him, not rolling anymore, but *flying*. The walls cracked in skittering bolts as the darkness pushed outward.

He dug in with his palms, his heels.

He still slid.

No one could resist that pull.

Kuh-RACK!

Something bit into the wrist of his outstretched arm. He stared up. A curl of leather cut hard into his wrist. He wrestled around onto his chest and grabbed the whip's end in the fingers of his trapped arm.

The whip trailed, taut as steel, back to a figure who stood with both his feet braced wide, leaning back hard, like a fisherman with a hooked marlin.

Good ol' Indiana!

Then Indy's heels began to drag across the floor, pulled as Mac slid. His friend jerked an arm out and snagged a pillar as he passed, momentarily stopping them.

But for how long?

Mac read the strain on Indy's face. His body was stretched as if on a torturer's rack. And at Mac's heels, the abyss yawned with the insatiable hunger of a dying star. And the vortex grew steadily toward him, pressure increasing with each breath.

Mac understood the truth.

"You gotta let go of me, mate!" he yelled.

Indy's voice was an overtuned violin string. "C'mon, Mac! We've been through worse than this!"

"No, Indy. Not this time."

Indy used his own words against him. "There's always a way out, Mac!"

"Not at the very end, my friend . . ."

The darkness called for him, a mirror of his own heart. He'd been a bad friend to Indy in life. But maybe in death, he could be a better one.

Mac let go of the whip with his fingers and twisted his wrist free of the leather.

"No!" Indy called to him.

Unhooked, Mac flew down the hall. He saw Indy, unburdened now, fall back safe.

Good luck, my old friend.

With nothing else to do, Mac turned away and faced the darkness and the unknown. Despite his doom, a small grin formed on his lips.

He had pockets filled with gold.

And the great unknown ahead of him.

Let's see where this goes!

SIXTY

INDY SCRAMBLED TO HIS FEET as Mac vanished into the darkness. He took a step after his friend, but in even that short distance he felt the dread power of what he faced increase tenfold. He not only felt it as a tug on his body, but also heard it silently screaming with forces beyond his comprehension, with energies not of this world.

He stood limned against that dark abyss.

And he took a step back.

Not in fear, but in simple certainty.

There was no rescuing Mac.

Not this time.

He heard a shout from around the corner behind him. "Indeeee!"

It was Marion.

Indy pushed backward against that pull, one hard step at a time. It was as if the air around him had become warm molasses, flowing toward the abysmal hole. He fought against it with all his will, driven not so much by pure survival as by something more important.

"Indeee!"

For the first time in his life, he had a *reason* to live—and no world-sucking vortex was going to stop him. With each step, he felt the pull of the abyss lessen. His pace increased, his feet stumbling in his haste.

At the rear of the hall, the walls buckled and huge cracks raced toward him as the underlying structure of the complex fractured. It was all coming down.

Reaching the far corner, Indy dashed around it and pounded along the next hall. He was pursued by skittering cracks in the walls.

Ahead, he spotted Marion. She stood at another corner of the interminable maze and pointed down the intersecting passageway.

"Indy!" Marion's voice rang with relief, frosted with anger. "About time! Over here! There's light!"

Bounding up to her, he scooped an arm around her waist and headed into the next passageway.

Here the tunnel walls had been dug out of black granite streaked with thick veins of crystalline quartz, and as Indy ran with Marion, the quartz veins widened—growing to encompass the walls, floor, and ceiling. In another few steps, the tunnel was pure quartz all around them.

Through the translucency, Indy noted water flowing behind the walls, heavy, turbulent, under high pressure. He pictured the giant reservoir over the city. They must be passing through the main feed for the metropolis's extensive aqueduct system.

Suddenly the ground quaked under them, another massive jolt.

Indy glanced behind him.

At the far end of the passageway, the walls fractured. Cracks reached for them like the black fingers of the vortex, scrabbling after its escaping prey.

"Move it, Jones!" Marion hollered.

"You're the boss!"

They fled faster.

Behind them, heavy grinds and deep groans followed. Rock

shattered and pulverized as strange gravities tore it apart. Then a new noise joined in.

Splashing and spraying.

With a glance over his shoulder, Indy spotted fissures opening in the quartz behind them. Water jetted into the tunnel through the cracks. The far end of the passage gave way and collapsed with a concussive *whomp.* A large block of quartz cracked from the ceiling and dropped under a massive deluge of water, like the floodgates on a dam.

"Go!" Indy shouted, realizing the new danger.

More sections crashed behind them.

Indy didn't look—just sprinted. Still, he heard the wall of water building behind them, pressured by the giant reservoir above.

They rounded a curve in the quartz tunnel, and Indy saw the source of the light. An exit must be near! Mutt and Oxley waited.

"Run!" he yelled at them.

"Where?" Mutt hollered back.

Then Indy saw Mutt's eyes widen in horror. The kid backpedaled away. Indy feared to turn around. He ran up to Mutt and Oxley and realized two things at once.

There was an exit.

Only it was a hundred feet *straight up* a sheer shaft.

Sunlight streamed down at them.

There was no escape.

Indy turned as a wall of water roared straight at them down the tunnel, powered by the weight of the reservoir.

He ran to the others. "Hold tight!"

They clutched as a group, arms clinging to one another. He held Marion, Marion clutched Mutt, they all held Oxley.

Then the water blasted into the shaft, swirling around them and sweeping them off their feet and upward.

Even so, Indy had underestimated the sheer power of the deluge. They flew faster and faster, spinning, choking, bobbing. The walls sped past. Debris churned with them. Indy spotted a burned husk of a skeleton swim past.

Then with a final flash of blinding sunlight, they exploded out of the shaft on a jetting column of water. It splashed against a hillside. They hit hard and tumbled apart from one another down its slope and came to rest at the bottom.

Waterlogged and dizzy, Indy gained his hands and knees, too weak to stand. He had only enough strength to pick up his hat and jam it on his head.

They had landed on a high plateau above the city, perched near the top of the ridgeline that encircled the valley.

Marion crawled over to him, soaked to the bone. Mutt followed, on his feet already with the stamina of youth. Though at least the kid had the decency to wobble and look sick to his stomach. Oxley simply lay where he had landed, dazed and drenched in his poncho.

Indy waved to the professor. "You might want to see this, Harold."

Reluctantly, Oxley sat up and shifted over.

Below their perch, the ruins spread out across the valley floor. In the center, the Great Stone Temple stood tall. Until now the pyramid had been a monument against the march of ages—*but no longer.*

As they all watched, the temple began to crumble, torn apart as it slowly turned upon its base, like the inevitable hands of a clock. Walls shattered and ancient blocks tumbled. It began to turn faster and slowly collapsed in on itself. From this center of the city, fissures and cracks extended outward, tearing apart the metropolis of Akator.

Indy imagined those same cracks going *down* as well, loosening the entire foundation of the valley. This proved true as the swirl of the temple ruins spread slowly outward, churning the whole valley floor as if it were water.

Homes ground to rubble, roads twisted and broke, and ancient statuary rode across the landscape, carried by the swirling movement.

In the center, the remains of the Great Stone Temple started to sink into the earth, vanishing completely, leaving a gaping hole.

And still the valley floor churned around it, faster and faster near the hole, slower at the edges. Soon the entire city was in motion.

Indy stared down toward the hole where the temple once stood. He knew what he was seeing: the new face of the vortex as those gravitational forces reached the surface. The entire valley had become a sinkhole, drawing down into the abyss.

"Look!" Mutt yelled.

Again with those sharper eyes, the kid had spotted it first.

From the center of the vortex came a flash of silver. Out of the heart of the vortex, it arose, so shiny that the reflected sunlight both burned the eye and seemed to flow over its sleek surfaces. It ascended slowly from the inky pit, an antithesis to the darkness of the abyss. But like the vortex, it spun, carrying debris from below and catching more above.

One of the roaming bits of statuary—a fractured chunk of a stone serpent—joined the debris field circling the sphere of silver.

As the craft climbed higher, hovering now directly across from them, its exact shape was hard to fix with the eye, spherical in the center, yet with changing rings of brilliance all around it, spinning along all axes, sometimes vertical, sometimes horizontal.

On the plateau, Indy stood and drew up next to Marion and Oxley. They all stared out as it spun before them, orbited by debris—then in a wink the image seemed to go flat before their eyes, losing dimensions, becoming like a photograph.

And as it slowly turned one last time, all Indy could discern was a single brilliant silver line, a photograph's edge. With a final turn, this, too, was gone.

Vanished.

All the levitated debris, no longer supported, came crashing down. The chunk of statuary in the shape of a serpent landed near them, upright, with the snake's head staring at Indy, its stone tongue protruding out at him.

It seemed some bit of the cosmos had a sense of humor.

A mighty grumbling crash echoed from the valley.

Indy turned in time to see the wall damming the high reservoir shatter, weakened by the passing of the vortex. The lake it held back came rushing out in a great tidal wave and swept over the city, flooding it completely until no trace remained.

Oxley sighed. "Like a broom to their footprints . . ."

As the churning water settled below and the sun sank toward the horizon, Indy hobbled over to a dry section of their hillside and collapsed. Marion fell next to him. Oxley sat on a boulder. Only Mutt remained at the edge.

"So where do you think they went?" Mutt asked. He pointed a finger upward. "Up there?"

Oxley shook his head. "Not into space. Into the space *between* the spaces."

To demonstrate, Oxley put his palms together to form an X—the same way the strange being had—then twisted them once, so the X inverted.

Into another dimension.

Indy spoke up, nagged by a question himself, one more practical. "Harold, how did you ever get past those skeletal guards at Chauchilla Cemetery, where you found the skull? We almost got killed."

"Hmm? Oh, I went in the daytime when they were asleep. No one in their right mind would ever rob graves in broad daylight."

Indy smiled with respect. "Never thought of that."

Mutt came to join them, sitting next to his mother. "I don't get it. Why the legends about a City of Gold? There wasn't much down there. Only what others brought here."

Indy pictured the gold coins and the bits of jewelry and decoration on the corpses. But the Ugha tribesmen had adorned themselves with no such riches.

"Misinterpretation," Indy said, drawing Mutt's eye. "The Ugha word for 'gold' translates as 'treasure.' The Spaniards assumed that meant gold, but it was really *knowledge.* That was the Ugha's true treasure."

Marion touched the gash on Mutt's cheek, the wound from his battle with Spalko. "You're going to have a nasty scar."

Aching all over, Indy groaned. "Plenty more where that came from, kid."

Shading his eyes, Indy stared to the west, to where the sun was just touching the ridgeline. End of the day. Settling in, he sprawled out on the grassy slope and tilted his hat over his eyes, ready to get a little sleep.

Marion leaned over and peeked at him under the brim.

He offered her a ghost of a smile and held out an arm to one side.

C'mere, babe.

She crawled into his arm, rested her head on his shoulder, and snuggled close and tight. Her warmth melted into him as Indy drew her even closer. They fit perfectly together, as if they were cut from the same mold.

Mutt stared down at them, disgusted, but not about his mother and Indy. He waved an arm toward the cliffs. "What? We're just going to sit here?"

"Night falls quick in the jungle, kid. Can't climb down in the dark."

"I could, old man." Mutt stood and headed toward the ledge.

Indy pushed his hat back. "Why don't you stick around, Junior?"

"I don't know . . . why didn't you, *Dad*?"

Indy sighed and stared up at the sky. "Somewhere an old man is laughing."

Oxley turned with a sweetly puzzled frown, staring between Mutt and Indy. *"Dad?"*

SIXTY-ONE

How could I have forgotten?

Charles Stanforth, the dean of Marshall College, hurried down the hallway lined by administrative offices. His polished oxford shoes tapped loudly on the marble-tile floor. He nervously straight-ened his tie and smoothed his navy-blue suit jacket. He would never live this down.

And on this of all days.

Ahead he noted a painter kneeling by the frosted glass door to one of the offices. The worker was painstakingly painting letters on the glass with the delicate care of an artisan.

Stanforth's feet slowed as he neared the painter. He read the top name freshly stenciled on the door.

Professor Henry Jones Jr.

The painter was finishing the last letter on the line below it. He glanced back at the dean with an inquiring expression.

Stanforth waved to him, not meaning to interrupt. "Oh, go on, go on. By all *means,* do go on."

Turning back to his work, the painter used his brush to fill in the last letter, completing the line.

Associate Dean

Satisfied, Stanforth hid a smile, hurried on to his own office, and ducked inside. He took a moment to collect himself. He noted a picture of the previous dean of the college, Marcus Brody, hanging on the wall.

He paused to touch two fingers to the frame. "You should be the one here, Marcus." He sighed and glanced toward the ceiling. "And perhaps you are, my good friend. I certainly hope so."

But Stanforth had his own duty. He reached his office library and searched the shelves. He found the Bible on the second row. It was bound in well-worn leather. The tome was as old as the college itself. It was said that Abraham Lincoln himself had taken the oath of office on this Bible. But more importantly, it had been in the Brody family going back generations, bequeathed to the college in Marcus's will.

The ceremony could not commence without it.

With the Bible in hand, Stanforth rushed out of his office with as much decorum as he could muster. It would not be fitting to have the dean be seen sprinting across the campus in his Sunday best.

So it took him a few minutes more to reach the Marshall College chapel. It sat in the middle of a green lawn, its walls constructed of gray stone quarried from the land here. Stained-glass windows glinted in the bright sunshine. The dogwoods that lined the main walkway were already flowering in shades of pink and white. But running late, Stanforth headed to the chapel's side entrance.

He pushed inside to discover that everything was as he had left it.

The minister still waited in front of the happy couple—though from Henry's impatient frown at him, *happy* might not be the right description. Henry, clean-shaven and scrubbed, was dressed in a fine suit with a bow tie. At his side, his wife-to-be, Marion Ravenwood, was resplendent in a simple white dress that set off her beautiful blue eyes. The remaining member of the wedding party, standing to Henry's right, was also in a fine suit, but he had unfortunately marred the look by wearing a scuffed pair of biker boots.

Youths today . . .

"'Bout time, Charles," Indy said under his breath.

"You know Marcus would not have wanted it any other way," Stanforth insisted, handing the Bible to the minister.

The impatience faded from Indy's eyes, and he offered Stanforth a grateful nod.

With the matter settled and his duty done, Stanforth returned to the pew where his wife and two children waited. They had arrived last night. No one wanted to miss the wedding. If only to verify it with their own eyes. The sheer impossibility of it had drawn guests from all around the world.

Indiana Jones was finally tying the knot.

Stanforth settled next to Harold Oxley, who mumbled under his breath, commenting on the delay. "Ahh, *how much of human life is lost waiting.*"

Indy had waited long enough for this moment—in fact, his whole life.

The minister opened the Bible and began the ceremony.

Indy took a moment to glance back to those in attendance, friends and family, going back years. Even General Ross had made it here from Nevada, outfitted in his dress blues and sporting a saber at his side.

Indy doubted he'd ever been happier than at this moment.

The minister continued, "—but it is also a declaration of love. I wish to read to you what Paul wrote of love in a letter to the Corinthians, who—"

Corinthians? Indy knew all about the Corinthians. He taught classes about the Corinthians. He could wait no longer.

Turning, he grabbed Marion, pulled her close, and kissed her.

She shifted back, lips still touching, just enough to speak. "Jones, I don't think this part comes till we're finished."

"*Finished?* Honey, I'm just getting warmed up."

He leaned in, kissing her more deeply, pulling her tighter, letting her know this time he was here to stay. He heard laughter in the background, but he didn't care. Here was where he belonged.

He finally leaned back and stared into Marion's eyes.

Let the Spaniards have their gold, let the Ugha have their knowledge . . . Indy had the only treasure he wanted right here.

Oxley called from the pews, "Well done, Henry!"

He grinned and called back, "Thanks, Ox!"—only to have it echoed from Mutt's lips.

Indy glared over at the kid.

Two Henrys in the family again . . .

Mutt gave him an innocent, questioning look: *What did I do?*

Indy stared upward. *Oh yes, someone was surely laughing.*

Mutt had to watch his mother kiss Jones a second time as the ceremony ended.

Oh brother.

But at least his mother was happy.

Happier than he ever remembered her.

The couple finally broke the clinch and headed down the aisle. The crowd cheered, called out, clapped. After a moment, he followed behind. He glanced around the chapel, sensing the weight of its age, imagining all the dignitaries who had once walked down this same aisle. Over the centuries the school's alumni had included both the famous and the infamous. And in the case of the man his mother had just married, Professor Jones was definitely *both.*

Mutt shook his head at the thought.

And this was his dad?

Down the aisle, the doors swung open for the happy couple. A stiff New England breeze blew into the church, scattering petals off the flowers that lined the pews and dancing the coats that hung on hooks beside the door.

A hat flew off a peg and rolled down the edge of the aisle.

Mutt blocked it with his boot and bent to pick it up. Straightening, he dusted off the brim of the old brown fedora. He studied it. Scarred and battered, the hat had held up pretty good.

Not bad really.

Maybe . . .

He lifted it up and moved it toward his head.

Before it touched a single oiled hair, a hand shot out and snatched it from his fingers. Mutt glanced up to find Jones giving him a dirty look.

Not today, kid.

Jones mashed the fedora atop his head, turned on a heel, and headed back down the aisle. Reaching the church door, he cocked out an arm, and Mutt's mother took it.

Together, the pair headed out into the brightness.

To points unknown.

About the Author

James Rollins is the bestselling author of nine previous novels: *Subterranean, Excavation, Deep Fathom, Amazonia, Ice Hunt, Sandstorm, Map of Bones, Black Order,* and *The Judas Strain.* He has a doctorate in veterinary medicine and his own practice in Sacramento, California. An amateur spelunker and a certified scuba enthusiast, he can often be found either underground or underwater. Visit his website at www.jamesrollins.com.

About the Type

This book was set in Caslon, a typeface first designed in 1722 by William Caslon. Its widespread use by most English printers in the early eighteenth century soon supplanted the Dutch typefaces that had formerly prevailed. The roman is considered a "workhorse" typeface due to its pleasant, open appearance, while the italic is exceedingly decorative.